THUNDER FALLS

THE EDUCATION OF LEOPOLD RED WOLF

Neil Perry Gordon

Contents

Chapter 1
The Battle of Carlisle
July 1, 1863

I was eight years old when a cannonball ripped Mother's body in two, leaving her legs shoved under the kitchen table and flinging her upper body to nestle against the wood stove. With the golden Star of David dangling from her neck, she seemed to stare at me with her piercing blue eyes, even though her soul had already passed on.

This horror occurred because a Confederate cannonball was fired through the front of our home. After it struck Mother, the errant projectile continued on until it found its way into the trunk of the old oak tree in our backyard. So began the Battle of Carlisle.

On that same fateful day, the infamous Battle of Gettysburg raged a mere thirty miles to the southwest. History barely mentions our own struggle in Pennsylvania, but I'll never forget it.

Father, along with a few of the other men in town, had joined up with a local militia led by Baldy Smith and did their best to defend Carlisle against General Stuart and his cavalry. In fact, their courage prevented the Confederates from taking our city. As Father explained it, the militia knew the city, its streets, alleyways, and best places to stage ambushes, and could therefore repel the invading enemy. Eventually, General Stuart had no choice but to retreat and join up with General Lee's army at Gettysburg.

The day following the battle, Father made his way home, weary, his face covered in gunpowder and dirt. I shared the news and showed him the coffin I'd built, where I placed Mother's remains. Father embraced me, as tears cut pathways down his cheeks, and told me how proud he was. This display of affection surprised me, since he was not a man to express his emotions. Apparently, the atrocities of war, along with the violent death of his wife, cracked his stoic demeanor.

Father wanted to bury her in the backyard, but I insisted on the importance of bringing her body to the cemetery behind the Harrisburg synagogue that she and I attended during the Jewish holidays.

From that day forward, it was up to me to take care of Father. Good thing Mother taught me everything about cooking, cleaning, and praying to Hashem. Though Father didn't much care for the Hebrew prayers, he liked to eat and appreciated my washing his clothes. That's not to say he was a bad father; he just had difficulty sharing his feelings. After a bloody war, I was comforted knowing he was there to protect me.

Father fought with the local militia until May 13, 1865, the day the war against the South ended. That is when he began to teach me the one thing he was good at—carpentry, which came in handy, because after the war, with much of Carlisle destroyed, demand for Father's woodworking services quickly rose. Soon enough he needed an assistant, and I was banging a hammer alongside him, learning the craft. Although I didn't particularly enjoy the labor, I loved working alongside Father.

Six weeks later, when returning from picking up supplies in town, I noticed Father working on something in the front yard, fairly close to the road. Upon my approach, I saw he'd hung a sign, cut from a large piece of oak and carved with block letters that read WOLF & SON WOODWORKING.

"What's this?" I asked, putting down the crate.

Father wrapped his muscular arm around my shoulder, pulled me in tight, and said, "This, Leo, is the new name of our business. From now on, we're partners."

Wolf and Son Woodworking prospered after the war, as homes and businesses rebuilt, then for many years afterward, as the city of Carlisle expanded. But when the economy turned sour in 1879, we were anxiously looking for work. So, on a summer morning when Captain Richard Henry Pratt knocked on our door and asked us to come work for him at his new school, we jumped at the opportunity.

On that sweltering day in July, while giving us a tour of an abandoned army facility, Captain Pratt told us that he planned to open the doors to the Carlisle Indian School in a few months. "These barracks will board hundreds of Indian children, both boys and girls, from across our great nation," the captain proclaimed, spreading his arms wide as we followed him into one of the empty barracks. "As you can see, the army left us with nothing, so I will need you to build everything, including bed frames for mattresses and cubbies for the students to store their things. We'll also need desks and chairs for the classrooms and long tables for the dining hall. Are you up to the task, Isaac?"

"Yes, sir," Father replied with a vigorous nod.

"What about you, Leo?" the captain asked me.

"Yes, sir, I am up to it," I said, mirroring Father's enthusiasm.

"You're a good boy, Leo," he said, ruffling my hair.

"Excuse me, Captain. I'm twenty-four years old. I like to think of myself as a man," I said, stroking my full red beard.

"Of course you are. It's just that you look young for your age. My apologies," he said.

I glanced briefly at Father's pursed lips and furrowed brow—a common expression he wore when he was frustrated with me. Later that day, he would tell me I talked too much.

"Now, Isaac, you and your son should get started right away. Our first group of students will be arriving on the first of November. I'm expecting nearly one hundred and fifty Indian children."

"Understood," Father said and extended his hand to the captain to seal the deal.

Wolf and Son Woodworking looked as if it would have plenty of work for the foreseeable future, and we certainly did for the summer of 1879. Every day, including the Sabbath, we toiled. Mother would have frowned upon this if she were still alive.

With the extra money, we were able to buy new tools and expand our woodshop. Father took me to a supply house in Harrisburg where we bought interesting things, such as a socket chisel used for carving, a plumb rule to make sure things were level, a mortise chisel, a plow plane, which I learned was for making grooves in the wood, and a bradawl to start holes for nails.

I don't remember a happier time than those summer months, working side by side with Father. We spent the bulk of our time renovating the old army barracks, which at first seemed an overwhelming task. After all, we were only two men and there were eight barracks. But Father prepared a daily work schedule and required us to complete certain tasks each day. Most times, these obligations kept us working well past sundown, though occasionally, when we finished early, Father would treat me to an ice cream in the city.

Much as I was involved in crafting every inch of those structures, what I didn't know was how my life was going to change once the Carlisle Indian School opened its doors, and how my narrowed outlook on the world would cease to exist.

Chapter 2
The Senator

I cannot say if I was ever told, directly, the purpose of the Carlisle Indian School. Most of what I learned was by working within earshot of Captain Pratt's tours for his array of distinguished guests.

The captain would greet visitors at his home on Claremont Street, which was a short walk from the barracks. I imagined upon their arrival they would be offered tea and biscuits before venturing over to see our progress. I knew about the biscuits from my Negro friend Abraham, son of his mother Alice, who did the housekeeping and cooking for the captain. Every now and then, Abe would sneak me a few biscuits from the kitchen.

On a late afternoon, while Father and I built cubbies in one of the barracks, the captain entered with an important-looking man whom he called "Senator." I pretended not to listen, but of course, I couldn't help myself.

"This is very impressive, Captain," said the senator, stroking his bushy, snow-white mustache. "Do you think you'll open on time?"

"I see no reason why we shouldn't be ready."

As they evaluated Father's and my progress, the senator asked, "Is it true that you convinced a few of the Lakota chiefs to send their sons here?"

"Yes," the captain said, nodding. "This was very important. Once they saw chiefs like American Horse amenable to sending his own son, they became convinced in the merits of our mission."

"American Horse! That ornery SOB," the senator growled. "How in the world did you convince him?"

"You know, Senator, the Lakota have a name they call the white man. It's *Wasichu*, which means *land-takers*. I'm sure you've heard this insult."

The senator nodded, offering an all-knowing grimace.

"I noted to the chief that if he were able to read and write in English, he wouldn't have been tricked, as he claims, into signing the treaty pushing his people off his land. Thus, I was able to make the point that his lack of education hurt his tribe."

The senator wagged a finger and said, "Don't forget about Chief Red Shirt. He also claimed his territorial boundaries were larger than he thought."

The captain nodded. "He's another one to whom I said he owes it to his people to send his son here in order to learn English, so they won't be made to look foolish again."

"You know, Captain, Chief American Horse has been a thorn in my side for years," the senator remarked with a smirk. "Maybe now that you'll have his son, he'll learn to behave himself."

I glanced over to the captain and caught him grimacing at the senator's remark. He quickly composed himself and said, "I hope you can join us for dinner tonight. Alice is a wonderful cook."

"I would be honored, Captain."

Captain Pratt turned to me and said, "Leo, I could use you and your father tonight. Alice will need your help to serve our guests."

I nodded and said, "Yes, sir. I'll tell Father."

*

Before heading over to the captain's home, I washed and looked at myself in the mirror, wondering if I would ever grow muscles like Father's. My arms were so skinny that I could wrap a finger and thumb fully around my bicep. The skin on my chest was stretched thin over my protruding ribs, and my legs looked like they would snap in half if I carried anything too heavy. It wasn't as if I was malnourished; I ate plenty. Father even liked to say I had a hollow leg. But when I stood next to him, my gaunt body accentuated his impressive physique. When he removed his sweat-stained shirt and torn trousers, I marveled at his thick layers of rippled muscles. I knew of no man who looked so powerful.

People often stared at Father, not just because of his tall and strong body, but also for his unusual face. His eyes were a pale blue and, in striking contrast with his olive skin, gave the impression of two glimmering stars in the evening sky.

The captain's home on Webster was a short walk from ours. Given his profession, Father commented on the homes he found praiseworthy, and criticized the poorly designed ones. The captain's, like most, was a mix of the two. Father appreciated the four tall wooden columns supporting the eave in the front, but didn't care for the lack of a porch. In its place was a patio of flat, blue slate stones, and in between these stones grew a ground cover of moss, due to the lack of sunlight. To this Father said, "Tsk, tsk," and shook his head.

When I offered only a forced smile in return, Father narrowed his eyes at me. I didn't have to tell him about my lack of enthusiasm for the building trade; he could see it for himself. Certainly, if Mother had been alive, she would have supported me in desiring more than from life than swinging a hammer. *Leo is smart and should do more with his life*, I envisioned her telling Father.

We entered the kitchen through the back of the house, where Alice and Abe were busy preparing for the meal. I greeted them, stood alongside Abe, who was peeling potatoes, and asked, "Can I help?"

Abe smiled and handed me a small knife.

The moment Alice laid eyes on Father, she let out a shriek. At first, I thought she was frightened, but her exuberance was just from seeing the man she adored. She ran over and wrapped her arms around him.

"Oh, Isaac, I am so happy to see you," she said, looking up into his eyes.

He grimaced, and said, "Let go of me, Alice."

Alice was the prettiest Negro woman I'd ever seen—and kind and loving on the inside to boot. She kept her hair pulled back, featuring a perfectly smooth, unblemished face, the centerpiece of which were her large, round, brown eyes.

I don't know why Father rejected her. I doubt it was because of the color of her skin, as Father never expressed such a prejudice. Maybe it was because he still loved Mother, though she had been gone for over sixteen years.

Father and I were given unstained white pants and jackets to wear. The pants were too big, requiring me to tie a rope around my skinny waist in order to keep them from falling down. While I appeared as a disheveled scarecrow, Father's outfit fit snugly. It looked as if, were he to inhale too deeply, his bulging chest muscles would rip the shirt apart at the seams.

Our job was to carry shiny silver trays filled with hot and cold servings of food. Alice warned me not to drop or spill anything. "Be careful, especially when you pour the wine," she instructed, guiding me to hold the bottle with two hands.

When idle, we were told to stand against the wall, and wait to be summoned. "And don't slouch," Alice warned.

I did my best to not fidget. But what got me through was overhearing an interesting conversation at the dinner table. The captain was sharing with the senator his philosophy about the school. "As you know, the Sioux wars have left the Lakota people broken and destitute. This is true for many of the Indian nations across the plains states. Sad to say, they are a vanishing race and their only hope for survival is a rapid cultural transformation." The captain paused in his pontification and took a sip of wine. "I want you to know, Senator, so you can share this with your colleagues back in Washington, that the Carlisle Indian School will Americanize the native. It will be a total immersion into our culture, our language, and our way of life."

The senator leaned back and tipped his chair onto its two spindly back legs. I thought I heard them creak as they strained under the large man's weight. I readied myself to catch him if the chair crumbled. Fortunately, that wasn't necessary.

"This sounds good in theory, Captain, but it may not be easy," the senator said. "I imagine that the older ones will be set in their ways by the time they arrive."

"Indeed, it will be easier with the younger children. But we intend to erase the Indian culture quickly and efficiently. Our mantra here is to kill the Indian in order to save the man."

The senator banged his chair back onto all fours and raised his glass. "Brilliant, Captain! Let's toast to that. *Kill the Indian, save the man!*"

Chapter 3
Arrival

"May I have your attention, please," the captain began, as we took our seats in the dining hall. The tall windows flanking the former army facility were swung wide open, allowing a gentle breeze to sweep across the large room.

"In an hour, our first group of students will be arriving," the captain said, glancing at his pocket watch. "Many of them, as you can imagine, will be frightened, a few traumatized. Your job is to help settle these children into their new lives."

As the captain continued, I looked around at the eight men and women who had arrived that morning. According to what was shared with me, they were all trained professional educators hired to serve as barrack counselors for the eight groups of boys and girls. That's why Father and I were surprised when the captain asked us to serve as counselors ourselves. After all, I never took care of anyone except for Father, and he never showed any interest in raising children, not even me.

But Captain Pratt told us our assignments were temporary until he found qualified counselors to replace us. "I'm trying to recruit from a few schools in Harrisburg," he explained.

So, along with the other new counselors, we sat and listened to his instructions.

"When the children arrive," the captain said, standing behind the wooden podium I'd built, "we will move them quickly into their assigned barracks and have them change into their new school uniforms."

"What do we do with their native clothing?" asked a pretty, blonde-haired woman with bright blue eyes.

"We'll collect and store it in the storage shed," the captain said, pointing to the building behind the auditorium where Father and I kept our tools.

This sent a charge through the counselors, resulting in numerous chatty conversations. Taking the children's clothes away on the first day seemed to be too much for these professionals to accept. But the next bit of news sent them into a tizzy.

"At some point throughout the day, the barber will visit each of the barracks to cut the children's hair," the captain announced.

This brought a few counselors to their feet.

"How can you do that on their first day?" shouted the pretty blonde.

"Don't you think the children need time to get used to things?" asked a tall, skinny man.

The captain spread out his arms, silencing the belligerent voices. "I've already explained to each of you, during our interviews, how we plan to proceed," he said, sweeping a hand across the room. "We need to assimilate these native youth into the white man's world swiftly, teach the boys a marketable trade, and the girls how to maintain and manage a household. The best way to do this is to remember our mission, our purpose, which is to kill the Indian in order to save the man. If you have a problem with that, now is the time to speak up. Otherwise, you'll follow our mandate without questions or debates."

No one said a word. I certainly knew of the captain's intent for the school, as I'd overheard his explanation several times. But with the reality of it about to unfold, even I worried how the children would respond to being torn from their homes, especially the young ones, who I feared would find this new way of life terrifying.

*

I was finishing some last-minute woodworking when I heard the wagon train rumbling down the road. I ran from the rear end of the barrack to the front door, shoved it open, and leaped from the porch to the grassy patch below just as the wagons came to a screeching stop. There they stood, twelve covered wagons drawn by forty-eight sweaty horses, snorting hard from the load.

The captain appeared, marching in his military uniform down the center of the grassy field we called the Great Lawn, which separated the two rows of barracks. Standing before the wagons, the captain clapped his hands together and announced, "Come, children, step lively now."

First, a few heads poked out from behind the canvas flaps, then an arm and a leg, followed by the rest of their bodies. Large and small, boys and girls emerged onto the Great Lawn. They stepped lightly as if they didn't want to harm the freshly cut grass; that's what I heard from two of the counselors. One said, "The Indians believe all things are alive, even the stones."

The children wore outfits of deer hides and other battered skins, marked with holes, tears, and curled edges, weathered from time. Even though these garments were probably handed down from older siblings, there were still hints of former glory peeking through the faded colors.

As I waited in front of my barrack, the captain organized the children into groups by gender and age. My group would be the boys between the ages of five and seven years.

My fellow counselors each stood on their porches, waiting for their children to approach. Father was at the other end of our row, three barracks down. His group was the fifteen-year-old boys. In between us were the other male counselors, and across the Great Lawn stood the mirror image of our barracks—our female counterparts, anxiously awaiting the girls' arrival.

Once the children began their walk down the lawn, I noticed their round, wide-opened eyes absorbing their new surroundings, while at the same time reflecting back their fearful souls. But seeing these children, many with tears rolling down their cheeks, reminded me of how I felt when Mother was killed. How she was violently torn from me, leaving an emotionless father to raise me, a man incapable of attending to my grief and confusion.

There was no doubt these native children were frightened, and who could blame them? Separated from their families, some as young as five years old, they were brought here by rail and wagon, traveling cross-country, joined by new children along the way, before finally arriving at the Carlisle Indian School.

Chapter 4
The Barber

As my boys entered the barrack, I gestured for each one to stand before a bed where a feather-stuffed pillow, a woolen army blanket, and a newly pressed uniform were all neatly folded, waiting for them.

I walked down the center of the two flanking rows and took a moment to make eye contact with each boy. They all stood frozen, not uttering a word. I approached the first child, offered my hand, and said, "Good afternoon, boys, my name is Leopold Wolf, but you can call me Leo. Welcome to Carlisle."

The boys looked at me with empty eyes, apparently clueless as to the meaning of my words. An older boy at the end shouted something in what I assumed to be his native language, and whatever he said seemed to encourage the young boy poised before me to say what I assumed was his name.

"Mato," he said.

I leaned down and asked, pointing at him, "Mato?" Then I straightened up and patted my chest and said, "Leo."

He stuck his little finger at me and said with a funny accent, "Leo."

"Yes, I'm Leo," I said with a broad smile and a laugh. I looked around the room at the other boys for their reaction, but they remained deadpanned.

"They don't speak," the boy at the end said, shaking his head.

"Oh," I said. "You mean they don't speak English."

The boy nodded.

"But you do," I said, approaching him quickly. "What's your name?"

"Hotah," he said. "Son of Chief American Horse."

Hotah couldn't have been more than seven years old. We gazed into each other's eyes for a moment before I said, "I'm honored to meet you, Hotah. Who taught you to speak English?"

"White man come to village to teach," he said, struggling to push out each word.

As he explained, I noticed strands of colorful beads woven into his black, silky hair, which hung well past his shoulders. He then pointed to the boy I'd just met and said, "Mato is also son of chief. Chief Red Shirt is father."

I recognized these boys' names, as the captain had personally reviewed with me the backgrounds of each of the children that would soon be under my care. He forewarned me that these "sons-of-chiefs" may have certain qualities lacking in the other boys, due to their privileged status within their tribes. But in the captain's opinion, that shouldn't matter, because the school's vigorous immersion program would soon eliminate this entitlement, making all the children equals.

I thanked Hotah and was ready to meet the other boys when the barrack door swung open and in strolled a thin, hunched-over man carrying a black leather bag. He pointed at me and asked, "Are you the one in charge?"

I nodded and said, "Yes, sir."

"Good, I'm the barber," he said. "Set up a chair over there." He cocked his chin toward the center of the room.

I put the only chair in the barrack in between the two rows of bunks. Someone needed to go first, so I looked over to Hotah and asked, "Would you be willing?"

Hotah looked at the barber, who held a large shear in his hand. The man said, with an exasperated sigh, "Let's go, son. I have many more haircuts yet to do today."

Hotah stood up and glanced at the other boys, who seemed unaware as to what was about to happen. He then looked at me and lifted one of his long braids and pretended to snip at it with two fingers.

"That's right," I said.

Hotah took a breath, nodded, and said, "Okay."

The young Lakota boy sat in the chair, his spine erect, his face calm, eyes solemn. Silence encompassed the room as the other boys sat wide-eyed and slack-jawed. The barber lifted one of Hotah's two long braids, and like a hot knife through butter, sliced through it with his shears, letting the bundle of hair drop to the floor, where it hit with an audible thud. Then he did the same to the second braid. When he was done styling the cut, Hotah stood up and pointed to Mato, who took his turn.

When all was done, my boys sported a traditional white man's hairstyle, short and combed over to one side. I allowed them to look at themselves in the small, cloudy mirror hanging on the back wall. When they returned to their bunks, their profound sadness was plainly evident in their solemn expressions.

The barber gathered his scissors and combs and hustled out the door to the next group of boys, while I swept up the clumps of hair, loose beads, and broken feathers.

When finished, I leaned the broom in the corner. I heard a few of the boys weeping. "Why are they crying?" I asked Hotah.

Hotah furrowed his brow as he tried to formulate his words. "We cut hair when people die. Very sad."

"Ah, I understand," I said. "Don't be sad. No one has died. You all now have the white man's haircut." With my abundance of red hair and beard, though, I was hardly a good example.

"I will teach boys English," Hotah said.

"Thank you," I said, patting his shoulder. I thought about Mother, who taught me how to read when I was about the same age as these boys. When I didn't know the meaning of a word, she pointed to the biggest book on the shelf and said, "Look it up in the Webster's."

After they wiped away their tears, I needed to get them dressed. The children's new clothes included woolen undergarments, white socks, black pants, and a white shirt—items that I never put much thought into in terms of how to put them on. But the boys, including Hotah, held each piece out in front of them, seemingly confused.

"Let me show you," I said, and proceeded to demonstrate how to put on the white man's clothes.

Ten minutes later, the boys were dressed, causing me to do a double take at their remarkable transformation. At least from their outward appearance, the Carlisle School's mission seemed to be coming to fruition. But there was no denying the torment each boy demonstrated through his furrowed brows and fearful eyes.

I gathered them around in a circle. As they all sat cross-legged on the floor, I began, with Hotah's help, the sharing of basic information. I learned that my group of boys were all of the Lakota peoples from the Dakota states.

In addition to Hotah and Mato, I met Mika, Chatan, Dakotah, Lootah, Teetonka, Wapasha, Chaska, Kangee, Appanoose, and Hanska. Twelve frightened boys sent to a strange land by their families, searching for a new way of life for their people. They had put their trust in Captain Pratt, who promised to transform these young boys into American citizens with equal status to the white man. A tall task indeed.

CHAPTER 5
THE CAPTAIN'S SPEECH

That evening, all one hundred and forty-seven students, ten counselors, eight teachers, four administrators, and six kitchen and grounds staff gathered in the dining hall for the first time. Each group of children took their places at one of the long wooden tables, with the youngest, my boys, sitting closest to the front, where the captain and his administration team sat facing us. Opposite us were the girls in the same age group as my boys. Seated at the head of their table was their counselor, the same blonde-haired young woman I'd gawked at during the first gathering. I would soon learn that her name was Sarah Cameron.

The next set of tables was for the boys and girls aged eight, nine, and ten years; then those aged eleven and twelve; and those aged thirteen and fourteen. Lastly sat Father's boys, the fifteen-year-olds, and a few older.

It was quite a sight: the assembly dressed in their black and white school uniforms, with the boys donning the white man's haircut, and the girls' coifs trimmed to a respectable length, falling just below their shoulders.

"May I have your attention," Captain Pratt said, standing before the students, his arms outstretched.

My boys sat in silence, some of them with their heads looking at their folded hands resting on the table. Others stared out the window, longing to be far away from here. I waved my hands and pointed, trying to get them to pay attention to the tall, gray-haired man towering over them.

"I would like to welcome you all to the Carlisle Indian School. I know most of you don't understand a word I'm saying, but you will soon, as we intend to teach you the only language you ever need to know in our country—the English language. For those who do understand, please share what I'm about to say with your fellow students." He paused a moment while a buzz of conversations circulated throughout the hall.

"Let me begin by saying it is a great mistake to think that you were born savages, as many white men claim. In my opinion, you were all born a blank slate, just like the rest of us. But," he said, holding up a finger, "growing up in the surroundings of savagery, you have learned to possess a savage language, a savage superstition, and a savage way of life, while we white people, who have lived in the surroundings of civilization, have been exposed to a civilized language, and a civilized life with a purpose. I suppose if we could, as an experiment, transfer the white infant into your savage surroundings, then that child would certainly grow up inheriting the same savage traits you all emulate."

I glanced at my sweet-looking boys and had a hard time thinking of them as inhuman, savage beasts.

The captain continued. "Carlisle will instill within each of you a spirit of loyalty to our great country, and then move you out into our communities and show the world, by how you conduct yourself, that the Indian is no different from the white man and is entitled to the same inalienable rights, liberties, and opportunities.

"Here at Carlisle," the captain said, sweeping his arm across his body, "you will learn that you are all capable human beings, and once provided with the proper tools to assert yourselves in a positive and productive way, will find the path to being truly civilized."

He stopped and looked at the boys seated at my table, then said, "I have spoken with the great Chief American Horse and have told this remarkable man that his name is praised across our country as the great leader of his people. Yet American Horse cannot read or write. He claimed to me that our government tricked his people by placing the boundaries of their reservation far off the lines they thought they had agreed to. I rebutted his complaint by saying if he had an education, he would have understood the documents he put his mark upon. I asked American Horse if he intends to allow his children to remain under the same conditions of ignorance in which he had lived, or will he allow them to learn and participate in the great American story?"

I looked over to Hotah, who among my boys had an inkling of understanding the captain's speech. Hotah offered me a smile and a nod, which I returned.

"I am confident," the captain said, looking out onto the audience, most of whom couldn't understand one word, "that with the staff and resources we have at here the Carlisle Indian School, we will succeed in killing the savage within you, and birthing a civilized, productive, and patriotic boy or girl."

CHAPTER 6
SARAH

Sarah Cameron and I often sat together watching our groups play on the Great Lawn. I doubt I would have ever met, or even spoken to, a woman like Sarah, had we not been colleagues at Carlisle. The people I knew before I was involved with the school were mostly neighbors I grew up with, all boring, and none who carried themselves with such confidence or had such exquisite beauty.

Sarah was so lovely that during our conversations, I would often lose myself in her sparkling blue eyes. When able to focus, I understood she came from Sporting Hill, a small town about two hours to the east. The town was famous for being the location of the northernmost battle of the Civil War, where General Lee's army had engaged in a short skirmish during the Gettysburg campaign.

Sarah went to Teacher's College in Harrisburg, not far from the synagogue Mother and I attended during holidays. She earned a degree that qualified her to get a job in education and heard about the Carlisle Indian School from her uncle, who was friendly with Captain Pratt.

"They offered me a better salary than the school in Sporting Hill," she said.

I speculated on what the captain was paying Sarah as a qualified teacher, compared to me, a simple carpenter standing in as a temporary hire. I assumed being a man, I was making more, but I never got the nerve to ask.

Whereas I lacked in boldness, Sarah excelled. She had no problem asking me personal or difficult questions. She would lean in, study me with her engaging eyes—as I all but gaped at her white, flawless skin, and her golden, sun-drenched blonde hair—and ask, "What was it like watching your mother die? How come your father never speaks to anyone? What do you want to do with your life?"

I did my best to answer, but then she would immediately follow up with more probing questions, which I found difficult and sometimes painful to even consider.

She enlightened me about the importance of something called *self-reflection.* "It's an internal way of dealing with bad things that occurred in your life," she explained.

Even with her education and confidence, Sarah faced the same challenges in disciplining the children that we all did. For example, when the children spoke in their native tongues, the counselors were instructed to insist that they only speak English. The captain said that any transgression, no matter how insignificant, must be punished by a spanking with one of the wooden paddles.

On the walls of the barracks hung four paddles, arranged in size order. The smallest paddle was twelve inches long and intended for minor offenses, like forgetting to speak English. As the offenses became more egregious, larger paddles were employed.

The fourteen-inch paddle was for such things as not keeping a bed made properly, or leaving a cubby disorganized. If a child was belligerent with a counselor, the eighteen-inch paddle would come down from the wall. The largest paddle was twenty inches long and used for major infractions, like stealing or causing physical harm to a fellow student.

During the first few weeks, I could have used the smallest of the paddles several times, but I had no desire to inflict corporal punishment—maybe because my father had never once raised a hand to me. Luckily, my boys were mostly well-behaved, and if they occasionally strayed, I would point with an outstretched arm at the objects of discipline hanging on the wall and warn them—*Don't you make me use a paddle on you.* Just the threat stopped them cold—at least so far.

During one of our first days, while the children played together on the Great Lawn, Sarah asked if I had trouble assigning the boys their American names. I shook my head and said, "I think they liked picking them out."

"I doubt that, Leo," Sarah said, with a twist of her full lips. "How would you feel if you were told your name was no longer Leopold Wolf?"

"That's true," I said with a grimace. "I guess I'm trying to look for anything positive."

"What about the sons of the chiefs?" she asked. "How did they react?"

"Well, Hotah looked up at me for a moment, which gave me pause, knowing his birth name had special meaning. But he just pointed to the blackboard and selected the name Samuel. So now he's known as Samuel American Horse. Taking his father's name as his last."

"At least that's a consolation," Sarah said with a shrug.

I sighed and said, "Hopefully they'll find their way of assimilating into the American culture, as the captain is insisting upon."

Sarah shook her head. "It's going to be hard. Being away from one's mother at any age can be psychologically debilitating, especially for the younger ones."

I tugged on my beard and nodded.

She raised a finger and whispered, "There's no doubt, Leo—within each of these children, there's a storm brewing. It's only a matter of time before we see it manifest itself into something ugly."

Chapter 7
School Life

"It's like being back in the damn army," Father would often complain.

In a way, he was right. Though I'd never served in the military, I could assume he was referring to how we organized our groups, with the counselors acting like officers. Each morning a bugle call awoke us at six. The children had fifteen minutes to wash up and dress in their uniforms. Then, in height order, the boys lined up and I would lead them out the door and onto the Great Lawn to where the school assembled facing the flagpole. We would then, in unison, pledge our allegiance to the flag and listen to the captain announcing the day's events before we marched single file into the dining hall.

After breakfast concluded, each child cleaned off their tray and headed to classes that consisted of reading, writing, and arithmetic for both the boys and girls. After lunch, the children were separated. The boys were taught useful crafts, such as carpentry, tinsmithing, and blacksmithing, while the girls spent their afternoons learning cooking, sewing, laundry, and childcare.

Father and I taught the carpentry class, where I was able to meet and interact with the older boys. It was also a way for me to observe the challenges of keeping them in order, as compared to the younger ones.

My boys were at least frightened enough by the prospect of being spanked by the paddles to behave as asked, whereas the teenage boys seemed to dare us to use the paddles on them. That was why for more serious infractions, such as fighting or stealing, they were spared the paddles and, instead, confined to the stockade, an ancient stone building with barred windows that was built for prisoners during the Revolutionary War.

There was one boy in Father's group who was constantly troublesome and a frequent visitor to the stockade. His American name was Tom. I'll never forget the day he arrived. It was the first significant snowfall of the winter. I was outside with the boys while they played in the freshly fallen snow when I heard a wagon approaching, its wheels crunching a path in the snow and ice along the road leading to the school. The moment before it came to a complete stop, out jumped Tom. Actually, he wasn't Tom yet. He was still the Navajo warrior Bidziil.

Up until that day, I had never met anyone who came close to matching Father's physique. While only fifteen years old, the Navajo seemed to be a few inches taller and about ten pounds heavier, due to his abundance of muscle. Everyone out on the Great Lawn that day stopped and stared.

Draped around his impressive, wide shoulders was a traditional Navajo coat embellished with geometric designs, and a black leather belt pinched at his waist. Each step he made in his fur boots was deliberate and purposeful. But most impressive was his long, shiny, beautiful black hair, falling halfway down his back.

He was ushered into Father's barrack and the next time we saw him was that night at dinner. I couldn't stop gawking at his transformation, which was remarkable as well as disturbing. His divine locks were cut off, and he was stripped of his golden earrings, beaded necklaces, and native clothing. But as we would soon learn, altering his outward appearance could not tame his inner torment. From that day forward, he was known as Tom, but we all knew that behind the scowl and fierce eyes was the untamable warrior Bidziil.

*

Each night, after the boys settled into their beds, I allowed a brief time for conversation before announcing *all quiet*. Most nights, they quickly nodded off to sleep, after which I was able to read.

Sarah had lent me textbooks from the classes she taught to her students at Carlisle. While Mother taught me many things and provided me with a wide assortment of books to read, I never learned the fundamentals children learned in school. So, by candlelight each evening, as the children slept, I read.

Occasionally, I would get a visit from one of the boys who awoke and needed to go to the outhouse. During the winter months, this would require both of us dressing for the cold, and then my waiting outside until they finished.

One evening, I lay awake reading *The Last of the Mohicans* by James Fenimore Cooper. It was about the French and Indian wars and its hero, a scout named Hawkeye. I was so enthralled with the adventure that I didn't notice Samuel standing at the foot of my bed.

Samuel whispered, "What you reading?"

By now, after several weeks of immersion into the English language, my boys were speaking fairly well. Samuel, with the head start he'd had, was nearly fluent.

"I didn't see you standing there. Do you need to go?" I asked, pointing in the direction of the outhouse.

"I already went."

"You're supposed to go with me, not alone," I whispered.

Samuel shrugged. "I always go alone."

"I guess you do, since I don't remember ever taking you," I said with a smirk.

Samuel nodded and said, "I think I can handle it."

"I'm sure you can. But if you get caught outside without me, I will need to give you a paddle."

He scoffed and said, "Then I'll make sure I don't get caught."

I shook my head and smiled.

"What you reading?" Samuel asked again, cocking his chin toward me.

"What *are* you reading," I corrected him.

He rolled his eyes and said, "What *are* you reading?"

I waved him closer as I swung my legs to the side of my bed so he could sit alongside me. "It's called *The Last of the Mohicans*," I said, handing him the book.

"Looks good," he said, looking at the illustration of the Indian on the cover.

"Once your reading improves, you can borrow it."

Samuel shook his. "Why would I want to read a made-up story? I am son of Chief American Horse. There is nothing in there that can match Father as a great warrior."

"Can I ask you something?" I said, taking the book and placing it behind me. "Do you know why your father sent you here?"

Samuel frowned and tilted his head as he looked at me. "He believes he will be the last chief of our tribe and the time has come for the white man to rule our lands. Father says I will never be chief," he said, with tears welling up.

"I'm sorry, Samuel," I said and put my arm around his shoulder. "We live in a time of great change."

Samuel rested his head on my shoulder and his tears released.

"You must never forget that you come from a line of warriors, great men, great chiefs," I said. "It's in your blood. They can take your name, your hair, and your clothing, but they can never take away who you are."

Samuel looked at me, his cheeks wet with tears, and offered me a pained smile.

CHAPTER 8
INDIAN ROCK

On one of the first warm days in early April, I took my morning break with a walk into the woods surrounding the school. In the middle of a clearing sat a boulder as big as the storage shed. My boys named it Indian Rock, as a way to claim it as their own.

I climbed up and sat upon its peak, allowing the sun's rays to soak into my soul. As I gazed out onto the woods surrounding me, I was excited to see tiny green shoots poking through the forest floor, one of the first signs of spring.

The snowy winter had been long, cold, and tough, with five children from the older groups taken ill with tuberculosis. Dealing with their deaths, along with being away from home, was challenging for my young boys. But I tried my best to comfort them, though their pain was real, and from what I could tell, damaging to their spirits.

Nighttime was especially agonizing, though they did find solace when I read to them. One of their favorites was *The Adventures of Tom Sawyer*. They loved the part when Tom and Huck wandered into a graveyard at night in search of a cure for warts. During their excursion, Tom and Huck witness the murder of Dr. Robinson by Injun Joe. The story takes off from there, as Tom and Huck swear a blood oath never to tell anyone what they have seen.

Luckily, Sarah was able to keep me supplied with ample books to keep the boys entertained. Each night I read to them until nine o'clock, when, according to school rules, they needed to go to sleep—and when the troubles usually began.

It seemed that a few times a week, there was a different boy making his way to my bedside. One of the youngest was William Red Shirt, the son of Chief Red Shirt. William was only seven years old when he arrived at Carlisle, and unlike Samuel American Horse, he was a troubled and easily frightened child.

One night, as the snow swirled and the winds howled, I was awakened by a repetitive poking on my chest. When I opened my eyes I saw, inches away, William's round, brown and frightened eyes.

"What is it, William?" I asked, sitting up.

"I had a dream about Father," he said softly.

The full moon reflected light off the snow and shone into the window by my bed, illuminating William's ashen face.

"Come here," I said, giving him a hug.

He turned his head and whispered into my ear, "Father told me I can never go home."

I grabbed his shoulders and look into his tearful eyes. "It was only a dream, William. You'll go home this summer, like all the children."

William shook his head, opened his eyes wide, and said in a serious tone as if his father spoke the words through him, "No, I am to go to live with a family on a farm for the summer, where I will learn how to grow food."

"I wasn't aware," I said, stroking my beard.

"I don't want to go, Leo," William said, shaking his head.

I shrugged my shoulders, not knowing what to say.

"Can I stay with you?" William said as his small hands curled into fists.

I furrowed my brow. "I don't know, William. This summer I'll be busy with carpentry work for the school."

William pointed at himself and nodded his head. "That's what I want to do. I don't want to be a farmer. Can I be a carpenter and stay with you, please?

"I don't know. But I'll ask the captain. Now go back to your bed," I said.

When I had the opportunity to ask Captain Pratt about keeping William with me for the summer and mentoring him in the carpentry trade, he said he thought it was a good idea, but would need to ask his father, Chief Red Shirt, for permission.

"How would we do that?" I asked.

He pulled a letter from his breast pocket and said, "I just got word that three Lakota chiefs, Red Shirt, American Horse, and Standing Bear, will be visiting us in May. We'll ask him then."

I climbed down from Indian Rock and as I walked back through the woods, I thought about that big day, which was now only a few weeks away. Two of the three chiefs, the fathers of Samuel and William, would be visiting my barrack. Luther, the son of the third chief, Chief Standing Bear, was an eleven-year-old boy in Major Lawrence's barrack.

Major Lawrence was a former Confederate officer. As a military man, he believed wholeheartedly in the captain's regimented style of governing. Because of this, all of the boys in his bunk were petrified of him—all except for Luther Standing Bear, who seemed to thrive on the attention to order and was often seen alongside the major as they marched across the campus while the rest of their group tried to keep up.

Luther Standing Bear became the role model for all the boys to emulate, according to the major, who proclaimed, "He'll make a fine American."

CHAPTER 9
THE NAVAJO

I awoke an hour before the bugle sounded on the day the three Lakota chiefs were to arrive. Meeting one real Indian chief was an exciting thought, but meeting three was creating a buzz between my ears like a hive of agitated bees.

The day before, the captain had spoken to the entire school during lunch about the upcoming visit. "Tomorrow at noon, we're expecting the arrival of three special guests: Chief American Horse, Chief Red Shirt, and Chief Standing Bear. These great chiefs of the Lakota Nation are fathers to Samuel, William, and Luther," he said, pointing to each boy.

I looked at Samuel, who sat tall in his seat, poised, with a plain expression, trying to look undisturbed by the sudden attention. William, who was by my side, blushed and covered his face with his hands. I offered him a smile and put my arm around the shy boy's shoulder.

Luther, sitting at Major Lawrence's table, stood up at the mention of his name, offered the captain a jerky, military-style nod, and sat back down. I looked over to Sarah, who gave me a slight smile and rolled her eyes. She knew that I would need to carry the large load of the next day's event, ensuring the chiefs found their visit worthy of their efforts and their sons well cared for.

The next day's morning classes were canceled in order to prepare the campus. After we spent the first few hours scrubbing floors, washing windows, and dressing the beds to military perfection, we headed outdoors to sweep the grounds for debris.

I had to admit, Carlisle never looked better. When I saw Father outside with his group, picking up trash, we shared a prideful smile. We knew we played a larger role than the rest of the counselors and staff because of our carpentry work.

At noon, all ten groups stood in formation on the Great Lawn in front of the barracks. The boys were neatly dressed in their school uniforms, their hair clean and combed to one side, while the girls wore dresses that reached to their ankles, with their hair brushed and shiny. At least on the surface, the Carlisle School appeared to have indeed killed the Indian in each of these children.

As the bell in the clock tower struck noon, the assembly held its collective breath, as if the wagons would magically appear. We all listened for the sounds of the wheels on the roadway. But as the minutes passed, it was obvious that the caravan of chiefs would be late.

Captain Pratt pulled out his pocket watch and glared at it, then took off his hat to scratch his head. I thought maybe the train bringing the chiefs into the Harrisburg station had been delayed.

We watched as the captain summoned over Abe. He spoke to the boy, who nodded and then ran off to the stables. Moments later, mounted on the horse we called Wili, he galloped down the Great Lawn in between the assembly of the boys and girls. We all stared as Abe held on tight and charged toward town. The children let out a cheer as if the kitchen boy we all knew was about to save the day. As the cheers simmered down, shouts from the far end of the barracks refilled the air.

When I looked down the row, I realized the commotion was coming from Father's group. That was when I saw Tom stumble out into the middle of the Great Lawn, visible to the entire school. He fell to his knees and looked up to the sky with outstretched arms, his hands curled into fists, and shouted what sounded like a prayer in his native language. I had no idea why Tom was upset.

Father appeared. He grabbed Tom by his shirt and pulled him back up to his feet. Tom shoved Father, causing him to stumble backward. Even from where I stood, I could see fear in Father's bulging eyes.

Father steadied himself and then charged into Tom, burying his shoulder into his chest, knocking him off his feet, and slamming him to the ground with a thud. Father jumped on top, trying to pin down his arms. But Tom would have none of that, and bucked like a wild horse, eventually tossing Father off him.

Tom quickly sprang to his feet and attacked with a fury of fists, connecting twice. Father fell back, stunned, but not beaten. He lifted his arms and blocked another battery of punches, then counterattacked, landing a powerful right onto Tom's temple. We all heard the cracking sound as Tom stood frozen, his arms limp at his sides. Then his eyes rolled back in his head, his knees buckled, and he collapsed to the ground.

"Here they come," Abe yelled, as Wili galloped back onto the Great Lawn.

From my vantage point at the far end of the grass, I gawked at Tom's ill-timed outburst and Abe's triumphant return.

Trying to salvage a potentially embarrassing moment with the three chiefs about to arrive, the captain ran over to Father, pointed to the unconscious Tom, and ordered, "Get him inside, Isaac."

I ran over to help Father lift Tom, who had begun to regain consciousness and was able, with our help, to walk. We ushered him inside the barrack just as the wagons pulled onto the school grounds. Father and I guided Tom to his bed, who at this point seemed content to lie down and cause no more trouble, at least for now.

"What happened?" I asked Father.

"Tom is troubled," he said, shaking his head. "Before we gathered on the lawn, I told the boys that this was going to be an exciting day. Then Tom started mumbling something about his father. When I asked him to tell me what was bothering him, he just waved me off."

I took a moment to look at Tom, who was now lying in his bunk, eyes closed. Apparently, the arrival of the three chiefs reminded him of his own father and a disturbing past.

As Father and I walked back outside, I saw the chiefs greeting the captain, and wondered what the rest of the day would offer.

Chapter 10
Three Chiefs

Captain Pratt and the three chiefs, American Horse, Red Shirt, and Standing Bear, paraded down the Great Lawn, while the boys and girls gawked at the magnificently decorated men.

I turned to catch Samuel's reaction to seeing his father for the first time in months. His eyes were locked on Chief American Horse, but his stoic expression betrayed no emotion. William, on the other hand, had no such veil. His mouth hung slightly open as if he was about to call out to his father, Chief Red Shirt, at any moment. His legs bounced, ready to race into his father's arms if summoned.

As for the other children, counselors, teachers, and staff, no one uttered a word. The only sounds were the birds and the sharp wind rustling the American flag perched high above us in the middle of the Great Lawn.

Captain Pratt stopped at the flagpole and looked up. He put his hand over his heart and began the recitation of the Pledge of Allegiance. Just as the first two words were spoken, the assembly joined in—all except for the chiefs, who glanced at each other awkwardly, but out of respect, placed their hands over their hearts as well.

I pledge allegiance to my flag and to the Republic for which it stands, one nation, indivisible, with liberty and justice for all.

As we concluded, the captain spoke to the chiefs while gesturing to my boys and then pointed to Major Lawrence's group. I took a breath as Chief American Horse and Chief Red Shirt approached, while Chief Standing Bear headed over to see his son.

I quickly turned and waved to Samuel and William to stand alongside me. With William on my right and Samuel on my left, I took a breath, trying to calm my nerves, while my heart beat like a war drum against my chest.

"You must be Leopold Wolf," the first chief said, offering his hand to shake.

I nodded and grasped it. As his rough hand squeezed mine, I admired the tall man's headdress. It was made up of hundreds of identical white feathers, their tips accented in dark brown, and hung like a sculpture down to his lower back. He wore this over a plain gray tunic and a brown deer-hide vest adorned with beads sewn in colorful geometric designs.

I swallowed hard, realizing my pause was too long, and said, "Yes, sir, I am Leopold."

"I am Chief American Horse," he said, looking directly into my eyes.

I put my hand over my heart and said, "It's an honor, sir."

The chief nodded and returned the gesture, then turned to his son.

Samuel took a step forward, but his father held his palm out, instructing him to wait. He then stepped aside, allowing Chief Red Shirt to approach.

He was slightly smaller in height, younger and clear-eyed, whereas Chief American Horse showed his age in his weathered skin. Chief Red

Shirt's face was shaven and unblemished. He wore no headdress. Instead, his hair hung in two long braids with feathers skillfully woven into them.

He leaned in and whispered into my ear, "I understand you are a Jew."

I nodded, not knowing what to say.

He pulled back and smiled. "This is good. You will have much to teach my son."

I nodded and glanced down the lawn at the hundreds of pairs of eyes staring at us, until I found Father, who gave me a proud smile.

The chief then turned and looked at William. "Come here, son," he said, reaching out his arms. William leaped into them, and the two of them shared a warm and loving hug. Their affection stirred me to tears.

At the same time, Chief American Horse offered his son a less demonstrative greeting, giving him a gentle pat on the back and a barely perceptible smile. I blew out an all-knowing breath, familiar with the chief's lack of emotion toward his son.

A commotion turned our attention to Chief Standing Bear, who was exchanging sharp words with Major Lawrence. We all hushed to hear.

"What have you done to my son?" the chief barked, inches from the major's face.

"I don't know what you mean, sir," the major said, looking past the chief for the captain.

Captain Pratt moved quickly to the confrontation. "What is it, Chief?" the captain asked.

"My son has been beaten," Chief Standing Bear said, loudly enough for everyone to hear.

The captain quickly herded the chief, Major Lawrence, and Luther back into the barrack and out of sight and earshot from the students, who were now gawking at the dispute.

The captain's assistant, Maggie, wasting no time, took control of the awkward moment and announced, "Okay, let's everyone make our way into the dining hall."

Maggie blew her whistle, which hung off a cord around her neck, as our signal to march in our practiced military fashion. Sarah led her girls to the center of the Great Lawn, turned sharply to her right, and headed for the dining hall. My boys followed the procession as the rest of the barracks formed in rows behind us.

In the meantime, Maggie ran over to the two remaining chiefs, who were left standing alone and obviously confused by the activity. "Captain Pratt will join us in the dining hall soon," Maggie said, trying to sound calm and confident as she escorted the men.

I shifted my eyes to catch a glimpse of Sarah, who gave me a look that most wouldn't recognize as anything, but I knew what she was thinking. The storm we were waiting for had arrived.

CHAPTER 11
MIDNIGHT VISIT

After a tumultuous day, my boys finally settled down and were asleep. I wasn't ready to close my eyes for the night, so I sat on the porch, recalling the day's events. I'd gotten a few moments to speak with Father earlier in the afternoon. He told me that Tom had apologized for his violent outburst. "He's a tormented soul," Father said.

I was surprised at Father's forgiveness. After all, he had been knocked to the ground in front of the entire school. But he seemed compassionate to the teenager's plight and shared the story of Tom's childhood.

As I understood it, Tom's father, Chief Manuelito of the Navajos, tried unsuccessfully to rally his people against the brutal oppression of the United States military, but were eventually forced to leave their lands and relocate to western New Mexico, in a place called the Pecos River Valley. In the spring of 1864, the Navajos were escorted by army soldiers to walk over four hundred miles to their new home. This event became known among his people as the Long Walk.

Tom described the trek as difficult, crossing harsh lands and pushing many of his people to the breaking point, which for many meant death, as the soldiers offered no assistance or sympathy for their plight.

Years later, after continuous struggles and difficulties that included disease and famine, Chief Manuelito learned of the Carlisle Indian School and decided to send his son. He explained to Bidziil, now Tom, that "education was a ladder our people must climb."

Father confided to me, "You must understand what Tom has gone through."

While I contemplated the plight of the Navajo, the clock tower struck the midnight bells, and a shadowy figure appeared out of the darkness. It was Chief Red Shirt.

"Good evening, Leo. I'm happy to see you're still awake," he said.

I shrugged and said, "I couldn't sleep."

The chief stood on the wooden step next to me, exhaled a long breath, and sat down. "Do you know why I sent my son to Carlisle?"

I thought it best to be cautious and not voice my opinion, so I just shook my head.

"My people will inevitably have to deal with the white man, even living among them," he said, sitting down and gesturing to the surroundings as evidence.

I nodded, sighed, and said, "It seems to be so."

"When Captain Pratt came to visit Pine Ridge last spring, I agreed with his reasoning that if we do not prepare our children for the inevitable, we will have no future. Our people will cease to exist."

"What does that mean for William? Will he ever return and become chief after you?"

"With the white man's knowledge, he can take whatever path he chooses, though there may not be much of a tribe to lead," he said, gazing out into the shadows spread across the Great Lawn.

I turned my head to look at the chief and asked, "But what do you want for your son?"

"I want him to have a choice. He may want to return to the reservation, and if he does, he will have the white man's knowledge, which I lacked."

"You are wise, sir," I said and offered a gentle smile.

The chief put his arm around my shoulder and said, "And your wisdom surpasses your age, Leo. My son is fortunate to have you as his counselor."

"Thank you," I said, blushing from the compliment. "William is a good boy and is helpful with the other children. It's obvious he learned a great deal from you."

The chief squeezed my shoulder, pleased with my words, and said, "The man I saw today, who is counselor to the Navajo, I understand he's your father?"

I nodded. "His name is Isaac."

"He'll have a tough time with that boy. When the children are young, like my son, there's less resistance to change, though it's harder on them being away from home."

"That's what Captain Pratt said."

"There's another reason I wanted to speak to you, Leo," he said, lowering his voice.

I leaned in to listen.

"What do you know about Major Lawrence?"

I shrugged. "I know he was an officer in the Confederate army."

"I'm curious. Why would Captain Pratt employ a soldier of the South?"

"From what I heard, the captain's father knew Major Lawrence's father before the war. They met prospecting for gold in California and became friends and business partners. One day, the two men were ambushed and attacked by another prospector after a dispute of a territorial claim. Captain Pratt's father was murdered and afterward the major's father made sure that the Pratt family got their share of the gold. So when the major came looking for a job at Carlisle, the captain felt that he couldn't refuse."

"Captain Pratt is an honorable man. But from what Standing Bear has told me, the major has been beating his boys."

I grimaced and said, "We're supposed to use the paddles when they misbehave."

"I'm not talking about paddles, Leo. He's using fists. I heard that Luther, Standing Bear's son, has bruises covering his body. So do some of the other children."

I nodded, as I, too, had witnessed the effects of Major Lawrence's violent nature. Once, when getting bandages in the infirmary, I had seen Luther shirtless. He had large, black and blue contusions on his upper arm and back.

Red Shirt put his palms together and said, "I have seen men like this before. Just because the war is over, doesn't mean the major can dismiss his hatred or bigotry. I want you to promise that you will watch over my son."

"I will," I said, meaning every word, though I prayed that I would never have to confront the major.

The chief stood up, looked at me one last time, and said, before disappearing into the darkness of the night, "Make sure you do, Leo, before it's too late."

Chapter 12
The Speeches

The first bugle notes of reveille began softly in my dream, but finished like a drill bit burrowing into my skull, forcing my sleep-encrusted eyes to slowly open. I sat up in bed and looked outside as the first rays of morning light illuminated the Great Lawn.

I took a deep breath, exhaled, and rose to my feet. As I walked down the center of the barrack, I noticed the boys seemed to be more talkative than usual. I figured this was because the captain arranged for the three chiefs to observe the student's classes and activities.

"How are you feeling this morning, William?"

William stopped tucking in the ends of his blanket, looked up at me, and shrugged. "Do you think Father is embarrassed by me?"

I ran my finger through my beard and said, "Of course not. He came to see me last night, and we sat on the porch talking about you."

"He did?" William said with his eyes opened wide. "What did you talk about?"

I smiled and said, "He's proud of you for the prospect of leading your people down a new path. Your father understands that takes courage."

William puckered his face and asked, "He thinks I have courage?"

"He does," I said and patted his back. "Come, let's get the boys ready. Today's going to be a big day."

*

With the lunch trays and trash cleared away, the assembly of students was abuzz with excitement for the upcoming speeches by the three Lakota chiefs. Our front-row table put us only a few feet from where the honored guests sat.

During lunch, the boys shared stories of the chiefs visiting their classes. But it was William who was the most excited. "I was standing at the blackboard doing a math problem when Father walked in—"

"Yeah, and I can't believe you got the problem right," yelled Samuel, causing the boys to break out in laughter.

"My hands were shaking so hard, I thought I was going to break the chalk into pieces," William said, as the boys continued their snickers.

"I'm sure your father was proud of you," I assured him.

Just as I was thinking that my boys seemed happy and well-adjusted, the captain stood up, clapped his hands together, and announced, "Students of Carlisle, may I have your attention?"

Like a dark storm cloud passing in front of the sun, silence followed the determined stare of the captain's eyes before he spoke again. He offered a subtle smile, then began. "Good day, students of Carlisle. Many of you have already met our distinguished guests," he said and paused to acknowledge the chiefs sitting alongside him. To his left sat American Horse, one seat over was Red Shirt, and to the captain's right sat Standing Bear.

"One day, when you're older and have children and perhaps grandchildren, you will look back upon your time here at Carlisle and realize you were part of history." He swept his hand across the room and continued, "You're playing a part in this great undertaking of assimilating the native Indian into the American culture. This is a time of great change, and those who do not recognize this reality, or shall I say opportunity, will be left behind, favoring the wrong side of history."

There was a buzz of commotion at the captain's remarks. A few moments later, he held up his hands to silence the assembly, gestured to the chiefs, and said, "These men here, these great chiefs of the Lakota Nation, understand this. That is why they have sent their sons to our school."

I glanced over to Samuel, who straightened his spine at the captain's words as if he anticipated the eyes of his fellow students to fall upon him. At the same time, William slouched in his chair. I twisted around to find Luther, who sat stoically, staring ahead.

"Students of Carlisle," the captain continued, "when our next speaker was only ten years old, he had herded several ponies to water when he realized he had been spotted by three bloodthirsty Crow warriors. Cleverly, he used his ponies as a diversion by sending them down their familiar path back home, while he hid in a thicket of willows. The Crows stole the ponies but could not find the young brave, who waited until morning before returning home, much to the delight of his worried mother."

A chuckle of laughter from the younger children interrupted the captain's story.

"This boy grew up, became a great warrior among his Lakota people, and soon became chief. He fought bravely and with honor at the Battle of Little Big Horn during the Great Sioux War of 1876." The captain paused a moment to allow the anticipation to build. "He strongly believes in our mission here at Carlisle, so much so that he has sent his own flesh and blood, his son, Samuel, into our care. Children, counselors, and staff, allow me to introduce Lakota chief and statesman—American Horse."

My boys applauded vigorously, and Samuel, as much as he tried, couldn't hold back a smile. The chief rose and stood before the assembly.

Even without the headdress he'd worn upon his arrival, his image was still proudly presented in his traditional Lakota elk-hide shirt that ended at his knees. Across his shoulders were geometric patterns woven upon a ground of turquoise beads. Loose brown fringe adorned his sleeves and the bottom of his shirt, which fell over buckskin boots.

I looked over to my boys, who expressed their confusion with pursed lips and furrowed brows. At that moment, I realized that even though their traditional way of life was coming to an end, the school's mission of "killing the Indian" could never erase what these magnificent men once represented.

Chief American Horse gazed out among the nearly two hundred pairs of eyes glued upon him and put his hand over his heart, acknowledging the honor of their attention. He looked at his son and offered a momentary smile, and then to me, where he finished with a brief nod.

"Students, faculty, staff, and Captain Pratt, thank you for allowing me to address you here today at the Carlisle Indian School," the chief began.

He then walked around to the front of the table where Captain Pratt, Red Shirt, and Standing Bear remained seated. American Horse stood so close to me that I had to look straight up from my chair to see his face, and to my surprise, he placed a hand on my shoulder as he spoke.

"When Captain Pratt came to visit with me last year, the Congress of the United States of America had decided just a few months earlier to divide up the remaining areas of the Great Sioux Reservation into five separate reservations. When I and my fellow chiefs realized what had been done to the lands, where our people have lived for many generations, we felt angry and betrayed."

The chief looked out at the audience, allowing his eyes to express the emotions behind his words. I recalled the captain's explanation to the senator that the chiefs felt deceived into signing the treaty and giving up their lands.

"But this was not the fault of the government; it was my fault, it was our fault." He paused and nodded to the chiefs seated behind him. "It was because we couldn't read or write English that we signed an agreement hurting our people. We have no one to blame but ourselves."

This moment of sadness shared by the chiefs produced an audible sigh of sorrow that washed across the room. American Horse then raised his hand with a finger pointing into the sky and said, "That is why I decided to listen to Captain Pratt and send my son Samuel to Carlisle, where he will be educated to—"

"That's enough!" a voice shouted from the far side of the hall.

I turned at the sudden outburst and saw Tom standing on top of a table. He towered over the assembly with pulsating veins bulging from his forehead, displaying an anger that seemed to stifle the breeze blowing between the open windows.

"These are lies and bogus claims," he said, pointing a finger at American Horse.

Father stood up and said, "Come down from there right now."

Tom ignored him and stepped further down the long table. Father followed, reaching out, trying to grab onto his arm. When Tom reached the end, he leaped onto the next table, where Major Lawrence sat with his boys.

"Tom, do not move!" the captain commanded.

My boys gawked, seemingly confused at Tom's outburst. I, too, tried to make sense of it. Could it be that Tom was upset by Chief American Horse taking blame for the white man's brutality? This was a justified argument to make, though not in the way Tom had offered.

"I do not recognize this name—Tom. My name is Bidziil, warrior of the great Navajo Nation." He raised his fists into the air and said, "You can cut my hair, take away my clothing, but you cannot take away the generations of great warriors who have come before me."

With that, Father surprised Tom by grabbing his hand, and, with a strong pull, yanked him from the table. Tom fell hard. Major Lawrence pounced on top of him to help, and between them, they pinned him to the ground.

These two men were too much for Tom, and he relented. He allowed Father and the major to lift him to his feet and escort him out of the dining hall and into the stockade.

Chapter 13
Abraham Lincoln

Abraham Lincoln was born on April 9, 1865, the same day the war against slavery ended. His mother, Alice, told me that she and her late husband, Luther, who was killed on the battlefield just a month earlier, decided to name their unborn child after the sixteenth president of the United States.

Abe and I became close, even though I was ten years his elder. Though he was a Negro and I was white, we had things in common. We both lost a parent to the war—and we were both sensitive to the plight of the native children enrolled at Carlisle. Our friendship developed during our mutually free time on Wednesday mornings after the boys were sent off to their classes.

On one of those days, we made plans to meet at Indian Rock. I arrived before Abe and was looking forward to seeing him.

As I reached the top of the rock, I saw him walking down the trail. I waved, sat down, pulled my knees to my chest, and waited for him to join me.

"Good morning, Leo," he said, climbing up the rock.

"Good morning," I said, reaching out and grasping his hand to pull him up. "I guess things will go back to normal with the chiefs gone."

Abe sat down and shook his head. "I don't know about that. Last night at the captain's home, we had quite a showdown."

"What happened?"

"You know that Standing Bear had words with Major Lawrence about him beating his son?"

I nodded. "Yes, the entire school heard him yelling at the major."

"Well, last night during the farewell dinner, they had it out."

"The major and the chief?"

Abe nodded. "It started off cordially, but when the captain asked for the whiskey to be poured, that's when the trouble began."

I hugged my knees tighter in anticipation of the fascinating details.

Abe continued, "The three chiefs sat side by side facing the captain and the major. I stood by the serving station, holding the carafe with the whiskey, ready to top off their glasses. After their third toast, the major raised his glass and said, *Here's to the Carlisle School and preparing the children for the future.* Everyone lifted their glass except Standing Bear. Instead, he pointed his finger at the major and said, *Why is this man here, Captain?* I watched the major's face turn as red as an apple. The captain put his glass down and said, *Come on now, Chief, the war has been over for fifteen years.* Standing Bear shook his head and said, *The war may be over, but that did nothing to dampen this man's hatred.* The chief rose from his chair, still holding his glass filled with whiskey, and with a flick of his wrist, doused the major's face in its contents, and said, *If you touch my son again, you and I will have more than just words to share.* The major jumped to his feet, knocking over his chair, and shouted, *How dare you!* I watched the chief's hand slide down to his knife, sheathed at his belt. The captain quickly rose to his feet, raised his arms, and said, *Gentlemen, let's calm down.* Standing Bear pulled his knife and pointed it at the major and then at the captain, and he said, *If I learn of one more incident, I will insist on you removing this man from Carlisle.* The major leaned across the table and said, *How dare you threaten me?* The captain turned to American Horse and asked him if he would take Standing Bear outside, which he did."

"This is unbelievable," I said. "Then what happened?"

"American Horse tried settling down Standing Bear," Abe explained. "And once the major retired to his bunk for the evening, the three chiefs spoke with the captain."

"What was said?" I asked.

"Standing Bear remained adamant about dismissing the major, but Captain Pratt explained he hadn't enough counselors and couldn't afford to lose even one. He actually made the point by you and your father, saying how he needed to hire carpenters to fill the ranks."

"He said that?" I asked, raising my eyebrows.

Abe nodded. "But Red Shirt said that if the counselors were half as good as you," Abe said, pointing at me, "Carlisle would be lucky."

I smiled. "Really?"

"It's true," Abe said, nodding.

"Thank you," I said. "But what about Standing Bear?"

"He eventually calmed down but left the captain with a warning: that if his son was ever beaten again, he would need to deal with the major in the traditional Lakota way. The captain said he understood and assured him that his son's safety and well-being would be his priority."

I shook my head and said, "I have a feeling that until the major is gone from here, there will be more trouble."

Abe nodded and said, "It's only the beginning, I'm afraid."

*

Later that day, after teaching woodworking class with Father, I caught up with Sarah walking up to her barrack. I hurried to catch her and asked, "How are your history lessons going?"

"Oh, hi, Leo," she said, her golden hair cascading into a swirl as spun around to greet me. "It's fine. Today we began our studies on the American Revolutionary War."

"That sounds interesting," I said wide-eyed, trying to drink in every nuance of her. "I wish I could sit in."

"Oh, are you interested in history?" she asked with a dimple-laden smile.

I wanted to say I was interested in everything she had to offer, but instead, I curbed my enthusiasm. "I am. Perhaps you can teach me privately," I said, feeling my cheeks blush.

"Privately?" Sarah repeated, raising an eyebrow.

I giggled and nodded.

"I'd love to," Sarah said, surprising me. With that, clutching her books in her crossed arms, she spun around and headed into her barrack.

Later that night, while the boys slept, I imagined Sarah sitting with me on Indian Rock. She would speak to me about the war against the British, while I sat mesmerized, hanging on every word. When she stopped, I would thank her for the wonderful lesson and ask if she would allow me to kiss her. Of course, in my mind, she agreed, and with my eyes shut, we kissed for hours.

59

My fantasy came to an abrupt end when a finger poked me in my chest. I opened my eyes and saw William staring at me. "I need to go," he said.

CHAPTER 14
RETURN OF THE SENATOR

As the semester drew to a close, William asked again about doing carpentry work with me over the summer months. When the captain first broached the idea with his father during his visit, Chief Red Shirt said he would think about it.

"Will you ask again?" William pleaded one Sunday afternoon while the boys were swimming in the pond.

I told him I had a meeting with the captain the next day to discuss my performance over the past year and perhaps that would be a good time.

"Thank you, Leo," William said and ran back to swim with his friends while I sat with Sarah on the grass watching the children.

"He's such a sweet boy," Sarah said, smiling as our boys and girls swam together in the pond.

"I do hope he can stay with me this summer," I said, picking up a few pebbles and tossing them into the water.

"I can't believe the school year is almost over," Sarah said.

I nodded and asked, "Do you have plans for the summer?"

"Well, I've been meaning to talk to you. I have an opportunity for an internship with my uncle in Washington."

"Your uncle?"

"Yes, I believe you met him last summer. Do you remember Senator Cameron? He's a good friend of Captain Pratt. That's how I got the job."

I tilted my head and looked at Sarah. "The senator is your uncle?"

"You didn't know?"

I shook my head. "I had no idea."

"Yes, he's my father's brother. I've been living with him and my aunt in Sporting Hill ever since the death of my parents."

"Sarah!" I said, putting my hand to my mouth. "I had no idea. I'm so sorry. Can I ask what happened?"

She sighed and said, "It happened eight years ago. They got caught in a shootout between the police and a gang robbing the Harrisburg National Bank. They were gunned down right in the street."

"That's awful," I said, shaking my head and reaching out to grasp her hand.

Sarah squeezed mine and nodded. "Thank you, Leo."

"Do you have any brothers or sisters?"

She shook her head. "I'm an only child."

"That must have been so hard for you," I said, keeping hold of her hand for another moment.

"It was, and still is at times," she said, looking out onto the pond. "But over the years, I've learned to manage with the grief."

"How's it been, living with your aunt and uncle?"

"Interesting," she said with a shrug. "My aunt is wonderful, but my uncle is always busy, as you can imagine. He's coming here on our last day of school and taking me with him back to Washington to work as his intern. Maybe if you get some time off, you can come visit me."

I felt myself blush at the overture. But I figured her offer was meant out of friendship and nothing more. Just then, as I was feeling a closeness to Sarah that I'd never known before, the major arrived with his boys.

I jerked my head, directing Sarah's attention to his presence. She rolled her eyes, reflecting my feelings for the man. We continued our conversation about the summer. Without so much as a hello, the major stepped right up to where we were sitting and said, "I see you two are becoming good friends."

I looked over to Sarah, then looked up to the major standing above us, and nodded. "Yes, Major, we are. Why do you ask?"

He crossed his arms over his chest and pursed his lips and said, "No reason."

I shrugged and held my tongue, though his remark caused me to wonder if the major had intentions of pursuing Sarah. Not that I was worried. Surely Sarah wanted nothing to do with the man. I stood up, gave him a sideways glance, and offered my hand to help Sarah rise from the ground. "Well, the pond is all yours, Major. Boys, it's time to go," I shouted.

"Come, girls, you too," Sarah called. "Quickly now."

I gave the major a brief smirk and a nod as we departed back up the path toward the school.

"You need to watch yourself with him, Leo," Sarah murmured. "Don't underestimate what that man is capable of."

"Ah, he's just full of bluster. I'm not worried."

Sarah stopped walking, gazed hard into my face, and said, "Don't be a fool. That man is capable of bad things, Leopold Wolf."

"All right, Sarah Cameron," I said with a smile, and for the first time realized that she and Senator Cameron had the same last name.

On the second to last day of classes, I received word from the captain that Chief Red Shirt had agreed to allow William to stay the summer with Father and me. Father wasn't in favor of the idea, but I promised to take care of the boy and assured him he wouldn't be a bother at all. Needless to say, William was ecstatic.

Also that day, Senator Donald Cameron was scheduled to arrive and address the full school assembly. This would be the last time I would see Sarah until the start of the fall semester. Besides Abe, she had become my closest friend, and I would miss her.

I let my imagination run wild once again, picturing myself taking her up on the invitation to visit her in Washington. Maybe this was her way of reaching out to me in hope of starting a romance, but I quickly dismissed it as far-fetched. For such a beautiful woman, with golden blonde hair, crystal blue eyes, and skin as fair as a flower petal, to be attracted to a tall, skinny Jewish boy with no future prospects, except as a simple carpenter, was unthinkable.

*

The captain stood before the assembly and smiled. Alongside him sat Senator Cameron, who was dressed in a buttoned-up black suit jacket, a crisp white shirt, and a black bowtie. His bushy, white mustache covered his entire upper lip. I imagined he looked the part of a United States Senator, not that I ever met any other senator to compare him to. I glanced over to Sarah, who kept her gaze focused on her uncle.

Captain Pratt took a deep breath, exhaled, and said, "Students, counselors, teachers, and staff of Carlisle, welcome to the final assembly of our inaugural year. I am proud to say—job well done."

Vigorous applause from nearly two hundred pairs of hands echoed throughout the cavernous dining hall.

"But before we bid our farewells to one another, I would like to introduce our illustrious special guest speaker," he said, and glanced over to the senator. "Four years ago, President Grant appointed him to his cabinet as Secretary of War, where he had to contend with a long list of challenges. The first one was from the southern states that threatened to secede from the Union for the second time. Next was in the summer of 1876, when the Great Sioux War took place that forever changed the future of the Lakota Nation."

I had no idea that the senator, while acting as Secretary of War, was in charge of the soldiers that defeated the Lakota tribes, forcing them to sign those controversial land treaties.

The captain continued, "The following year, in March of 1877, Senator Simon Cameron resigned and was succeeded by his son—Donald Cameron, and then in the fall of 1878, Donald was duly elected, by the people of our great state of Pennsylvania, to the United States Senate."

Another scattering of applause rang through the hall, until the captain held up his hands asking for silence and said, "Before we give a warm Carlisle School welcome, let me add that we are also fortunate to have the senator's niece as one of our counselors—Sarah Cameron."

I looked over to Sarah, who was blushing a pretty shade of deep tomato red. She offered a smile and a nod at the acknowledgment.

"Students, counselors, staff, and friends, let's offer our warmest, heartfelt greeting to the senator from Pennsylvania—Donald Cameron!"

It's not a stretch to say that the applause was less than enthusiastic for the man. Especially after the captain's introduction describing him as the one responsible for tens of thousands of dead Indians and the subsequent defeat of their tribes in the Lakota wars. But the senator rose and responded as if he was being cheered wildly. I imagined that was a sign of a polished politician being able to carry on in the face of a public snubbing.

"Thank you, students of Carlisle," he began. "When Captain Pratt first approached me about the idea of this school for Indians, I thought it to be a questionable venture at best."

As the senator spoke, my mind drifted from his words, which seemed a replay of what I had already heard many times before. Instead, my attention focused on Sarah. I couldn't help myself from staring. The way she gently placed her elbow on the table with her hand under her chin sent a rush of warmth through me. She was not only the loveliest woman I'd known, but in some ways, she also reminded me of my mother. The way she seemed attentive to my well-being, her remarkable intellect, and her always wanting me to further my education. There was no doubt that I was in love with her.

But with summer now upon us, and our departure just hours away, I would have no chance to act upon my yearnings. I would need to wait until the autumn, and in the meantime, to be content with my dreams and to search for ways to suppress my desires.

Chapter 15
The Long Walk

William and I stood on the lawn, waving our farewells to the last wagon of children as they departed. Some were heading back home, while others were destined for the Carlisle Summer Outing Program. This program was arranged for the students to work in people's homes as domestic servants, on farms as hands, or, like William, as apprentices in a business like ours—Wolf and Son Woodworking.

A few of the older children were sent to summer camp in the forest north of Carlisle, to a place called Tagg's Run. From what we were told, the students would live in tents there and be required to hunt and gather for their food. This sounded to me like a pleasant summer for those teenagers longing for their former way of life.

I put my arm around William's shoulder, gave him a squeeze, and said, "Let's go to the house."

With the barracks closed for the summer, the plan was for William to stay with Father and me. I had set up a bed for him in my room and was looking forward to his companionship. After spending ten months living with William, waking with him every morning, and comforting him during those dark and scary homesick nights, he looked up to me like a son would to a father, and I have to admit that I developed an affection for the boy, and would without a doubt protect him from harm.

"Do you live far?" William asked me, grunting with the effort of carrying his belongings.

"No, it's only a few minutes' walk. Are your things too heavy? Would you like me to help?"

"I've got it," he said, giving his blanket and pillow an extra squeeze to prove his point.

When we arrived, I saw Father on the front porch repairing a railing that had split from the ice creeping into the cracks during the winter. I stopped dead in my tracks when I saw another man working alongside him.

"Tom, what are you doing here?" I asked. Both men were shirtless and displayed the muscular physiques that the Almighty must have intended for men to look like when He created them.

"Good morning, Leo. Hello there, William," Tom said, in a surprisingly jovial manner.

"Hi, Tom," William said, excited at the Navajo's greeting.

"What's going on?" I asked Father as I stepped onto the porch.

Father stood up, wiped the sweat off his forehead with a cloth he pulled from his pocket, and said, "Tom is staying with us for the summer."

I looked at Tom, who was at times as aloof as Father, then over to William, who offered a big smile that displayed the gap of his missing front teeth. I shrugged my shoulders, gave William a gentle push to encourage him to step forward, and we entered the house, leaving Father and Tom to their work.

*

We started the summer with plenty to do. Father was right about Tom. Having someone to match his strength was useful, especially for the work on two new barracks that Captain Pratt hired us to construct. Apparently, there would be more students coming to Carlisle in the fall, and the current facilities needed to be expanded.

While Father and Tom worked on framing the large structures, William and I focused on constructing beds and cubicles. Even though he was only eight years old, he enjoyed the work, never uttered a complaint, and became a good assistant.

A few weeks into the summer season, after a full day's work in the blazing sun, all four of us sat on the front porch enjoying the cool breeze blowing in from the west. Rumbles of thunder told us a storm was coming, a welcome relief.

I turned and smiled at Father, who was sitting in his favorite chair. Alongside him was Tom, leaning against a post that supported the eave over the porch. I sat on the front step with William alongside me.

Tom was the only other person I knew who spoke less than Father. That was why, when he decided to share his life's most significant event, we were all taken aback.

As the thunder approached and lightning streaked across the summer sky, Tom offered, without provocation, the tragic story of his people.

I leaned back and asked, "Do you mean the Long Walk?"

Tom nodded and took a seat next to Father, while William and I sat cross-legged on the wooden deck of the front porch.

Tom offered a slight smile before he began. "My story actually started a few years before my birth. Like so many of the native nations across this country, we were invaded by the white man looking to push us off our ancestral lands. This, as you could imagine, led to violent conflicts, first with the settlers, and eventually against the United States Army."

As Tom spoke, I noticed he was more thoughtful than he portrayed himself as the angry Navajo warrior—Bidziil.

"To end the fighting, the army forced my people off our homeland. This happened during the dead of winter in 1864, when Mother, who was pregnant with me, marched along with eight thousand of our people under the escort of the army, over three hundred miles to a place along the Pecos River in New Mexico called the Bosque Redondo Reservation. This was where the army had an outpost called Fort Sumner. Over two hundred Navajo died of starvation or exposure to the cold."

I lifted my hand to interrupt Tom and asked, "The army did nothing to help your people?"

Tom shook his head. "My father, Chief Manuelito, was sickened by the treatment from the soldiers. When halfway through the journey Mother went into labor with me, he insisted we stop and allow her to give birth. The soldiers refused, saying the caravan must proceed. Father told the heartless soldiers that he would stay behind to attend to his wife and would catch up."

"Your father delivered you? How did you all survive?" I asked, spellbound by Tom's story.

"My father was not only chief, he was also a medicine man, experienced in childbirth. As the caravan and soldiers disappeared into the forest, Father found an outcropping of rocks offering a stone overhang for shelter, and built a *hogan*, a sacred home of the Navajo people, for Mother to give birth in. With a campfire and an ample supply of water from a nearby river, I was born. Father and Mother agreed on naming me Bidziil, which means—*He is strong.*"

I smiled and nodded, thinking how well his birth name suited him.

"Would you prefer to be addressed as Bidziil or Tom?" I asked.

Tom tilted his head and furrowed his forehead. "I think while I am here at the Carlisle School, I will be Tom. When this is over and I return to my people, then I will be Bidziil once more."

"Tom?" William interrupted with pursed lips.

"What is it, William?"

"Why would the warrior Bidziil come to Carlisle?"

Tom nodded and said, "You are a wise little brave to ask this question."

A toothless smile spread across William's face.

"Not all battles are fought by the fist. A warrior's strength comes from here," he said, pointing to his forehead. "As Father taught me— *Education is the ultimate power.*"

Father stood up from his chair, took a step toward the railing, turned around, and said, "You've come a long way since your words in front of the school when you shouted about cutting your hair and taking away your clothes, but never taking away the real you."

"And I meant every word, Isaac. Nothing has changed. I've just decided to honor the decision of my father. It's the way of the warrior."

"Is your father dead?" asked William meekly.

Tom nodded. "He died the day I left for Carlisle."

"What happened?" I asked.

The few tears that flowed down Tom's face before were just a prelude to what followed. He was barely able to speak as emotion choked his words. "I believe he died of sadness. It was too much, seeing the death of our way of life."

I stood up and sat myself next to the large young man, reached my long skinny arm around his bulky shoulders, and said, "I'm sorry, Tom."

"Father's last words to me were, *Go to the white man and learn. Then when you're ready, return and take your place as chief of our people.*" We all sat in silence as Tom straightened his spine and took in a deep breath to compose himself. "I will fulfill that final wish of the Great Chief Manuelito."

I stared at Tom and wondered if the crossing of our paths was a coincidence, or if the Almighty had placed Tom, or should I say Bidziil, in my life for a purpose.

Chapter 16
Chief Red Shirt

I was surprised when, during an overcast morning as Father and Tom were shingling the roof and William and I were adding a few finish details to the new barrack's interior, Captain Pratt stopped by. While a visit from him wasn't unusual, what he had to say to me was.

The clomping of his boots on the newly laid wooden floor brought my attention to his presence. "Leo, I need you and William to come with me right away."

I looked over to William, whose goggling eyes mirrored my reaction to the captain's request. "Of course," I said.

We put down our tools and followed him out of the nearly completed barrack and onto the Great Lawn. I had no idea what he wanted us for, but I was fairly confident that it had nothing to do with the work we had done the past eight weeks.

The Wolf and Son Woodworking team had built two barracks, ready to house the arrival of the new students. I was proud of our work and equally proud of William. He had proven to be a reliable assistant and a jovial companion.

We followed the captain up the narrow wooden staircase to his office in the administration building. As we entered the reception room, Maggie greeted us with a warm smile and a nod, which, I realized afterward, was a clue to the surprise waiting for us.

The captain opened his office door, and that's when we saw Chief Red Shirt standing with outstretched arms, inviting his son to embrace him.

"Father!" William shouted and ran to him.

The captain asked us to sit at a round table set off in a corner of his office.

"I'm surprised to see you, Chief," I said, shaking his hand.

"I was in Washington and decided to divert my trip home to see my son."

The mention of Washington triggered an image of Sarah. "You were in Washington?" I asked, probably sounding more enthusiastic than I intended.

The chief nodded. "I'm a delegate of the Lakota tribes. We meet in Washington several times a year to discuss important issues concerning our people."

"Did you see Senator Cameron?" I asked, hoping for a casual mention of his niece.

"I did. He's the chairman on the Senate Committee for Indian Affairs. That's who we made our presentation to."

I nodded my head and thought of Sarah sitting near her uncle, perhaps writing notes of the meetings for some official government document.

"The chief didn't come here to discuss his business in Washington," the captain explained.

"That's right." Red Shirt began by putting his arm around his son while looking at me, and said, "I'm here to take both you and William back to Pine Ridge."

"Pine Ridge?" I repeated with a furrowed brow.

"It's the reservation where my people live."

William jumped to his feet. "You're taking me home?"

"For a few weeks. Then you'll return to Carlisle with Leo to begin the new year."

William threw his arms around his father's neck and squeezed him tight.

I looked to the captain and asked, "Is this all right with you, sir?"

He nodded and said, "It looks like your work is mostly done, and your father and Tom can finish what's left."

"But why would you want me to come?" I asked Red Shirt.

Red Shirt leaned forward in his chair, looked at me with his sparkling brown eyes, and said, "I would like you to come and meet my people, Leo. You'll see how we live and then you can bring back the knowledge to Carlisle. This is something Captain Pratt and I have agreed upon."

William grabbed my arm and shook it. "You'll come, Leo, yes?"

I looked over to the captain, who nodded. Then I patted William's little hand gripping my forearm and said, "Yes, I will come."

*

"You're going where?" Father asked, pinching the skin on his forehead when I told him the news.

"It's called Pine Ridge. It's the reservation where the Lakota people live," I said, surprised at Father's ignorance.

"But there's work to be done here," he said.

I sighed. "I know, Father, but we're almost finished, and Tom can help you with the rest. I'd really like to go and learn how they live."

"For what purpose?" he said with a grimace.

"I don't know," I said, struggling for an answer. "So that I can better understand my boys, I suppose."

Father shook his head and sighed. "Fine, Leo, go. I'll find a way to make do," he said, as he turned and walked away.

Chapter 17
Pine Ridge

It took a week by train and then wagon to arrive at the Pine Ridge Reservation. During the long hours heading west along newly laid rails, traversing the cities of Pittsburgh, Cleveland, Chicago, and eventually Rapid City, Chief Red Shirt told me the story of his people's tragic history.

"Several years ago, gold was discovered in the Black Hills," he said, as we glided across narrow tracks that hardly seemed suitable for these massive iron horses, traveling at unimaginable speeds.

"As word spread of fortunes to be won, prospectors flocked to the Black Hills, making claims on the land where our people had lived for generations. This was soon followed by Lieutenant Colonel Custer leading an army of one thousand soldiers to investigate the spectacular claims of gold in our mountains, and to decide upon a suitable location for a military fort.

"As you can imagine, our people felt threatened; we worried for our survival. But the real trouble started when a journalist wrote—wait a moment while I pull it out—" the chief paused to remove a folded paper from his pocket. He handed it over to me.

I looked at it and shrugged.

He jerked his chin at me and said, "Read it."

"All right, Chief," I said, unfolding the paper, remembering he couldn't read. It was an old and weathered newspaper clipping from the

Rapid City News. He reached over and pointed to the spot where I should begin. I nodded and read aloud to the chief and William.

> *A wall of fire, not to mention a wall of Indians, could not stop the encroachment of that terrible white race. At the news of gold, the grizzled Forty-niners shook the dust of California off from their feet and started for the far distant "Hills." The Australian miner left his pack and started by saddle and ship for the same goal, the diamond hunter of the Cape, the veteran prospector of Colorado and Montana, the reduced gentleman of Europe, the worried and worn clerks of London, Liverpool, New York, or Chicago, the sturdy Scotchman and the light-hearted Irishman, who drinks the spirit of adventure with his mother's milk, the miners of Wales and Cornwall and the gamblers of Monte Carlo came trooping in masses to the new Eldorado.*

I finished, folded up the paper, handed it back to the chief, and shook my head, thinking of the utter devastation the Lakota people experienced and how they fought for their survival. I asked, "What did you do?"

The chief pursed his lip before answering. "The whites needed towns and settlements to be built. As you can imagine, Leo, these intruders angered us. We fought back, hoping to frighten them away."

"Did it work?"

The chief shook his head and smirked. "It only made things worse. Four years ago, over one hundred and fifty miners created a militia to protect the settlers from us. Of course, we ended up in bloody fights. This rail," the chief said, patting the wall of our cabin, "the Northern Pacific Railroad, moved tens of thousands of white people to our lands. Red Cloud and Spotted Tail traveled to Washington, in order to persuade President Grant to stop the flow of these treasure hunters, and do you know what the president told us?"

I shook my head and glanced over to William, who was also shaking his head, equally anxious to hear the reason.

"The president called it the *manifest destiny* of the United States to take the Black Hills away from our people. As if that were some sort of divine right. The army ordered us to give up our lands and accept life on the reservation or face military action."

"What did you do?" I asked.

"We fought back, of course, causing the United States government to declare war upon my people, and after many bloody battles we were defeated, driven from our ancestral birthplace to Pine Ridge, where we were prevented from hunting the buffalo beyond the boundaries of the reservation, though that was nothing compared to the great hardship of the army nearly wiping all of the buffalo clean off the earth." The chief turned his head and gazed out the window.

In the silence that followed, I looked over to William, who had rivers of tears running down his cheeks, seeming to express the collective sadness of his people's demise at the hands of greedy, gold-seeking white men.

CHAPTER 18
BLACK ELK

After arriving at Pine Ridge, I soon realized that the chief's invitation had an *ulterior motive*, a term I had learned from Sarah. He did want William to visit with his mother, siblings, and friends. Though I think his true purpose was to reveal to me his people's fall from grace, and in doing so, convert me into an advocate. Someone who understood their pain and anguish. But to what end? That was something I expected to learn soon.

My first impression, as I disembarked from the wagon and looked out upon the village from an elevated vantage point, was of one of a peaceful setting. Large, puffy clouds hung in a brilliant, sunlit blue sky over hundreds of tipis scattered across a rugged landscape. White smoke twisted upward from campfires, while horses gathered by a large river meandering across a wide-open, barren landscape.

"This is our home," the chief said, with a hint of frustration and a sweep of his arm across the valley below us.

I smiled, nodded, and said, "Lovely."

William pointed to a pack of boys running nearby and asked, "Father, can I go?"

"Of course, son."

As William ran off to greet his friends, the chief turned to me and said, "I've brought you here to show you how we live. This may look lovely to you, but underneath we're a broken, defeated people, Leo. The white man has taken away our sacred home and forced us here." He paused a moment and looked out upon the activity of his people, busy with their daily chores. "We were hunters and gatherers within the great Black Hills," he said, pointing to the mountains off in the distance. "What the white man fails to understand is that you cannot demand that a people abandon their homeland and expect them to continue a way of life without the resources that supported them for generations."

I nodded, listening to his words.

He lifted his palms skyward and said, "I had no choice but to make peace with the white man. There are many among us who accuse me of cowardice for expressing such an idea. But I saw it as a matter of life or death, and I choose life for those still too young to decide for themselves."

I nodded while looking at his son William and the boys running wild in a pack of carefree playfulness across the village.

*

The first few days I spent at the Lakota village were pleasant. At first, I was a curiosity. People stared and pointed fingers at me. Having a white man wander about the village caused legitimate concern. But that was quickly dismissed once they learned I was William's counselor at the Carlisle School, which the Lakota considered as a position of honor.

What I found interesting was William's friends' initial reaction to his haircut and clothing. They mocked him as he no longer looked as they did, with their long hair and loincloths. But within a few days, after receiving permission from his father to wear his traditional native clothing and allowing his hair to go unkempt, he quickly blended in with the boys of the village.

As I followed the chief and observed him, he seemed committed to sharing with his people that if William received a white man's education at Carlisle, one day he would be able to lead them with pride as chief into the white man's world. It was obvious that several of the younger men considered this a form of capitulation, but Red Shirt insisted their very survival as a people depended upon it.

At the end of the first week, I thought over and over again of Father's displeasure, causing me to worry if this visit to Pine Ridge was worthy of my time. After all, there were still several carpentry projects needing completion at Carlisle and I was sure Father would express his further displeasure with me upon my return. However, my guilt evaporated once I met Black Elk.

*

The next morning, I awoke just before daybreak and wandered down to the banks of the creek that passed through the village. As I made my way down the embankment to the riverbed, I noticed the waters running strong due to the mountain runoff from the rains that had soaked the Black Hills for the past few days.

These waters, while an important element to the tribe's survival, were also a sad reminder of what the people were forced to give up. They used to harvest this resource directly from the waterfalls cascading down the mountainside. It was hard to understand how they acquiesced to this eviction from paradise and continued to have faith in the chief's wisdom and directive to integrate into the white man's world.

A series of flat stepping stones that rose inches above the rushing waters offered me a convenient pathway across the river. After a few short jumps, I reached the other side and turned to look downstream. I noticed a shadow shifting in the darkness of an outcropping of rocks.

I leaned into the breeze tunneling upriver and as I squinted to focus, I realized someone was moving about. The figure appeared to be gliding toward me, as if skimming across the surface of the rushing waters. This vision caused me to take a step back, not in fear, but in awe. With the sunlight now swallowing the shadows, I clearly saw this strange Lakota man standing before me. He swept a hand across the space between us, let it land upon his heart, and said, "I've been waiting for you."

I tilted my head, confused at his familiarity, and asked, "Have we met?"

"My dreams have foretold our friendship," said the man. His skin was as smooth as a river stone. He appeared quite young, perhaps not yet twenty years of age. A fur hat sat upon his head like a nest, with feathers sprouting out of its top. I stared at it for a moment, perhaps expecting something to chirp from within.

"Who are you?"

"I am Black Elk," he said with a smile that lit up his face.

"Black Elk." I repeated the strange name. "My name is Leopold Wolf."

"Come, Leopold. Let us sit," he said, gesturing to a shady spot under a tree.

Once seated, he smiled and said, "May I tell you a story?"

I shrugged and nodded.

"When I was a young boy, I was taken ill," Black Elk said, so softly that the birdsong drifting down from the branches of the oak tree threatened to drown his words. I leaned in closer so I could hear.

"As I slept, the Buffalo Calf Woman came to me in the form of the Thunder Beings and brought me before the six grandfathers that represent the sacred directions—north, south, east, west, above, and below," he said, pointing to the six orientations. "Not unlike my own grandfathers, these spirits were kind and loving, offering me their wisdom. They brought me deep inside the caverns of the Black Mountains, where both stillness and movement resided, the central axis point of the six sacred directions. I saw that the sacred hoop of my people was one of many hoops making up one circle. It was wide as the daylight and the starlight, and within its center grew one mighty flowering tree to shelter all the children, and I saw that it was holy."

Each of his words floated like soft petals, as if descending softly to the earth from the flowering tree he described.

"What did the Thunder Beings offer you?" I asked.

Black Elk held out his open palms and invited me to place my hands on his. The moment we touched, he clasped mine tightly and said, "I was given the gift of healing."

My hands felt as if they were too close to the flames of a bonfire. I tried to pull them back, but Black Elk held on tight. I cringed as the searing heat crept through my hands and traveled up my arms.

"What's happening?" I said, my voice rising to a pitch that amplified my pain.

Black Elk released my hands and the burning sensation subsided. I looked at my hands, expecting to see them scarred, but they were fine. I shook my head and asked, "What did you do to me?"

Black Elk smiled for the first time and said, "I looked inside you, Leopold."

"Inside me?" I said, touching my chest.

"Don't worry, you're healthy," he said, showing me his palm. "But I have seen what has been foretold in my dreams."

"Which is what?"

"Do you believe that you are here, sitting before me, by chance?"

I shook my head and said, "I don't know."

Black Elk put his slender fingers upon his chin, nodded, and said, "The White Buffalo Calf Woman has brought you here to help restore what has been lost."

My eyebrows rose to express my surprise. I shook my head and asked, "Who is the White Buffalo Calf Woman, and what have you lost?"

Black Elk leaned forward, patted my knee, and smiled.

CHAPTER 19
THE SACRED PIPE

On the eve of our departure back to Carlisle, I was invited to partake in the Sacred Pipe ceremony. When I shared the news with William, he asked if I knew the story of how his people were given the pipe. I stopped packing and turned to look at him, surprised at his engaging and thoughtful question. I smiled and said, "No, I don't. Can you tell me?"

William sat cross-legged on the ground of the tipi and gestured for me to join him. I obliged, taking my place across from him, and nodded, ready to hear his tale.

William took a breath and began. "Two warriors were hunting when they saw someone walking toward them. As this person approached, they realized it was a maiden wearing a white buckskin and holding a bundle wrapped in a buffalo hide. As she got closer, she sang a song." He proceeded to sing, in his child's pitch. "*Behold me, I am the White Buffalo Calf Woman, I am the sacred one walking.* Then one of the men was said to have evil thoughts about the woman and wanted to run to her."

"The White Buffalo Calf Woman?" I repeated, as Black Elk just the day before had spoken the same name to me.

William nodded and continued. "The good warrior tried to stop him, but the evil warrior pushed him away. Then," William paused and lowered his voice, forcing me to lean in even closer, "a dark cloud came down from the sky, covering the evil one like a blanket, and when the cloud lifted, his body was a skeleton, his skin eaten by worms." He grimaced.

Wide-eyed, I asked, "What happened next?"

"The good warrior fell to his knees in fear. The maiden told him not to be scared, to go back to his people and tell them she would be coming soon. He did that, and then one day, she did come." William nodded quickly for emphasis. "When our people saw her, she placed the bundle in front of them and unwrapped it." William looked down to the space before us, as if the bundle lay there, and whispered, "And inside was the sacred pipe."

I nodded, encouraging him to continue.

"She then taught our people the prayer. Would you like to hear it?"

"Yes, I would."

William closed his eyes for a moment, took a deep breath, and said,

"With this sacred pipe, your voices will reach the Great Spirit,
your Father and Grandfather.
With this sacred pipe, you will walk upon the Earth,
your Mother and Grandmother.
All your steps will be holy."

William opened his eyes, looked at me, and said with a shrug, "That's it."

I smiled and gave him a hug. "That's a wonderful story and you tell it well."

"Thank you, Leo," William said and hurried off to say his farewells to his friends while I went to see Chief Red Shirt. As I walked across the hardened pathways carved out by the tribe's people, I thought about my encounter with Black Elk and his words. *The White Buffalo Calf Woman has brought you here for a reason.*

Perhaps the chief would help me understand if these words were a prophecy, or perhaps just wishful thinking on part of Black Elk.

As the sun set in the western sky, I stepped into the chief's tipi. The campfire was already blasting sparks upward, offering a playful array of light and shadow upon the animal skins and colorful blankets draped about. I saw the chief, who gracefully invited me to sit. Black Elk followed me inside and took his place around the fire. Several Elders were already seated, forming a circle.

"Would you do us the honor of smoking the Sacred Pipe with us?" the chief asked.

I nodded, not realizing that there was an actual Sacred Pipe.

As I took my place, Black Elk was handed the pipe by a young man, who was also feeding the flames with logs. Displaying the pipe to me with both hands, Black Elk explained, "The bowl is made of red stone which represents the earth." He pointed to the figure perched on top and continued, "This carving of the buffalo calf is from stone, symbolizing the four-legged creatures." He then tapped gently on the stem. "This part is made of wood, representing all things that grow, and these feathers," he said, gently stroking the array tied to the end of the pipe, "are from the spotted eagle and speak for all of the winged brothers who live among us."

Black Elk reached into a pouch attached to a strap that hung across his chest and removed a pinch of tobacco. "Each pinch represents the four winds," he said while loading the pipe, with a pinch for the north, south, east, and west. "We honor the sky and the earth," he said, adding two more pinches.

The attendant paused from tending the fire and offered a wrapped bundle of burning twigs at the bowl's edge as Black Elk puffed on the pipe. Satisfied, he exhaled a stream of white smoke that drifted upward. He handed me the pipe and said, "All elements of life are joined when we smoke, and all of our voices are sent as one to the Great Spirit."

I gently placed my lips on the mouthpiece and inhaled. Warm smoke filled my lungs, though, with caution, I tempered my intake. Once satisfied, I tilted my head back and blew out a feeble breath of smoke, which hardly compared to Black Elk's voluminous cloud. I looked at him with a furrowed brow, feeling myself flush at my paltry attempt. Black Elk smiled and cocked his head, indicating that I should pass it on.

As the pipe made its way around the circle, filling the tipi with its sharp, earthen aromas, Black Elk spoke. "The White Buffalo Calf Woman's Sacred Pipe binds our people to each of the seven generations that have come before us."

With the pipe back in his hands, Black Elk pointed to the design carved into the red stone. "There are seven circles on the stone, each representing one of the seven rites: prayer, respect, compassion, honesty, generosity, humility, and wisdom."

The pipe was set aside. Chief Red Shirt lifted his hands into the air with his palms facing the flames and said, "The smoking of the Sacred Pipe is our way of honoring you, Leopold."

I placed my right palm over my heart and smiled, acknowledging the respect.

"Black Elk has shared with me your encounter by the creek. He believes that you are the one to seek out the Sacred Pipe and return it to our people."

My eyes darted over to Black Elk, whose vision stayed focused on the dancing flames. I pointed at the pipe now in the hands of the chief and said, "I thought that was the Sacred Pipe."

"Yes, Leo, this is a sacred pipe," the chief said, nodding. "But not the one of our grandfathers' grandfathers."

I rubbed my chin and said, "I don't understand."

"The Sacred Pipe of our people was handed down for many generations. It's the one given to us by the White Buffalo Calf Woman. This one," he said, pointing to the pipe in Black Elk's hands, "is a replica."

"You're saying there's actually a pipe given to your people by this spirit you call the White Buffalo Calf Woman?"

Chief Red Shirt nodded. "Of course. It's not a children's bedtime story."

I swallowed hard, trying to make sense of what I was being told. "So, what happened to the original one?"

"Lame Johnny stole it," the chief said, with a tilt of his head.

I squinted at the strange name and repeated, "Lame Johnny?"

"Yes, but Lame Johnny no longer possesses it."

I stared at the chief and asked, "Then who does?"

"After it was stolen, we believe he hid it in the caverns somewhere within the Black Hills," he said, pointing to the tipi's open flap.

"And you want me to find it?" I said, placing my hand on my chest.

The chief nodded.

"Even if I believe everything you're telling me, I can't do what you're asking. I know nothing about the Black Hills, these caves, or this Sacred Pipe. Shouldn't it be one of you?" I said, gesturing to the men seated around the circle.

Black Elk put a soft hand on my shoulder and said, "As a child, I was visited by the Thunder Beings. At first, I was frightened by their thunderbolts brightening the black clouds and shaking the earth. But soon the rains came, which flooded our lands. Eventually, the storms passed and our world was green. This, Leopold Wolf, is how we must understand the truth. It comes wearing two faces. One is terrified during the storm, while the other is joyful, laughing in its aftermath, realizing that only through suffering can one receive authentic joy. But we know both of these expressions come from the same face."

I squinted my eyes and said, "What does that have to do with me going on some quest for a lost pipe?"

Black Elk sat back down, saying nothing.

"Please," Chief Red Shirt said, gesturing for me to exit the tipi.

I took a breath and nodded.

"Allow me to tell you the story of Lame Johnny, then you decide."

Chapter 20
Lame Johnny

Once William was asleep, I gazed out the window onto the beauty of the Dakota countryside while our train steamed home toward Carlisle. I took this quiet moment to think back upon Chief Red Shirt's words about Lame Johnny and the fate of the lost Sacred Pipe.

"Lame Johnny was what the white man calls an outlaw," the chief said, walking with me alongside the riverbank. "He and his gang were notorious in the Black Hills for stealing horses, but with the discovery of gold, he soon ventured into robbing strongboxes from stage routes. For a long time, he and his men were never caught, until last year when he set his sights on the Homestead Mine gold shipment."

"What happened?" I asked, riveted by the chief's story.

"This shipment was held within a special coach used for treasure; they called it the Deadwood Stage. It was this impenetrable, ironclad fort on wheels—that is, until Lame Johnny and his gang held it up thirty miles south of Deadwood. They shot the crew, killing two of them, and made off with the entire stage into the woods, where they were able to pry open the strongbox and discover thousands of dollars in currency, diamonds, and gold."

"Wow," I said, holding out my hands. "But what does that have to do with the Sacred Pipe?"

The chief stopped walking, took a breath, and said, "Along with this bounty was also the Sacred Pipe."

I grimaced and asked, "Why was the Sacred Pipe on the Deadwood Stage?"

"I brought it to Deadwood for a ceremony honoring our people who were killed in the Sioux War and thought it prudent to return by stage rather than our delegation of wagons. So I made the arrangements with the company before we left for Pine Ridge."

I rubbed the back of my neck and said, "So you're saying that some outlaw named Lame Johnny stole your Sacred Pipe?"

The chief nodded. "Of course, he had no idea what he had."

"Then what happened?"

The chief explained that soon after the news of the heist spread throughout the territory, Lame Johnny and his gang were captured at a place called Buffalo Gap by one of the several posses chasing after him and his gang. "Most of the loot was recovered, except for two large gold ingots and the Sacred Pipe. On their way back to Deadwood to stand trial, they were grabbed by a vigilante mob who threatened to hang the lot, unless they confessed what they did with the missing gold. Lame Johnny told them that the gold was hidden in caverns under the Black Hills."

"Along with the Sacred Pipe?" I asked.

"We believe it's there with the gold," the chief said, pointing to the mountain range far off in the distance.

"And that's where you want me to go and search for it?"

The chief nodded.

"I'm sorry," I said, holding out my hands, "I can't find your pipe, I don't—"

"It's okay, Leo," Chief Red Shirt interrupted with a smile. "I understand if you're not ready yet."

I nodded and said, "But why would you think I could do such a thing?"

The chief put his hand on my shoulder and said, "Because Black Elk has foreseen it. You are to be the one to return the Sacred Pipe to our people, but not yet."

I shrugged and said, "Ready? How will I know I'm ready?"

"You will know when the Great Spirit calls upon you."

CHAPTER 21
BACK AT CARLISLE

Upon the day of our arrival at Carlisle, Father greeted me with a hug, squeezing me tight, and whispered, "I'm glad you're home."

"Really?" I said. I'd expected him to express anger at how I abandoned him.

He released me and jerked his thumb behind him to where the new barracks stood. He said, "Tom and I finished a few days ago."

"I see. Nicely done," I said, looking at the pair of buildings that would provide housing for the new students set to arrive tomorrow.

"We make a good team," he said, sounding proud.

Later that day, upon entering through the large double doors into the dining hall for our counselor orientation meeting, I saw Sarah speaking to Maggie, Captain Pratt's assistant. Even with her back to me, I knew it was her, though her blonde hair looked more golden than I remembered, perhaps from the rays of the summer sun. I waited a moment for the conversation with Maggie to end before tapping her shoulder.

"Hello, Sarah," I said, as she turned to face me.

Her eyes widened, and a broad smile brightened her face. "Leo," she said, leaping forward, wrapping her arms around me, and pulling me close.

My entire body warmed at her demonstrative greeting. "It's good to see you, Sarah."

She took a moment to look at me, then said, "You've changed, Leopold Wolf. You're not so skinny anymore. You're growing muscles like your father." She reached out to squeeze my arm.

"You think so?" I said, feeling my cheeks blush. I knew my body was changing, getting stronger, but I didn't think it was noticeable. I appreciated the compliment, especially from Sarah. "You look good, too. Your hair, it, um—looks nice," I said, nervously stumbling over my words.

She touched her golden locks and smiled. "Thank you, Leo," she said and turned to enter the dining hall.

Once inside the large room, I looked about at the array of long tables where over two hundred students would be gathered the next day. I greeted a few of the other returning counselors and staff, but kept an eye on Sarah, making sure to sit next to her once the captain's presentation began.

*

Later that evening, the captain hosted a dinner party at his home for the ten counselors. This was going to be the first time I was considered a guest, rather than one of the staff serving food and drink. As I took my seat at the long, fabric-covered table, set with the elegant dinnerware and glassware, Abe gave me a look that expressed his confusion at my sudden elevated status. I smiled and greeted him, trying to show that I was still the same humble man he knew. Abe leaned in and whispered, "Don't let it go to your head."

I chuckled and replied, "Not likely."

Father also seemed uncomfortable with his shift in roles. I caught him offering Alice an awkward but friendly smile, which caught my attention. I wondered whether something had changed between them.

I thought the captain would have found professional educators to replace Father and me by now, but apparently he was pleased with our performance with the children last year and decided to keep us on. As for the other counselors, all had returned, plus two new ones.

One counselor in particular whom I was not pleased to see again was Major Lawrence. He seemed as serious and angry as I remembered. I also think he was especially annoyed at being seated between Father and me.

Sarah sat directly across from us, and I couldn't help staring at her throughout the evening.

Once Abe made his way around the table, pouring wine for each of the counselors, the captain said, "Ladies and gentlemen, I would like to make a toast."

I remembered from my time as a server that this was a cue to lift my glass and hold it out in front of me while the captain spoke.

"I would like to welcome back our counselors from last year," he said, looking at each of us, as we all offered some acknowledgment in return. I smiled, while Father grunted some sound and nodded. When he looked at Sarah, she elevated her glass a bit higher and flashed her charming, dimpled smile. "I am pleased to see all of you and wish the best for the upcoming school year," he said, and everyone drank.

The first taste of the wine slipped smoothly down my throat. Certainly better than the foul-smelling whiskey Father kept in the cabinet. It had a wonderful depth of flavors that seemed to stimulate and awaken my mouth. I quickly took another gulp and felt a warmth begin to fill me from deep within.

As Abe refilled the glasses, the captain began his next toast, honoring the two new counselors. Between the anticipation of my second glass and watching Sarah's lips turning the same deep burgundy color as the wine, I paid little attention to the captain's words.

Before we had finished the main course, I was feeling pleasantly drunk, and rather loose with my attitude. That's when the major, who seemed equally intoxicated, became annoyed with my flirtatious behavior toward Sarah.

When she shared her story of the summer with her uncle in Washington, I nodded, laughed, and clapped my hands as if she was a performer on stage. That's when the major grabbed my wrist and squeezed it tight. I grimaced and demanded, "Let go of me, Major."

His cheeks were as red as Sarah's lips. "I've had enough of you, Jew," he snarled.

"Hey!" people shouted as I tried to pull my arm away, but his grip was too strong. Suddenly Father rose from his chair, towering over the seated major, and tapped on his shoulder. The major turned his head to look up at Father, but kept his tight grip on me.

Father looked down at the major. His bloodshot eyes swirled like two flaming torches. "Let go of him now," Father demanded.

The captain, who was now on his feet with his arms outspread, said, "Gentlemen, please calm down."

"Are you going to allow this Jew to behave so inappropriately in front of Miss Cameron?" the major demanded.

"It's fine," Sarah said, trying to defuse the tension.

Father grabbed the major by his free arm and tried to pull him away from the table. But in one swift motion, the major released my wrist, grabbed the steak knife placed upon the table for the upcoming main course, and drove it deep into Father's belly. Father's eyes looked like they were about to pop out of their sockets. He let go of the major and put both hands over the wound. Blood gushed between his fingers as he fell forward, hitting his head on the table before collapsing to the floor.

I ran over to him. He was curled up in a tight crunch, his knees to his chest.

"Let me look," I pleaded. But by the time Father rolled onto his back, his eyes had begun to cloud over. Blood soaked his once-white dress shirt and started to spread onto the wood plank floor.

I looked up at the major and cried out, "What have you done?"

He shrugged and dropped the bloody knife, displaying no remorse.

Alice was now down on the floor next to Father. Tears rolled down her cheeks. "Isaac," she cried, caressing his face.

I felt a hand squeezing my shoulder, so I looked up and saw Sarah's tearful eyes looking down upon me. I placed my hand upon hers. When my gaze returned to Father, he exhaled his last breath and was gone. Silence enveloped the room. Father was dead, killed at the hands of Major Lawrence.

CHAPTER 22
THE AFTERMATH

My hands shook uncontrollably as I sat in the kitchen of the captain's home, trying to come to grips with Father's gruesome murder. A police detective, a retired army officer of the North, interrogated the major and seemed to relish the testimony of the multiple eyewitnesses that would likely result in the major's punishment by hanging.

After the undertaker removed Father's body, Alice did her best to scrub the blood and tears from the dining room's wooden floor.

Sarah tried comforting me. "I'm so sorry, Leo," she said, stroking my back.

My hands didn't stop shaking until at last my tears began to flow. Sarah pulled me close, and I buried my face in the cradle of space between her neck and shoulder. I took a deep breath, seeking to compose myself, lifted my head, and said, "The only positive thing to come out of this is that Major Lawrence will finally be gone from Carlisle."

Alice, her pretty face smeared with Father's dried blood, got to her feet and took a seat alongside Abe and me at the table. Sarah, showing her concern, walked over to the washbasin, grabbed a cloth, dipped it into the basin, wrung out the excess water, and gently cleaned the streaks of blood off Alice's forehead, nose, and cheeks.

I reached over and touched Alice's hand. As I did, she looked at me and said, "There's something you should know, Leo."

I tilted my head and held out my hands.

"I loved your father," she said, the words sputtering out in between her sobs.

I looked over to Abe, who offered a pained smile, then back to Alice and said, "Please continue."

"This past summer, while you were away, we spent time together. You know, like a couple."

I shook my head. "I didn't know," I said, unaware of their romance.

"Your father was a shy man," she said, trying to smile.

"Mother, you should just tell him," Abe interrupted.

Alice nodded, took a deep breath, squeezed both of my hands in hers, and looked at me with a determined focus. She said, "I'm with child—Isaac's child."

I jerked my head back and my jaw dropped, but no words spilled out.

I glanced over to Sarah, whose hand was over her mouth, her eyes as wide as river stones.

"Oh, my Lord," I said.

Abe stood up and tugged at my arm, encouraging me to join him, and as I did, he hugged me tight and said, "We're going to be a family."

*

Later that day, I caught up with Tom at the barrack. He was sitting on the floor, his back pressed against the wall. "Hey there," I said, letting the screen door slam behind me.

"Leo," he said, looking up, "I'm so sorry. Your father was a good man."

I nodded and slid my back down the wall and sat alongside him.

"I want you to know that the major will pay for this."

I twisted around to look at Tom. His bloodshot eyes spoke of the tears he had shed, but they also told the story of a hot anger ready to boil over. "You know that the major will pay for his crime. The detective said he will be hung."

Tom scoffed. "He won't make it out of the stockade alive."

"What do you mean?" I asked, gripping his arm.

"I'm breaking into the stockade tonight," he said holding up his two hands. "Swift justice."

"No, Tom, you mustn't," I insisted.

But Tom dismissed me with a wave of his hand.

Unable to dissuade his need for vengeance, I returned to my barrack. While I struggled to absorb the fast-changing landscape of my life, as well as to prepare for the arrival of the children, the screen door slammed, causing me to jump in fright. I spun around and saw the captain.

"How are you holding up, Leo?"

I shrugged and said, "I guess I'm okay—considering."

"I want to ask you something. Come, sit down," he said, pointing to one of the bunks.

The captain leaned forward, placed his elbows on his thighs, and looked into my eyes. "Your father was a good man. I'm deeply sorry for your loss. I want you to know that you can count on me if you need anything at all."

I gave him the best smile I could muster and said, "Thank you, sir."

"Leo, be honest and tell me if you are able to carry on. If you need time off, I completely understand."

I jerked backward. "Please, Captain, don't take this away from me," I said, gesturing to the space surrounding us.

"No, Leo, I'm not. I just want you to know that if you need to take a break, I'll find someone to replace you."

"No. My boys need me, sir. I don't need a break."

The captain held up his hands and smiled. "Understood. Then let me ask you something else. As you know, the loss of two counselors on the eve of opening day is a problem I must address immediately. For the group of boys under the major's care, I was able to reach out to Dr. James McCauley, the president of nearby Dickerson College, who offered us one of his instructors to replace the major. But we still need a counselor for your father's group of boys."

"So what are you going to do?"

"I have an idea of a counselor for your father's group."

"You do?"

The captain nodded and said, "I was planning on asking Tom. What do you think?"

I furrowed my brow and thought of Tom's intention to kill the major. But instead of dismissing the idea, I said, "I think you should ask him."

The captain clapped his hands together, which gave me another start, and said, "So do I. I'm going to do it right now. Come, let's go see him together. It might help to have you there."

"Sure," I said, and we both rose and walked across the Great Lawn to where Tom was now working on some last-minute carpentry on the front porch of one of the barracks.

"Tom," the captain said, getting his attention as we approached.

Tom looked up and gave a casual wave.

When the captain and I stood before him, though, he seemed less agitated than before. Perhaps this offer to be counselor would change his vengeful mind.

Tom took a seat on one of the steps leading up to the porch of the barrack. The captain stood on the lawn while I leaned against the hand railing.

"I'll come right to the point, Tom," the captain began. "I'm in a bit of a quandary with the unfortunate event that occurred last night. As you know, we lost two counselors. I was able to hire an instructor from the university in town to take over for the major's group. But I am still searching for a replacement for Isaac."

Tom glanced over to me for a moment, perhaps looking for a clue about where the captain's remarks were headed.

"Tom," the captain said, "I would like you would take over as the group's counselor."

"Me?" Tom said, touching his chest.

The captain nodded. "You're a natural, and you've come a long way since you arrived. Isaac, God rest his soul, spoke highly of you many times over the summer."

Tom looked down to his feet and said, "I don't think so."

"But why not?" the captain said, holding out his hands. "It's a chance to demonstrate your leadership skills. Once you get out into the real world, such experience will help you find a good job."

Tom stood up, took a deep breath, and exhaled. "My answer is no," he said and headed into the barrack.

The captain grimaced, and without saying another word, turned and marched away.

I climbed the stops and entered the barrack where Tom was sitting on the edge of a bed. I sat down beside him and sighed. Without looking at me, he rubbed his hands together and said, "I'm taking care of the major tonight."

"You don't need to do that," I said, shaking my head. "He'll hang for sure; there were plenty of witnesses."

"Your father deserves more. You don't need to be involved, Leo. I just wanted you to know."

I swallowed hard, knowing his words were not coming from the Carlisle School's version of the man, but from the warrior buried within—Bidziil. I also knew if the major had plunged the knife into me instead, Father wouldn't have hesitated to take justice into his own hands.

Chapter 23
Bidziil's Revenge

I had not seen William since Father's murder. He remained at the house and wasn't scheduled to move to the school's barrack until later in the day when the caravan of students arrived. I assumed Tom had delivered the bad news the night before, and wished I could have been there to comfort him, but I spent a sleepless night with Alice, Abe, and Sarah as they did their best to console me, and discuss the future of the child growing inside Alice's belly. When I finally went to fetch William for the funeral service, I spotted him on the tree swing in the front yard.

"William," I called out.

The moment he saw me, he hopped off and ran toward me. He jumped into my arms and squeezed me tight. "Tom told me what happened," he said, weeping.

I held on to him and carried him back to the porch. "We need to be strong," I said, placing him down on the wooden bench.

"Why would the major do such a thing?" he said, in between his heaving sobs.

I sighed and said, "He's a man filled with hatred."

William nodded, giving me the impression he understood. I put my arm around him, doing my best to comfort the young Lakota child. Soon I heard voices calling out. I got to my feet and hurried to the road, where I saw, heading toward the house, the captain leading a procession of several police officers.

"Leo," the captain said, pointing to the house. "Is Tom inside?"

I looked over to William, who nodded.

"What's this about?" I asked, as they ignored me and headed for the front door.

I ran to William and took his hand, pulling him out of the way of the three police officers who were now, along with Captain Pratt, standing on the front porch.

"Tom," the captain shouted while banging on the wooden door frame, "come outside now."

"What's he done?" I demanded to know.

Captain Pratt turned to me, placed a hand on my shoulder, and said, "Last night, Tom broke into the stockade and murdered Major Lawrence."

I put my hand to my mouth and said, "Oh no."

*

I had trouble sleeping that night. So, when the floorboards creaked, I was aware that someone had entered the house. I looked over to William, who hadn't stirred. I quietly got to my feet and opened the bedroom door, where I was met by Tom.

Before I could say a word, he put his hand over my mouth and cocked his head toward the front door, beckoning me to follow. Once outside, he looked around the yard, then whispered, "I've come to say goodbye."

"How did you get out of the stockade?" I asked, pointing down the road.

"Abe brought me the key," he said with a sly smile.

"But what about the guard?"

Tom shook his head. "There's no guard, never was. That's how I got to the major."

"But he would have been hung. You didn't need to risk your life."

Tom shrugged and said, "It's the way of the warrior."

"How did you do it?" I asked with a grimace.

Tom held out his hands to demonstrate and said, "I strangled the life from him."

I stared into Tom's red-rimmed eyes and shook my head. "We need to figure out a way of getting you out of here."

Tom nodded. He reached into his pocket, pulled out a folded paper, and handed it to me.

"What's this?" I asked, taking it.

He gestured for me to look at it. I unfolded it and perused the flyer's faded colors. Across the top, printed in bold red letters, I read *Buffalo Bill's Wild West Show*, above a colorful drawing of Indians in full war dress attacking a wagon train.

"Buffalo Bill?" I said with a furrowed brow.

"It's where I'm going," he said, shifting his brow. "I have a horse tied up in the woods."

"And you plan on doing what?" I asked with a furrowed brow.

Tom smiled and said, "I'm joining the show."

"You're not serious."

Tom nodded.

"I thought you would return to your people and become chief."

"Not yet," he said with a shrug. "There's more to learn."

"Who gave this to you?" I said, returning my gaze to the paper.

"Chief Red Shirt, the last time he was here."

I lowered my voice and said, "The chief gave you this?"

Tom nodded.

Confused, I looked again at the paper. "What's a Wild West show?"

"It's a show about cowboys and Indians," he said, tapping the paper, then looked around. "I've got to go."

I sighed. "All right, Tom, I wish you good luck," I said, offering my hand.

He shoved it away, embraced me, and whispered into my ear, "Don't dwell here too long—follow your heart."

Before I could respond, Tom handed me another folded note.

"What's this?" I asked.

"A prayer for your father," he said and ran off down the road and disappeared into the darkness.

*

When I arrived at Carlisle's cemetery the following morning, I paused to look at the headstones surrounding Father's grave. Buried there were the five Indian children who had died from an outbreak of tuberculosis during last year's harsh winter. So much death lingered around me, especially within the past two days, after Father's senseless murder and Tom's impulsive revenge upon the major.

When the captain arrived, he placed an arm around my shoulder and said, "I know this is hard. But do you think you can say a few words honoring your father?"

I shrugged. "I wouldn't know what to say."

"Just speak from the heart, Leo. You'll be fine."

Before the captain stepped away, I reached out, grabbed his arm, and asked, "Where's Major Lawrence going to be buried?"

"Don't worry, Leo," he said, patting my shoulder. "Far away from here. I'm having his body sent down South to his family in Virginia."

There were nearly thirty people, including Sarah, Alice, and Abe, huddled around Father's grave. I had hoped to have a rabbi conducting the service, but the captain said the closest one he knew of was in Harrisburg, which was too far away. Instead, the school's minister said a few nondenominational prayers before the captain shared some nice words about Father, and then it was time for me to begin. I stepped forward, only inches away from the open grave, where the plain wooden coffin lay. I took a moment to stare, with my hands clasped, and then I looked up at the congregants and spoke.

"When I was a child, Mother read Bible stories to me. My favorite was Samson and Delilah. Of course, as a young boy, I couldn't understand the hero's obsession with the alluring woman, but I certainly appreciated his incredible strength. I remember lying in my bed, listening to Mother tell the fable of the great Samson killing the mighty lion with his bare hands. As she read, I would close my eyes, imagining the heroic battle between the ferocious lion and my powerful hero. His tales of courage and strength conjured up fantastic images. Even now, I can picture him in my mind. I see the same face of the champion I once did when Mother read to me so many years ago. It was and will always be the face of Father," I said, gesturing to the coffin resting deep in the grave.

"Father was my Samson, my hero. His hands were the hands of God placed upon the earth to defend the poor and the meek. Yes, he was a man of great physical strength, but he was also a gentle, kind, and quiet man who taught by example, never needing words to demonstrate what it meant to live an honorable life." I paused and pushed the tears off my face with the back of my hand.

"What about the prayer Tom gave you to read?" Sarah said, reminding me of the note Tom had handed me before he disappeared.

I nodded. I pulled out the paper and read the Navajo prayer for the dead.

"As I walk, as I walk. The universe is walking with me. In beauty it walks before me. In beauty it walks behind me. In beauty it walks below me. In beauty it walks above me. Beauty is on every side. As I walk, I walk with beauty.

"Rest in peace, Father. I love you. You will be missed."

Just as I finished, Maggie came running toward us and whispered something to Captain Pratt. The way he jerked his head back, wide-eyed, I knew what she'd told him.

"I'm sorry, Leo, but I need to go," he said, and charged off with Maggie.

"What's happened?" Sarah asked.

I turned, making sure the captain and Maggie were far enough away, and said, "Tom escaped last night."

*

While making a last-minute inspection of my barrack, I tried making sense of why Tom would want to be part of a show that seemed, by its advertisement, to denigrate the Indian. But maybe, as he said, it would offer him the education he was seeking, as well as a way to get a good distance from the law who was no doubt searching for him.

While contemplating Tom's future, I heard the front door squeak open. I turned my head and saw William. He joined me and said, "Do you think the captain will send the police after Tom?"

"Yes, but I doubt they'll catch him," I said with a sigh.

"Where do you think he went?"

Not wanting to share Tom's secret, and even more surprisingly, Red Shirt's, I shrugged and said, "I wish I knew."

"I'm glad he killed the major," William said, looking up at me.

I took a deep breath, slowly exhaled, and said, "So am I."

We stood together for a moment without saying a word. The silence was soon pierced by sounds coming from the distance.

"What's that?" William asked, wide-eyed.

"Shush," I said, cupping my hand behind my ear. "I believe I can hear—"

"It's the wagons!" William shouted. "I hear them!" He ran off to greet his long-lost friends.

Chapter 24
The Kiss

"Do not go into the water until we get there!" I shouted, as Sarah and I hurried to keep up with our twenty-eight rambunctious boys and girls who wanted to run ahead and leap carefree into the pond. I couldn't blame them, as sweltering heat and humidity settled upon Carlisle for several days and our only relief was the afternoon swims. By the time we reached the pond, the children were creeping into the water, some already in as deep as their knees. Once Sarah and I released them, it was only the blink of an eye before they were thoroughly submerged, laughing and splashing.

For the rest of the afternoon, while the children swam, Sarah and I shared stories of what we had done over the summer months. She told me about her internship with her uncle, Senator Cameron. "The last few weeks before school started, I was home, since Congress was in recess for the month of August. But before that, I experienced a frenzy of what life was like for a United States Senator in Washington," she boasted.

As she spoke, I imagined Sarah wearing a dress with her hair pinned up and her face painted with makeup, highlighting her bright blue eyes, while she assisted her uncle as he wielded power in the nation's capital. She shook me out of my bliss by telling me disturbing reports of what was happening in the former Confederate states.

She leaned in, lowered her voice, and said, "Of course, with the abolition of slavery, one cannot deny that life for the Negroes has improved, but there are stories coming from the South that men are being lynched."

"Lynched?" I asked, unfamiliar with the word.

Sara pursed her lips, shook her head, and said, "There are men called white supremacists who terrorize Negros with their version of justice known as *vigilantism*, which means they take the law into their own hands. When they learn of a colored man accused of a crime, they'll apprehend him, perform a mock trial, and of course find him guilty, even if the accused was already cleared of the crime by a proper court." Her brow furrowed. "Their version of justice is quick and brutal. Sometimes they'll hang the poor soul or whip him into a bloody mess. It's a barbarous act, meant to intimidate an entire community by reinforcing their self-proclaimed hierarchies of race."

My mouth hung open. How could men be so cruel to one another?

She raised a finger in the air and continued, "I heard this story about a Negro man named Bill Gilmer who lived in Tennessee. He was whipped for using offensive language in the vicinity of the wife of Thomas Wood, a prominent attorney."

"He was whipped just for using bad language?"

Sarah nodded and said, "Then, by chance, someone shot and killed Thomas Wood. Naturally, the first suspect was Bill Gilmer. He was tried in a Tennessee court, but found innocent because he had a solid alibi that held up in court. He was freed.

"A few days after the trial, a group of men came, at night, dressed in white robes, and white hoods covering their faces. They dragged Gilmer from his home and brought him to a nearby farm, where flaming torches lit up a barn, serving as a mock courtroom. They had their own judge and a jury, and after a few questions and a brief reiteration of the accusations, Gilmer was found guilty and sentenced to death by hanging, which was immediately carried out in a field where a large oak tree stood."

"How do you know all this, Sarah?"

"The government embedded a lawman in the group who witnessed it all. They were able to arrest several of the men."

"Who were these men in the white robes?"

"They call themselves the Ku Klux Klan, and trust me, Leo, you don't ever want to cross their path."

I rubbed the back of my neck while quietly watching the children and thought of what it must have been like for Bill Gilmer the moment the noose was slipped over his neck and the horse he sat upon kicked away. I imagined him swinging back and forth as the men in the white robes rejoiced.

"Enough of these gruesome stories. Tell me about your summer," Sarah said, breaking my nightmarish thoughts.

I smiled and nodded, appreciating the change in the subject matter. I told her how William and I traveled by train to Pine Ridge to see Chief Red Shirt, my unusual encounter with the Lakota people, and, in particular, with the mysterious holy man known as Black Elk. "I never met anyone like him, and there was something strange that he said to me."

Sarah opened her palms, inviting me to continue.

"Black Elk is known to have visions, and he saw me in one of them."

"He saw you in a vision?" she said, with her eyes wide open in anticipation.

"He said I would be the one to find their lost Sacred Pipe."

Sarah furrowed her brow and asked, "What pipe?"

I told Sarah the story of how the Lakota people were gifted the pipe by the White Buffalo Calf Woman, then how the outlaw Lame Johnny stole it and hid it in a cavern somewhere in the Black Hills.

Sarah shook her head, expressing her confusion, and asked, "And you're the one who's supposed to find it?"

"I know it sounds crazy. But Chief Red Shirt believed it to be true as well."

Sarah smiled, leaned over, and gently kissed my cheek. "Well, you are a special person, Leo. Apparently, I'm not the only one who sees it."

I touched the spot where Sarah kissed me and, without allowing another thought to stop me, I leaned in and kissed her lips. To my surprise, her mouth accepted mine and as we lingered in the moment, a warmth exploded within me; I was lost in a delightful world of unique pleasures.

When our lips parted, I stared into her eyes, and the pleasurable warmth cascaded through me. *This must be what love feels like*, I thought. Seconds later, the spell was broken by the giggling and snickers of a few of our boys and girls who were standing before us, gawking at their counselors kissing. I looked back at Sarah, whose cheeks were flushed.

"Go away," I said, waving a hand. The children scattered back into the water.

I turned back to Sarah and whispered, "I love you, Sarah."

She smiled, adjusted her seated, cross-legged position to look directly at me, and said, "I love you too, Leo. But you must realize, like

Romeo and Juliet, our love is forbidden, destined for a tragic ending. We mustn't allow our passions to take us down that path."

"I don't understand," I said, as her words drained me of the passion that had pumped through me only a moment before. "I read the play, thanks to you, and it's true, what you say—how it ended badly. But what's to say we're destined for the same?"

"Just like Romeo and Juliet, we are from different tribes."

I jerked my head back and furrowed my brow. "Different tribes? You mean, like the Indians?"

Sarah sighed, leaned forward, and said, "Do you seriously think my uncle would permit me to marry a Jew?"

My jaw hung open while I gathered my scattering thoughts. "That's a problem?"

"You are naïve, Leo," Sarah said, shaking her head. "According to him, Jews, Indians, Negroes, they're all problems. If William Shakespeare knew my uncle, he would have been inspired to write a tragedy that would make Macbeth seem like a children's bedtime story."

CHAPTER 25
THE STORM

A late April snowstorm was the last thing anyone expected, as the past several days had teased us with promising signs of spring. Nevertheless, it snowed all day and well into the night, burying the Great Lawn under a foot of powder. The boys didn't complain, spending the entire afternoon blissfully tossing snowballs, and building forts and snowmen. We returned to the barrack after dinner as darkness fell and readied ourselves for the bedtime story. The boys were exhausted, and it wasn't too much later before they fell asleep.

As the winds swirled the snow into towering drifts against the barrack and the cold seeped in through expanding cracks in the wallboards, I added a few more logs to the stove. I then propped myself up in bed and pulled my blanket up to my chin, trying to warm up.

I thought about Sarah, wondering if she too was lying in her bed, cold and alone. How I wished I could have comforted her, kissed her, and even dared to make love with her. Though such thoughts occupied my mind nearly every night, for some reason they were especially potent tonight, causing me to consider—*What if I crossed the field of snow, snuck into her barrack, and slipped into bed with her? How wonderful it would be to caress Sarah's body, kiss her lips, and stroke her golden hair.*

As I allowed myself to fantasize, my virgin body warmed considerably. Then, like a cold shower, Mother's face appeared, engaging my guilt about having relations with a woman not of our faith. But at the moment, with my loins on fire, I dismissed my contemplations of disappointing my deceased mother.

Father, on the other hand, would have had no problem with my sinful musings, perhaps even encouraging me. After all, he had made love with Alice, a Negro woman, and given her a child.

It wasn't often I allowed myself to dwell upon my parents, as such thoughts stirred up the grief I struggled to keep suppressed. I tried pushing away the images of seeing them both violently killed before my eyes. Instead, I focused on happy times, like when Mother and Father first met.

I remembered being a young boy, lying in bed and begging Mother to tell me the story once more. "Again?" she would ask with a smile. "I've told you hundreds of times."

"Yes, please," I said, staring into Mother's blue eyes.

"Very well," she conceded. "I was attending classes at the synagogue when I saw your father for the first time. I, along with every girl, turned our heads as he walked by our window. After all, he was tall, muscular, and very good looking. But he didn't even know I existed until he came to our home one day with his father, Jacob, your grandfather. My parents were planning to build an extension on to our home in Carlisle, and asked Jacob the carpenter to come take a look. He arrived with Isaac, who had just turned seventeen years old. They were hired, but I didn't see them again for several weeks, when they began the work. I can still remember your father with his tool belt cinched to his waist, swinging his hammer. He was so handsome, so strong. I would stare at him for hours. Since your father was too shy to speak to me, I needed to think of a way for us to meet privately."

"What did you do?" I asked, though I already knew the story by heart.

"Well," Mother said, shifting her eyebrows, "I waited for your father to be sent into town for supplies. While he headed off on foot, I quickly hitched our horse to the wagon, caught up with him, and asked, 'Would you like a ride, Isaac?'

"He blushed the color of an apple," Mother said, with a grin and a sparkle in her eyes, reliving the moment. "He was so nervous that he turned to look back at the house, worried someone would see us. Then he nodded and climbed onto the seat next to me."

"What did you talk about?"

"We spoke about school and what we wanted to do with our lives— though I did most of the talking. You know how quiet your father is."

I chuckled and nodded.

Just thinking about their love story put me in a happy mood. So much so that I got to my feet, dressed, and decided to act upon my urges to sneak over to see Sarah.

I knew the consequences should I get caught. Captain Pratt, as he demonstrated with others who disobeyed his strict rules, would dismiss me on the spot. Though at this point, with the end of the school year only four weeks away, I doubted he would leave my group without a counselor.

Without awakening any of the boys, I dressed and headed outdoors into the raging storm, pushing my way through the wind-driven snow. Once I reached Sarah's barrack, I took a moment to glance around, making sure no one saw me as I climbed the steps to the front porch. This would be the first time I dared to enter the barrack while Sarah and her girls were inside, awake or asleep.

The creaking of the wooden door was swallowed by the whistling of the winds. I stepped inside but couldn't see much of anything, though I could sense the dozens of little girls asleep in their bunks. While I stood there, staring into the darkness, I heard Sarah whisper, "Leo, over here."

I turned to the voice and saw her silhouette in the shadows. I approached and sat down on the edge of her bed, where I was able to see her face. Without hesitation, she lifted her blanket and invited me to crawl in.

Once I was lying alongside her, she said, "What took you so long?"

I thought my heart would burst through my chest, and didn't wait for another invitation to kiss her. We remained locked in each other's arms for hours, while our lips and tongues mingled, our hands caressing each other.

Before morning broke, I returned to my barrack, nearly gliding over the snow in a state of perfect bliss. We had not gone all the way, but certainly more than I'd experienced before. She was the only woman I could ever imagine myself with.

Chapter 26
Alice Gives Birth

Abe charged into the barrack one morning in early May just as the sun rose over the tree line, flooding the Great Lawn with a warm light. "Leo! Wake up, the baby's coming," he shouted, loud enough to stir the boys from their slumber.

I sat up, rubbed my eyes, and groaned, "Are you sure?"

"Of course I'm sure. The captain called the midwife. She's there now. We're going to have a brother. Hurry, Leo."

"You know, it could be a girl," I reminded Abe, as I pulled up my pants and slipped on my shoes.

Abe shrugged.

"Samuel, get the boys ready for the day. I'll catch up later," I said, as we bolted out of the barrack and across the Great Lawn.

I could hear Alice screaming, a startling cry that echoed throughout the Carlisle infirmary as we ran through the hallways. Abe turned to look at me, his hand covering his mouth, and said, "What's happening?"

"She's giving birth. Sarah told me that it's painful for the mother."

The thick plaster walls where we waited in the adjoining room did little to muffle the agonizing cries. Except for the occasional momentary, wide-eyed glance over to Abe, I kept my gaze glued to the door, waiting for someone to walk out and announce the news of the birth.

It took about a half-hour more before the door opened and out walked the midwife. She looked at us and said, "It's a boy! Both mother and baby are doing well."

Abe jumped to his feet and boasted, "I knew it!"

"You were right. We have a brother," I said, as we embraced.

Once allowed inside the delivery room, we saw the baby wrapped in a cloth, snuggling in the arms of Alice.

"Come and meet your new brother. I'm naming him Isaac," she said, looking directly at me and brushing back a sweaty strand of hair.

Tears swelled in my eyes, and then, as if a dam were breaking, they cascaded down my cheeks. I hesitated to step forward, unsure of the protocol for a newborn.

"You can come closer, Leo, he won't bite," Alice said, in a weary voice.

I looked at Abe, who graciously stepped aside for me to approach before he did. I nodded and moved alongside the bed. Alice grabbed my hand, squeezed it, and said, "Isn't he beautiful?"

"Can I touch him?" I said, rubbing the tears from my eyes.

Alice nodded and said, "Of course."

The moment I reached out and gently stroked his smooth-as-glass skin, Isaac stopped sucking, turned his head, and looked at me. We held each other's gaze for a moment, then a sensation, as best as I can describe it a chill, shook me. It was as if the baby knew me and reached out in the only way he was able to, through his newborn eyes.

I turned to look at Abe, pointed at Isaac, and said, "Did you see that?"

Abe shrugged, unsure of what I was referring to.

"That's amazing," I said, smiling broadly.

After we had a chance to greet our new brother, the midwife asked us to leave so Alice could rest. We offered our farewells, and I walked over to the dining hall where the children were having breakfast, while Abe went to the kitchen to help out with the serving.

*

Later that day, while the children played on the Great Lawn, I told Sarah about the birth. "It was remarkable," I said, keeping an eye on some roughhousing between a few of my boys and two from the eight-year-old group. "When Isaac caught my eyes, it was as if he recognized me."

"That's wonderful, Leo. I'm so happy for you," she said, sounding distant.

Ever since our late-night intimate encounter, Sarah never allowed me to speak of it. Whenever I hinted at the subject, she quickly dismissed it by changing the conversation. To my disappointment, it appeared Sarah would stick to her conviction of considering me nothing more than a good friend. But that didn't mean that I was able to control my fantasies. As a result, a pent-up desire was storing itself somewhere deep inside of me, and I worried if there was a limit to what I could suppress.

CHAPTER 27
THE TELEGRAM

Before I knew it, the school year was swiftly drawing to a close. Next week, the children would be sent off to their summer assignments, while I had yet to solidify my plans. Without Father or Tom to work alongside, any possible carpentry work seemed menial, as I could only manage small projects on my own. Of course, William wanted to stay with me no matter what. This indecision was about to come to an end when Captain Pratt sent word that he wanted to see me.

When I arrived, Maggie offered me a nod and said, "He's waiting for you, Leo."

I took a breath, trying to calm my nerves, worried that someone had seen me sneaking into Sarah's barrack. "Good afternoon, Captain," I said, pushing the door open.

Captain Pratt ignored me, keeping his eyes focused on a telegram. Awkwardly, I stepped over to one of the spindle-back chairs in front of his desk and sat down.

"What do you know about this?" he asked, handing it to me. I reached out and took the telegram and read it aloud.

LEOPOLD WOLF=

=PLEASE ADVISE YOUR EXPECTED DATE OF DEPARTURE FROM CARLISLE. WE WILL ARRANGE FOR YOUR TRANSPORTATION FROM CARLISLE TO PINE RIDGE.

=AWAITING YOUR PROMPT REPLY. OUR PEOPLE ARE GRATEFUL FOR YOUR DECISION.

=CHIEF RED SHIRT=

When finished, I looked up at the captain. He tapped off the ashes clinging to his cigar and asked, "Can you tell me what this is about?"

I sighed and glanced once more at the telegram. "*Um*, I think it has to do with last summer when the chief asked if I would help find something they lost. I didn't think I could, so I said I would need to think about it."

The captain squinted and leaned back in his chair. "What did they lose?"

"A pipe," I said.

The captain took a puff of his cigar, blew it out the side of his mouth, and said, "The Sacred Pipe?"

"Yes," I said nodding. "How did you know?"

"I've heard those same stories about the White Buffalo Calf Woman's gift to the Lakota people and how it was stolen."

"By Lame Johnny," I added.

"Yes, I read about the robbery and how that lowlife was lynched. But why do they want you to search for the Sacred Pipe?"

"According to what Black Elk said, there's—"

"You met Black Elk?" the captain interrupted.

I nodded. "Yes, when I was at Pine Ridge. He had a vision that I would be the one to help find the pipe. They said it's hidden in the caves up in the Black Hills."

"You?" the captain said, pointing his cigar. "Why you?"

I shrugged and said, "It sounded strange to me, too."

"Well," the captain said, snuffing out his cigar, "I trust you're not going."

"I don't know. Though I've—"

"Well, Leo, let me help you out," the captain said, interrupting me. "You're not going. The last thing we need is to give hope to those people that their way of life has a chance of surviving. Especially after all the things we do here in order to kill those fanciful fairy tales. We must remain true to our mission and bring the Indian into the world of the white man."

I stared at the captain, unable to conjure up a response.

"It's better off lost, for everyone's sake," he finished.

I sighed and looked down at the telegram. "But I don't think it's a fairy tale," I said, shaking my head. "When I met Black Elk, he seemed like a prophet with spiritual powers, like Isaiah."

"Isaiah?" the captain repeated.

"Yes. My mother told me the Bible story of how Isaiah was God's messenger. He too had visions."

"That's fine, Leo," he said with a sigh. "Regardless, I forbid it. You can stay on here for the summer. We have plenty of carpentry projects to keep you busy."

"But what if I don't want to be busy?" I said, in a bombastic tone.

The captain squinted and asked, "What are you trying to say?"

"Maybe I want to go to the Black Hills and search for the Sacred Pipe," I said, surprising myself with my own audacity.

He blinked and shook his head. "I already told you, Leo, I won't allow it."

I tugged on my beard and said, "But you really can't stop me."

The captain's jaw fell open, and he stared at me for a long while before he replied, "That's true. Just don't expect to have a position here when you return in the fall."

"What if your premise about the Indians is wrong?" I asked, cocking my chin at the captain. "They lived in peace for hundreds of years before the white man came and destroyed their way of life. Why can't you leave them be?"

The captain leaned back in his chair, folded his arms across his chest, and said, "Do you want to know why I founded the Carlisle Indian School?"

"To kill the Indian and save the man?" I said, repeating what had become known as the school's mantra.

The captain sighed. "Yes, but that's not just a clever slogan I conjured up. Before Carlisle, I spent eight years out in the Great Plains fighting with the army in the Indian Wars—first at the Battle of the Washita River with Custer, then later in the Red River War, where we pushed several tribes into reservations. It was from those experiences that I understood that there must be a better way to achieve peace, which I believed and still do to this day—that the Indians should receive an American education and be absorbed into American society." He rose to his feet and walked over to the window overlooking the Carlisle campus.

"After much convincing, I gained support from my superiors on this view, and in 1875, I was given command of seventy-two Indian prisoners at St. Augustine, Florida where we began, through education, to transform the most savage of men into law-abiding citizens. We succeeded in the process. This was the seed that eventually resulted in all of this." He held out his arms.

"That's all well and good," I said with a shrug. "But it was still done against their free will."

The captain smiled, walked toward me, put his hand on my shoulder, and said, "Apparently there's much you need to learn about the world. Go and find your own way, make your mistakes, and hopefully learn from them. I wish you good luck, Leopold Wolf."

With that, I said goodbye to the captain, and on my way back to the barrack, I saw Sarah with her girls seated in a circle on the Great Lawn. When she looked up, I offered a smile and a wave, hoping to get a moment to speak with her later and share my impulsive decision to return to Pine Ridge. But first, I would need to tell William, who would no doubt be ecstatic at the prospect of going home to his family.

Chapter 28
Farewell

Sarah squeezed my hand and smiled. "Do you think we'll see each other again?"

"I hope so," I said, relishing her soft palm pressed against mine.

"What's going to happen with the house?" she asked, glancing around the kitchen.

"I'll close it up for now. When I return in the fall, maybe I'll get Wolf and Son back in business—though I don't have a son," I said, with a shrug.

"Not yet," Sarah said, lifting her brow.

"This would make a wonderful home to raise a family," I said, with the uplifting thought of Sarah being my wife and mother to our children.

"It would," she said, without encouraging me further, and just as swiftly deflating my fantastical musings.

"Have you heard back from your uncle about interning this summer?"

"Yes, just this morning." She lifted an envelope from her jacket pocket. "He wants me to meet him in Washington as soon as school is dismissed."

"That's good," I said, with an exasperated sigh.

"What's wrong, Leo? You sound sad. Don't you want to go to Pine Ridge?"

"I want to go," I said, staring into Sarah's eyes. "But it's just—I'll miss seeing you."

"Leo," Sarah said, wrapping an arm around my waist. "You are sweet."

I placed my hand behind her neck and gently pulled her close, kissing her pink lips. As we parted, I felt my legs wobble a bit. "You're the love of my life, Sarah."

Sarah placed a palm on her chest and smiled. "I know, Leo, and I love you too, but we mustn't act on our urges."

A sudden fit of rage flooded my thoughts, forcing me to shout, "Dammit! Why are people so screwed up? All this hatred. I wish we could just run away to some place where no one cared. Just the two of us."

Sarah stroked my beard and said, "You know that's not possible."

Just as I was about to press her further, William barged in and said, "Oh, hello, Sarah. I didn't know you were here."

"Hello, William. I understand you're heading back home. Are you excited?"

"Yes, very," he said with a dimple-laden smile.

Sarah turned to me and asked, "When are you boys leaving?"

"We're catching the 6:40 train tomorrow morning."

"Well, I guess this is farewell, then?" Sarah said, with a tilt of her head.

"Not just yet. Would you mind walking with me to the cemetery? I'd like to see Father's grave one more time."

Sarah nodded and said, "Of course."

The campus was nearly empty of students as Sarah and I crossed the Great Lawn. As we walked, Sarah grabbed my arm and said, "Why don't you ask Alice to move into the house with Abraham and the baby? At least until you get back. After all, they're nearly family."

"Well, Isaac Junior is my brother," I said, considering the idea.

"This way, they'll have more room than they do at the captain's home."

I nodded. "That's a great idea."

Just as we approached the cemetery, Alice came running toward us with eyes bulging and called out, "Have either of you seen Abraham?"

"No," I said. "Is something wrong?"

"I sent him into town early this morning to pick up a few things and he hasn't returned."

"That's hours ago," I said with a grimace.

Alice nodded. "I'm worried something has happened. Would you go look for him?"

"Of course," I said. "I'll go right now."

Sarah put a hand on my shoulder and said, "I'm coming with you."

"Would you watch William?" I asked Alice. "He's at the house."

Alice nodded. I ran to the stable and hitched Wili to the wagon and within minutes, Sarah and I were heading into town in search of Abe.

*

When we reached Gruber's General Store on Main Street, Mr. Gruber was standing on the sidewalk with his hands on his hips. The moment he spotted us, he waved to me and said, "That boy of yours, what's his name?"

"Abraham?" I said.

Mr. Grant nodded. "Yeah, yeah, him."

"Has something happened? Is he here?" I asked, looking around.

"He was, until he was taken away by some man who claims to know Major Lawrence."

"Major Lawrence?" I repeated, feeling my stomach churn.

"What does this have to do with the major?" Sarah demanded.

"Abraham was in my store picking up supplies when this man, who I didn't know, walked in and seemed to become agitated at the sight of him. After he pushed him around and said a few foul things, he snatched a bag of beans off the shelf, held it high in one hand, and with the other, dragged Abraham by the collar to my counter and accused him of stealing."

"Was he?" I asked.

Mr. Gruber shook his head. "No, of course not. I know Abraham. He comes into the store several times a week."

"So, what happened?"

"I told the man to leave the boy alone. I said he's not a thief and that he works over at the Carlisle Indian School. When he heard that, the man became hostile, and asked if Abraham knew Major Lawrence. Which he said he did."

I shared a look with Sarah, who appeared frozen in place.

"He was upset with what happened to the major, saying he was murdered by one of those savage Indians at that school of yours. The next thing I knew, the man dragged Abraham from the store. He threw him into the back of a wagon and before I could stop him, he drove away."

"Which way did they go?" I asked.

"They headed west," Mr. Gruber said, pointing.

"Mr. Gruber, it was Major Lawrence who killed my father."

"Major Lawrence was a soldier of the South," Sarah added. "If this man was a friend of his, then I'm afraid Abe's life is in danger. Leo, do you remember what I told you about lynching? We must find him."

"Who's this man that took Abe?" I asked Mr. Gruber.

He shrugged and said, "All I know is he was taken away in a wagon from McClure's Pig Farm. The name was painted on its sideboards."

"McClure's Pig Farm?" I said, unfamiliar with the enterprise. "Where's that?"

"It's a mile straight out of town," he said, cocking his chin.

"Thank you," I said.

Mr. Gruber grimaced and said, "I'd think twice before mixing it up with those boys."

"Why is that?" Sarah asked, wide-eyed.

"Because they're troublesome. To say the least. If I were you, I'd forget about it and head on home."

"*Pfft,*" I said. "We can't do that."

"All right, it's your decision. But you'll need more than the two of you to get your boy back," Mr. Gruber said.

"But there's no time," Sarah said, gripping my forearm.

"Thank you, Mr. Gruber," I said, and gave Wili a snap with the crop.

CHAPTER 29
TROUBLE

A weathered, hand-painted wooden sign was nailed to a fence post, advertising McClure's Pig Farm.

"Maybe we should leave Wili here and walk in," I whispered.

Sarah looked around, nodded, and said, "All right."

We proceeded along a dirt road surrounded by thick woods until the smell of pig manure seeped into my nostrils. The stink reminded me of what Mother once said, about why Jews weren't permitted to eat pork. *They're unclean because they don't chew their cud, and they live like scavengers, prone to sickness,* she would say.

I tapped Sarah on her shoulder, pointed to the woods, and whispered, "We should stay hidden."

She nodded. We held hands as we slid down the embankment into a marsh and sank ankle-deep into the softness. Though it soaked through our shoes and socks, we were able to advance without too much trouble, while remaining hidden from the road.

About ten minutes in, we heard pigs squealing, which I assumed meant they were being fed. "Come on," I said, hurrying Sarah along, figuring this would be a good time to observe the farm, with the McClures distracted by their chores.

We soon found ourselves a few feet away from the tree line with an unobstructed view of a log home and a barn with a fence, slick in mud, where a tall skinny man was attending to the pigs engaged in a feeding frenzy.

"Maybe Abe's in the barn," Sarah whispered, pointing.

I nodded. "Okay, but we should wait until dark, or they'll see us."

Sarah sighed and nodded. So, we settled in, while keeping an eye out for any sign of Abe.

*

By the time darkness fell, Sarah and I had lain on the damp forest floor for hours. While tired, hungry, and covered in mud, we agreed to emerge from the marsh and search for Abe. As we rose to our feet, ready to step out onto the open field, we heard voices coming from the log cabin. Suddenly the door opened, allowing the light from the lanterns within to spill out onto the porch, and four men emerged, one of them the skinny man we had seen feeding the pigs earlier.

They gathered a moment as each picked out a pine tar torch from a basket. One of the men lit one with a match and then shared his flame with the others. The four men, with torches held high, proceeded to the barn. When their backs were turned toward us, Sarah and I emerged from the woods and followed.

As they made their way, we stayed back, unable to see their faces, but close enough to hear their conversation.

"Johnny, did you fix the rope?" a graveled voice said.

"I did," said a man with a southern drawl. "It's ready to go."

"Once we're done with the trial, let's hang this nigger and get him chopped up," Stanley said. "The piggies will have a feast."

"Oh, my Lord, Leo," Sarah whispered, "they're going to murder Abe and feed him to the pigs."

I rubbed the back of my neck, trying to think of ways we could save him. But with just the two of us and no weapons to challenge four men, we were outmatched. "Maybe there are guns in their cabin," I said.

Sarah nodded vigorously.

"Stay here while I go look," I said and ran toward the cabin. With my heart pumping more from fear than exertion, I reached the porch, where the door was left slightly ajar. I held my breath, pushed it open, and stepped inside. To my relief, the one-room cabin was vacant except for an old beagle slumped on the floor, who lifted his tired eyes to look at me.

I moved with caution, wanting to keep the dog settled, but instead, he rose to all fours and approached, wagging his tail. As I bent down to pet him, he sniffed my hand, just as I noticed a shotgun leaning against a wall. Luckily, it looked like the same type of Winchester that Father had taught me to use when we went hunting.

I grabbed it and checked to see that it was loaded. Satisfied, I looked around and saw, on a nearby shelf, a box of cartridges. I was about to pocket a few when the dog became agitated and growled. As I reached down to comfort him, his eyes widened, and he barked, causing me to jerk backward.

Without trying to settle him down, I left the cabin and ran across the field with the beagle yapping at my heels. The sudden break in the silence caught Sarah's attention. But before she approached, I held out my hand, hoping she would stay back while I made my assault on the barn.

Halfway there, the dog gave up chasing me, but continued his incessant barking. The moment I reached the barn door, it slid open and the skinny man stood there facing me, goggle-eyed. "Who the hell are you?" he demanded.

I pointed the shotgun at him and said, "I'm here for Abraham."

The skinny man turned to look behind him, where a man dressed in a white robe stood before a wooden table staring at me. Two other men, dressed the same way and seated facing my friend, twisted around to see the disturbance. Abraham, with his hands folded on the table, stared back at me.

"Abe," I called out. "Hurry!"

In the blink of an eye, Abe realized what was happening, jumped to his feet, and sprinted toward me. Just before reaching the barn door, the skinny man blocked his way and pulled a knife. "Take another step, nigger, and I'll slit your throat."

Abe froze and looked at me, his mouth hanging open.

"Let him pass," I demanded, pointing the rifle at him.

The skinny man looked at me and scoffed. "You don't have the guts to shoot me," he said and thrust the knife toward Abe. Without hesitation, I fired, shooting the man in his side. He collapsed to the ground and moaned before falling silent. Abe and I stood there frozen until Sarah screamed, "Run!"

CHAPTER 30
ESCAPE

We fled down the dark road while voices rang out behind us, letting us know the men of McClure's Pig Farm were in close pursuit. I'd dropped the rifle the moment I shot the skinny man, and feared if they were able to catch us, we would all be lynched.

Wili snorted his greeting as we reached the end of the road and climbed on board the wagon. Abe sat next to me, while Sarah found a spot in the back. "Hurry, Leo," she urged. "They're coming."

I heard the shouting as I cracked the whip on Wili's hind. The sharpness of my snap caused him to jerk forward, nearly knocking Abe and me off our perch and sending Sarah tumbling onto the wagon's floorboards.

I gripped the reins, doing my best to encourage Wili, though I knew with the weight of the three of us he couldn't move as swiftly. Just as I considered ditching the wagon and running, shots rang out. The McClures were firing at us.

"Keep your head down, Sarah," I shouted.

The gunfire spooked Wili into a full gallop, nearly bouncing us out of the wagon. But we managed to hold on, as the McClures eventually gave up the chase. We sped through town and didn't stop until we made it back to Carlisle.

When Wili came to a full stop on the Great Lawn, I let go of the reins, dropped my face into my hands, and sighed.

Abe grabbed my arm and said, "Leo, I think there's something wrong with Sarah."

I twisted around and saw Sarah lying on her side, her hands clutching her stomach. I climbed into the wagon and gently shook her, and said, "Sarah, it's okay, it's over. We're home."

She groaned as she tried to lift her head and said, "I've been shot."

"What?" I said, looking down at her body.

Sarah slowly turned over, and I saw a large patch of blood staining her blouse.

"Sarah!" I cried out and turned to Abe. "Take us to the captain's house."

Abe snapped the whip on Wili's hind and within a few minutes, we pulled around back to the kitchen entrance. "I'll get Mother," Abe said. He leaped from the wagon and ran inside.

In the meantime, I rolled Sarah onto her back and placed my hand on the gunshot wound, trying to stop the bleeding. Sarah grasped my hand and asked, "Am I going to die?"

"No, no. Alice is coming and she'll mend you up, I promise."

"I want you to know something, Leo," she said, struggling with each word.

"Don't speak. Save your energy."

"I must tell you, in case I die."

"You're going to be fine," I insisted.

"Come closer," she said, breathing heavily.

I leaned in, bringing my face inches from hers. She blinked her bloodshot eyes and said in a whisper, "I love you, Leo."

Those words nearly made my heart burst forth from my chest. "I love you, too," I said, barely able to get the words out.

"Out of my way," came the voice of the captain, who appeared with Alice.

"Sarah's been shot," I said.

"Let's get her in the house," Captain Pratt ordered. "I've already sent someone to fetch the doctor."

Abe and I lifted Sarah from the wagon and carried her into the kitchen. We placed her on the dining table, where Alice had laid out a sheet and a pillow.

"What the hell happened?" the captain demanded.

"Those men out at McClure's Pig Farm were about to lynch Abe. Sarah and I saved him, and as we were making our escape, they shot Sarah."

Captain Pratt looked down at Sarah, who was losing consciousness but still breathing. He poked a hard finger into my chest and said, "She better not die, Leo." Then he turned and left the kitchen.

Once out of earshot, Alice said, "He's such a bastard."

My eyes welled up while I kept my gaze on Sarah and asked, "Is she going to be all right?"

"It's hard to know," Alice said while keeping pressure on the wound.

*

"She's in here," Abe said, holding open the door for Dr. White, a man familiar to us at Carlisle. He was the staff doctor who treated the children when they came down with various ailments, including the tuberculosis that had been so deadly.

"Let me see her," Dr. White said, entering the room.

After he'd examined the wound for a minute or so, I asked, "What do you think?"

Dr. White shook his head. "The bullet is too deep. She needs to go to the hospital. Let's move her to my wagon," Dr. White said. "There's a stretcher in the back."

"I'll get it," Abe said and ran off.

A moment later he returned, and Abe and I lifted Sarah off the table while the doctor slid the army-style stretcher under her. "Follow me," Dr. White said, leading us through the back door and out to the wagon.

Once Sarah was settled, the doctor said, "One of you needs to ride with her."

"I'll go," I said.

"You're not going anywhere," Captain Pratt called out.

"But I want to," I said, placing a hand on Sarah's shoulder.

"You and Abe are coming with me to the police station," the captain said, pointing at us. "Alice will ride with her."

"Is that necessary right now?" I asked, my face turning red with anger.

"We need to get those McClure boys arrested. I can't have things getting nasty in Carlisle," the captain said.

"Can I go to the hospital afterward?"

"It's best you keep your distance from her. I just sent a telegram to her uncle, who I doubt wants you by her side. You may have gotten the poor woman killed. Say your goodbyes now, Leo. Whether she survives or not, I doubt you'll see her again."

On the day I returned to Pine Ridge, I still had no idea whether Sarah had survived the gunshot wound. Abe said he would try to send word if he heard anything. I sat with Black Elk, sharing the tragic news about Sarah's condition and Father's murder, and he listened, doing his best to comfort me.

"I understand your anguish," Black Elk said. "Many of my people had violent deaths."

I pinched the bridge of my nose and asked, "What do you think happens when we die?"

"I don't use that word—*die*," Black Elk said, shaking his head. "Instead, I prefer to say *walk on*, like a continuation of our journey." He waved his open hand outward across the horizon.

I furrowed my brow and asked, "Walk on? To where?"

"Into the spirit world," he said with a matter-of-fact shrug.

"That sounds comforting for those who have passed," I said. "But how do the living cope? How do I deal with my grief?"

"For our people, we find comfort through ceremony," he said with a gentle smile. "It's how we understand loss, and at the same time, it helps those who have walked on."

I nodded, absorbing Black Elk's words, and realized I'd done nothing like this for Mother or Father. Hoping it wasn't too late, I asked, "What can I do to help my parents?"

"From what you told me, your mother died long ago."

I nodded.

"Then she has already journeyed among the stars," he said, holding his hands in the air and wiggling his fingers. "But your father's death is recent, and therefore he may be searching for his place."

"What place?" I asked.

"When we are killed, like your father was, our soul is not prepared, as it would be when dying of old age or a prolonged sickness. He could use your help to transition into the spirit world."

"How do I do that?"

Black Elk stared at me for a moment, then asked, "Do you have a lock of his hair?"

"No, I don't," I said, remembering when Father was placed into the wooden coffin and buried at the Carlisle cemetery.

"That's all right. You can take a lock of yours," he said, reaching out and tugging at my red hair. "You have plenty."

I squinted at Black Elk and said, "At Carlisle, when we cut the boys' hair, a few of them cried, believing someone had died—I mean walked on."

"This is not surprising, for the Lakota children," he said, leading me to a shady spot under a rocky outcropping. "It's what they learn of our customs at an early age."

I sat down, crossed my legs, and asked, "Can you tell me of your ceremony?"

Black Elk nodded, closed his eyes, and took a few deep breaths, then said, "I can do better. Let us honor your loss and your grief with our custom."

*

Tika, a young Lakota man with two long braids and soft, round brown eyes, stepped toward me, holding out a large knife. He reached and grabbed a healthy lock of my hair and sliced it off. With the several Elders of the tribe observing, including Chief Red Shirt and Black Elk, he held the clump over a woven strand of burning sweetgrass.

"This is to purify," the chief said, sitting next to me.

Tika, once satisfied with the purification, wrapped the hair in a piece of cloth, handed it to me, and said, "This we call the *soul bundle*, and you, Leopold, are the *soul keeper*."

I took the bundle and asked, "What do I do with it?"

"Keep it safe," the chief said with a nod. "As soul keeper, you must take a vow to live a harmonious life for a year. At the end of this year, you are to take the bundle outdoors and open it, allowing the soul to be released. If the hair blows to the right, the soul is judged worthy and your father's spirit will join the Great Spirit. If, however, it is carried to the left, it will be considered tainted, and your father will be unable to begin his journey."

"Tainted?" I asked with a furrowed brow. "What does that mean?"

"Do not worry," the chief said, patting my knee. "I'm sure you'll live a harmonious life and will prove your worthiness."

I placed my hand on my chest and said, "My worthiness? Isn't it Father's soul that must move on?"

"That is so, but you are now its keeper," he said, pointing to the bundle in my lap. "Your father's eternal soul rests in your hands."

I looked down at the bundle, cinched tight with a cord, and sighed. "But how do I live a harmonious life to ensure this?"

"That has yet to be determined. In the meantime, we will smoke," the chief said and gestured to Tika to light the Sacred Pipe.

I pointed to the pipe and asked, "Is that it? Have you found it?"

Chief Red Shirt bowed his head and said, "Sadly, no."

While the pipe was being passed around, I thought of the chief's request. I looked at the men seated in the circle, including Black Elk, and said, "What if I decided to search for the stolen Sacred Pipe? Would that prove my worthiness?"

Black Elk closed his eyes, nodded, and said, "Most certainly."

*

"Is that the soul bundle?" William asked, pointing to the wrapped cloth lying next to me.

"You know what this is?" I asked, lifting my head off my pillow.

William crawled into his bed beside me. "Of course, I've seen people with it."

I suppose I shouldn't have been surprised at William's intimate knowledge of his customs. But at his age, I hardly knew what the Jewish rituals were when someone died, and even now, I wouldn't know what to do without the guidance of a rabbi.

"Those who you've seen with it," I said, pointing to the bundle, "have they lived a harmonious life?"

"I don't know, I suppose so," he said, turning over, and within a few minutes, was asleep.

For the summer, William and I were to live together, but beyond that, I had no idea of my life's direction. Certainly, a return to Carlisle seemed unlikely, especially after what happened to Sarah, as well as my disobedience in the eyes of Captain Pratt at returning to Pine Ridge.

I sighed and wondered whether, maybe, Black Elk was right. Perhaps if I sought out the lost Sacred Pipe, and proved myself worthy to the Great Spirit, that would ensure Father's soul would commence his journey.

CHAPTER 32
LEOPOLD'S QUEST

While attending to the supplies on the wagon, Chief Red Shirt approached with another man. "Looks like you have everything you need," he said, patting the neck of one of the two horses.

"I hope so, though I have no idea where I'm going," I said, tucking the soul bundle into a safe spot behind the buckboard.

"Leo, I would like you to meet my wife's brother Red Dog," he said, gesturing to the shorter man. He had a round face and a large frown that pulled down upon his baggy cheeks. "I chose him because he speaks English."

I shook the man's rough hands and said, "It's good to meet you."

Red Dog nodded his reply.

"He will accompany you into the mountains and show you the way to the cavern's entrance," the chief said.

"Oh, that's good," I said, scratching at my beard. "But what then? Will I be on my own?"

The chief nodded. "This is your journey, Leo, not Red Dog's."

"All right," I said, looking at the chief's brother-in-law. "I'll be ready to go as soon as I say goodbye to William."

"He's waiting for you by your tipi," the chief said.

As I walked through the village, many of the Lakota people approached, offering their gratitude in my quest for their lost Sacred Pipe. One elderly man hobbled over to me, grasped my arm, and asked, "Have you been told why you're the chosen one?"

"The chosen one?" I repeated.

Not waiting for an answer, the old man pulled me in closer, stared at me with his blurry, colorless eyes, and declared, "It's because Black Elk has seen it."

The moment he released me, I heard William calling out, "Leo!"

I turned and saw him running toward me.

"Hello, William," I said. "It's time for me to leave."

"Father said that Red Dog will show you the way. He's old, but tells good stories."

"Does he?" I said with a smile.

"I wish I could go with you," William said.

I patted his back and said, "That would be good, but your father would never allow me to take you."

"I know," he said and dropped his gaze down to his feet.

"Don't be sad. I'll be back before you know it."

"I know," he said again, with a sniffle. "I was just thinking about Sarah. Is she going to be okay?"

"I'm sure she's fine," I said, though I still had no knowledge of her fate. For all I knew, she could have died.

I reached out and lifted William's chin and saw him crying. He turned his head, and with the back of his hand, wiped the tears away.

"It's okay to cry," I said. "I wish I could."

"It's easy for us, because children's hearts are pure."

My jaw dropped upon hearing these words coming from an eight-year-old. "That's so true. Where did you learn that?"

"From Black Elk."

I nodded and said, "He is wise."

"That's not all of what he has taught our people," the chief said, approaching. "Black Elk's actual words were—*Grown men learn from our children, for their hearts are pure. Therefore, the Great Spirit may show them many things that older people miss.*"

I sighed, absorbing the wisdom. "This is true. During my two years as counselor at Carlisle, I have learned many things from my boys. Especially from William." I laid a hand on the boy's shoulder.

"Wisdom does not only come from the Elders," Chief Red Shirt added and turned to William. "Now, son, say goodbye to Leo. He must begin his quest."

"Quest?" William repeated.

"A quest is where we test ourselves against great obstacles, and if we succeed, our life is given a purpose," the chief said.

"I want to have a purpose. When will you send me on a quest?"

Chief Red Shirt nodded. "You will have your chance, son. But not today."

William nodded, turned to me, and said, "I hope you find the pipe, Leo."

"Thank you, William," I said.

CHAPTER 33
THE CREATION STORY

With the hot sun on our backs, we left the Lakota village and headed north on an eighty-mile journey toward Rapid City. Once there, Red Dog said the Black Hills were another fourteen miles due west. If we were able to make our way without delays, we would arrive at the cave's entrance by tomorrow afternoon.

About twenty minutes after we left the Lakota village, I said to Red Dog, "William tells me you spin a good tale."

Red Dog turned his head, looked at me with a narrowed squint, and said, "Spin what?"

"I'm sorry," I said with a chuckle. "I meant to say that you're a good storyteller. Can you share one with me, as a way to pass the time?"

Red Dog nodded, keeping his gaze straight ahead. "Perhaps," he said, taking off his hat and scratching his head, "I could tell you the story of my people's creation."

"Yes, I would like that."

"It began before man walked upon the earth. The only things in existence were plants and animals," he said, gesturing to the expansive landscape before us. "The people at this time lived underground, waiting for the Creator to prepare the earth for them to dwell upon. At this time, two spirits, Iktomi and Anog-Ite, roamed the lands. Iktomi, the spider, was a trickster spirit, while Anog-Ite, the woman spirit, had two faces. One face was beautiful, while the other was a twisted, hideous creature," he said, twisting his own face to demonstrate.

"Since they were alone on the earth, they had only each other for company. Iktomi amused himself by annoying Anog-Ite, never allowing her a moment of peace. But this eventually got boring for the spider, and he looked toward the humans to play his tricks upon."

"The humans living under the earth?" I asked.

"Yes," Red Dog said, nodding. "He was excited to try his mischief on someone new and asked Anog-Ite for help. She said she would if he promised never to torment her again. He readily agreed.

"Iktomi told Anog-Ite of his plan. She agreed and filled a leather pack with buckskin clothing, porcupine quills, ripe berries, and dried meats. Anog-Ite then summoned over her wolf companion and strapped the pack to its body. Iktomi led the wolf into the mountains and down a hole in the ground with instructions to find the humans. The wolf entered the caves and disappeared into the darkness, following long and meandering passageways.

"Eventually he found the people, spoke to them of the wonders upon the earth's surface, and instructed them to remove the items from the pack. One man took out the buckskin clothing and was in awe when he touched its soft leather. Someone else found the meat and tasted it. Wide-eyed and pleased, he passed it around. The others devoured the meat, wanting more since they had never eaten anything so delicious.

"The wolf told them to follow him to the earth's surface, where they could eat as much as they wanted. But the leader of the humans, a man named Tokahe, refused, saying the Creator had instructed his people to remain underground until called upon. Most stayed, but those who tasted the delicious meat couldn't resist and followed the wolf to the surface.

"After a long and perilous journey, they reached the earth and were taken aback by the vision of the glorious blue sky. The people were in awe of the plants and flowers in bloom and thought it to be the most gorgeous place they had ever seen.

"When they met Anog-Ite, a shawl concealed her horrible face, revealing only her beautiful side. When asked about the clothing and food, Anog-Ite said she would teach the people how to hunt, and then to butcher and tan the hides of animals.

"But the work was hard, and these people of the cave were not used to such effort, and were unable to complete their tasks. So, when winter came, and the snows fell, they hadn't enough clothing or food.

"They returned to Anog-Ite, begging her for help. But instead, she pulled the shawl from her head, revealing the hideous side of her face, and laughed at the foolish people. Frightened, they ran away with the wolf snapping at their heels until they found the place from where they first emerged. But this time the hole was covered, leaving them trapped upon the earth's surface."

"What did they do?" I asked.

"They sat down on the frozen ground and wept, and as they continued crying, the Creator heard them and asked why they left the caves. Once they explained, the Creator was angered and said, 'You should not have disobeyed me. Now you must be punished.'"

I reached out, grasped Red Dog's arm, and asked, "How so?"

"The Creator turned the cave people into great wild beasts. They became the first herd of *tatanka*."

"Tatanka?" I repeated.

"Our name for buffalo."

"Ah, buffalo?" I repeated, putting my hand over my mouth.

Red Dog nodded and continued, "When the earth was finally ready for people to live upon it, the Creator instructed Tokahe to lead them through the cavern's passageways and onto the surface. When they arrived, the people saw the hoofprints of the buffalo. *Follow the beast*, the Creator advised. *For it will provide everything you need—food, tools, clothes, shelter—and will lead you to water, allowing you to survive upon the earth.*

"When they left the caverns behind, the Creator shrank the hole so small that the people could never return," Red Dog said, and paused.

"Is that the end?" I asked while he looked off into the distance.

Red Dog nodded and said, "That is our creation story."

I thought a while as we drove on in silence, then asked, "Do these caverns still exist?"

"They do," he said.

"Do you know where?"

Red Dog pointed into the heat rising off the road in front of us and said, "Up in the Black Hills. The same caverns where the Sacred Pipe was hidden."

Chapter 34
Alvin McDonald

As we stood before the grand entrance to the cavern, a young, clean-shaven man emerged from the shadows, surprising both Red Dog and me. The man, tall and thin with skin as pale as if he hadn't seen the sun in months, said, "Welcome, gentlemen. My name is Alvin McDonald. Are you here because of the news?"

I looked over to Red Dog, who shook his head and asked, "What news?"

"About the prospectors up in these hills, who heard a whooshing sound coming out of the ground," Alvin said, pointing toward the trail leading up into the woods.

"What was it?" I asked.

"It was a hole in the ground, though too small for a man to squeeze his body through. But according to your people," he said, pointing to Red Dog, "this appears to be quite a discovery."

I turned to Red Dog. "What is he talking about?"

Red Dog stared at Alvin for a moment, absorbing his words, then asked, "What do you mean, a whooshing sound?"

"You know, like your creation story," he said with an engaging smile. "When the people came out of the caves for the first time."

"Is this true?" Red Dog asked softly.

Alvin nodded, placed his hand over his heart, and said, "Yes, my Lakota friend, it is true."

"What's true?" I asked breathlessly.

Red Dog sighed and said, "There's a part of our creation story I didn't tell you."

I nodded, encouraging him to continue.

"The place underground where our ancestors came from was known as the *Tunkan Tipi*. To reach it, there was a passageway called *Oniya Oshoka*, the breathing earth. Somewhere deep inside these caverns," he said, gesturing to the entrance behind Alvin, "is the way into the spirit world, where the earth breathes."

"It actually exists?" I asked.

Red Dog held out his arms and said, "Of course it exists. The story of our creation is not a child's fairy tale."

I thought of what Mother had told me, of how God created the world in six days and rested on the seventh, and wondered how both stories could be true.

Red Dog pursed his lips, pointed to Alvin, and asked, "Can you show me?"

"Sure, it's not far. But we should hurry," he said, looking up into the dark clouds overhead. "It looks like a storm is coming."

After a fifteen-minute walk down a winding, steep trail, we came upon a heavy growth of blueberry bushes spread across a landing. "It's through here," Alvin said, pushing through the thorny bushes.

Without hesitation, Red Dog followed, wide-eyed and nearly on Alvin's heels. By the time I reached them, a little bloodied by the thorns, Red Dog was on his knees, stretching his arm deep inside a ten-inch wide, round hole. "You can feel the wind!" he cried out.

"Really?" I said.

"Come," Red Dog said, stepping aside, "stick your hand inside."

As I got to my knees, I could feel a breeze blowing at me from within. "Oh," I marveled, and buried my arm as far as I could, reaching into the blackness. "How did the people get out from here? It's too small."

Red Dog squeezed his hand into a fist and said, "I already told you, it's because the Creator shrank it so the humans couldn't return."

"But there must be another way in," Alvin said, "and that's what I've been searching for."

"Oh, you mustn't," Red Dog said with a snarl. "Tunkan Tipi is holy."

Alvin, wide-eyed, put his hand to his mouth and said, "I just thought it would be interesting to find."

Red Dog took a step closer to Alvin, pointed a finger at him, and said, "It's the spirit world and not a place for the living." He then turned his attention back to me and said, "I must return and let the chief and Black Elk know of this."

"But how will I get back to Pine Ridge?"

"There's plenty to worry about before you concern yourself with that," he said with a shrug. He pushed his way back through the prickly bushes and proceeded down the hill. Alvin and I followed, and when we reached the wagon, Red Dog was already unloading my pack.

As I stood there, my mind was flooded with fears. "Red Dog, this is crazy," I said, waving my arms in the air. "How do I know which way to go? I could get lost—then what would I do? I'll die in there!"

Red Dog sighed, walked toward me, put his beefy hands on my shoulders, and said, "Leo, there are many unknowns. But rest assured, the

Great Spirit is everywhere and will guide you to your destiny, whatever that may be."

Mother had spoken similar words about God being everywhere at the same time.

"Here's pine pitch for making torches," he said, handing me a small wooden box.

"There's no need," Alvin said. "I've found simple candles provide me with enough light."

Red Dog scoffed. "Candles?" he said and looked at me with brows drawn. "It's up to you, Leo. You can always use the pitch to mark the walls so you can find your way out."

"I use this," Alvin said, holding up a ball of twine.

"Very well," Red Dog said, shaking his head. "I'd best be going. Maybe I can outrun the storm."

"I guess this is goodbye," I said, as Red Dog climbed up to the seat on the wagon. He waved and gave his horses a smack with the crop, and I watched until the wagon disappeared down the trail. At that moment, I had an inkling to run after him, but instead stood my ground. Whatever path my life would take from here on out, I knew I had to embrace it if I had a chance of surviving. While finding the Sacred Pipe was the purpose of my mission, I sensed much more was at stake.

CHAPTER 35
DAY ONE

Hands on my hips, I stood upon the grassy knoll and gazed at the massive rock wall soaring overhead. About a third of the way up, where the outcroppings ended, pine trees stood tall, their roots clinging to the mountain's edge, while their crowns reached skyward, piercing the dark storm clouds. I dropped my gaze and peered into the cave's entrance, but could only see a few feet in due to the overhang blocking the light. I took a breath and readied myself before stepping into the dark unknown.

"What are you waiting for?" Alvin said, startling me from behind.

I turned to look at him and bit my lower lip.

"There's no need to worry," he said, putting a hand on my shoulder. "Come, I'll give you a tour. No charge!"

I followed Alvin. The moment I entered through the stone archway, a cool dampness seeped into my nostrils and down the back of my throat, causing me to swallow and grimace at the grit. Slowly my eyes adjusted to the depths of the darkening shadows, as Alvin swung his arms outwards and announced, "Welcome, Leopold Wolf, to my world."

"Your world?" I repeated, curious about the man's claim.

"Come on," he said, pointing into the depths beyond, "follow me."

With each step we took, the light dimmed. Soon we were in near-total darkness. "How can you see?" I asked, squinting.

"After a while, your eyes adjust and you see just enough. But for you, I'll light a candle."

I watched as Alvin reached into a pocket. Like he was performing a magic act, he withdrew a ten-inch long, tapered candle from his animal skin coat, along with a box of matches.

He lit the candle and, cupping the flame, cocked his head, beckoning for me to follow as we proceeded down the stone corridor, until we emerged into what I sensed was a large space. The candlelight only provided enough illumination to see for a few feet before the darkness swallowed it up.

"Want to see something spectacular?" Alvin asked.

"Sure," I said.

He pointed to my pack and said, "Light one of your torches."

I untied the rope binding the branches to my pack and pulled out the box holding the pitch. Red Dog had already split the ends of the branches, onto which I would dab the pitch. Once prepped, I held it over the candle's tiny flicker and lit it.

With the torch burning bright, the expanse of the cavern blossomed before my eyes. I gasped at its magnificence, where thirty feet above us, clinging to the ceiling, hung a multitude of long, tapered stone spikes. "What are those?" I asked.

"These caverns live and breathe," Alvin said, pointing above. "Notice how each one drips its substance, forming its mate below."

I followed his finger down to the mirror image of each spike, rising upward toward its maker. "I've never seen anything like this."

"Isn't it wonderful?" he said with a smile.

Absorbed, I stood wide-eyed, watching the shadows dance about.

Breaking my trance, Alvin asked, "Why is your last name Wolf?"

I looked at Alvin and shrugged. "Because it was my father's father's name."

"I once knew a Running Wolf," he said with a sigh.

I hadn't thought of my name that way and smiled at the idea of it.

"What do you think of my home?" he said.

"Do you really live here?"

He nodded and said, "Yes, Leopold Wolf, this is where I dwell."

"So, you see people coming and going all the time," I said.

"Sure, I do."

My breath quickened and I asked, "What about Lame Johnny? Do you know who he is? Have you seen him?"

Alvin laughed. "Do you think this is the only entrance?" he said, holding out his hands. "There are many, and once inside, you're met with a web of interlocking tunnels that go on forever. But to answer your question—sure, I see people come and go, though they're mostly miners prospecting for gold. Maybe one of them was this Lame Johnny, the one everyone's talking about."

"Has anyone died down here?"

Alvin scoffed. "Sure, there are many who have made these caverns their final resting place."

I swallowed hard, thinking of stumbling upon a human skeleton, and considered turning back.

"Tell me, Leo, what's the purpose of this exploration of yours?"

I explained the exploits of Lame Johnny, and how the Sacred Pipe was stolen along with the gold and then hidden somewhere within these caves.

"I heard about the gold," Alvin said, raising his brow. "That's something I've been on the lookout for, but this pipe, no one has ever mentioned it."

"I've been asked by Chief Red Shirt to find it, as it holds significant importance to the Lakota people."

"The natives are quite verbose with their tall tales, like the creation story and the breathing earth."

I furrowed my brow and asked, "You don't believe them?"

Alvin scoffed. "Do you?"

I thought about what Red Dog shared, and he seemed sincere, though as I thought about the story of those who emerged from caves and followed the buffalo, who used to be humans, it did sound made up. But then, with the recent discovery of the breathing hole, who knows, this too could be true.

"But what do I know," Alvin said, not waiting for my reply.

With so much mystery, I sighed and said, "Maybe I should go back home to Carlisle."

Alvin pointed a finger at me and said, "You, my friend, are what I would call being at a crossroads."

I grunted and said, "That's for sure."

"Perhaps I can offer you some advice," he said, holding out his hands.

"What's that?" I asked, dubious of Alvin's wisdom.

"As I see it, you have two choices. You can turn around and return home. But if you do, you'll live the remainder of your life full of regrets. Or you can walk into the darkness, where there's a good possibility you may perish. But, if by the grace of the Almighty you complete this task and survive, then your name will be spoken for generations. The legend of Leopold Wolf," he said, waving an open palm, "the man who found and returned the Sacred Pipe to the Lakota people."

I sighed, thinking at first Alvin was mocking me. But in a way, he could be right. So, I asked, "What's it like down there?"

"Besides being dark, it's freezing cold," he said, wrapping his arms around himself. "The type of cold that seeps into your bones, causing your teeth to chatter. It's also quiet, except for your breath, and the endless droplets of water dripping from the stone ceiling."

"Would you help me?" I asked with a grimace. "If I find the pipe, I'm sure the gold will be there too. You can have it all. All I want is the pipe."

Alvin took a step backward, folded his arms across his chest, and said, "How do I know I can trust you?"

I shrugged and said, "I suppose you don't, but I could ask the same of you. Anyway, it seems that the risk is worth it, as the rewards are plentiful for both of us."

"I like your reasoning," Alvin said, sticking out his hand. "Consider me your partner."

We shook hands as I forced a smile, hoping I hadn't made an agreement I would eventually regret.

CHAPTER 36
ALVIN'S STORY

While we sat on a rock ledge, sharing pieces of smoked deer meat from my pack, I asked, "Where do we begin?"

Alvin sighed and thought for a moment. "Some say the place where Lame Johnny entered was the same as where these caves were discovered three years ago," he said, scratching at his black, greasy hair. "Do you know the story?"

I shook my head, anxious to hear something that might lead us to where the notorious stagecoach robber hid the treasure.

"A little ways from here," he began, "a log flume broke, and the loggers noticed the water was being sucked down into a hole, like a stopper being pulled from a drain. When they dug out the mess, they found an entrance into these caverns."

"Maybe we should go there?" I asked, holding out my hands. "Is it far?"

"If we go outside along the mountain trail, it will probably take a day or two. But it's only a day if we go through here," he said, pointing ahead.

Not wanting to waste time, I said, "The caves, of course. I should start getting myself acclimated to this new world."

"That's right," Alvin said, with an avuncular nod. "This is a new world, at least for us. I'm sure humans have sheltered in these caves for thousands of years."

I got to my feet, swung my pack around, slipped my arms through the straps, and said, "Okay, Alvin, show me your underworld."

Alvin led me into the caverns by candlelight. After a few steps, I noticed something he was fondling. "What's that in your hand?" I asked.

"Oh, this?" he said, holding up a set of beads on a cord. "I use this to count my paces."

"Count paces?" I repeated with a curious squint.

Alvin nodded. "That's how I track. Here, let me show you," he said, handing me the candle.

"Okay," I said.

He held out the beaded string and with his finger, slid over one bead. "I slide a bead to the knot for every ten paces I take. Then, on the tenth pace, I slide one from the other side of the knot. This way I know how far I've gone. I also drew a map," he said, patting his pocket. "This is where I've marked down the number of paces. But at this point, I've memorized the counts, so I don't need to look."

"How did you end up living down here?" I asked.

Alvin smiled and said, "My father was hired two years ago by the South Dakota Mining Company to oversee their claims. While exploring the area, he recognized an opportunity to offer tours of these caverns. Without hesitation or much forethought, a trait my mother often complained about, he quit his job, started a business, and asked me to work alongside him."

A sudden pang of sadness washed over me, as Alvin's words reminded me of Wolf and Son Woodworking. I missed Father.

"So, we began enlarging passageways and building ladders and steps to assist visitors' access. That's how I became aware of the wonders down here."

"Does your family still give tours?"

Alvin stopped walking and turned around to face me. "Father gave up on the enterprise and headed back home to Ohio with my mother and sister. I stayed on. The business wasn't enough to support a family of four, but it's plenty for me, especially since I have no need for a homestead."

"Because you live down here," I offered.

"That's right. The only costs I have are matches, candles, coffee beans, and occasionally I treat myself to a meal when I go into town for supplies."

"Sounds like a simple life," I said and followed Alvin up a steep incline. "What about companionship? You must get lonely being all by yourself."

"Ah," Alvin said, stopping again. "But I'm not alone. Once you're here a while, you'll see."

I furrowed my brow and asked, "Are there other people who live down here?"

Alvin glanced at me sidelong and said, "It's not the living I run into."

I stared at him for a moment, trying to grasp what he was implying. "Do you mean like human remains?"

"Oh, there are quite a few skeletons. But what I'm speaking of are the spirits who dwell within this elaborate web," he said, sounding joyful as we stepped into a new cavern, as large as the first one.

"Spirits?" I repeated with a grimace. "Do you mean of the dead?"

Alvin guffawed, his laughter echoing across the cavern. "Are there any other kind?"

CHAPTER 37
THE RED WOLF

"How do you know when it's nighttime?" I asked after I'd followed Alvin through channels of stone and across wide open caverns for several hours.

"Are you tired?" Alvin asked in a mocking tone.

"Yeah," I moaned. "When do we sleep?"

Alvin stopped, handed me the candle, reached into a pouch tied around his waist, and pulled out a pocket watch. He flipped it open, brought it closer to the light, and said, "Ah, it's past ten. You're right, Leo, it's time. Let's walk a little further—there's a good place up ahead where we can rest."

About fifteen minutes later, we came upon an elevated stone porch tucked under a large overhang, forming a seemingly protected space. "This is it—it's a nice spot," Alvin said, pulling out a blanket from his pack and laying it out.

"Should we make a fire to keep warm?" I asked, feeling a chill.

"Fire?" Alvin said, wide-eyed. "Not unless you want to die of smoke inhalation or cause that rock shelf overhead to come crashing down on us."

I looked up to the cracks in the low-hanging ceiling and imagined a tremendous chunk of stone breaking off and crushing me in my sleep.

"You'll be fine," he said, pulling out a small basket. "Would you like some berries? They're fresh—I picked them this morning."

I nodded and held out my hand, while Alvin dropped ripe blueberries into my cupped palm. I popped a few in my mouth and bit down, allowing the juices to coat my tongue before swallowing. "That's good," I said, as my stomach rumbled aloud.

"Still hungry?" Alvin asked.

I scoffed. "A few blueberries is hardly a meal."

"In the morning, we'll head out into the woods and hunt for rabbit or squirrel," he said, patting his bow. "That should hold us for a few days."

"Does that mean we need to cook outdoors?"

"Oh no," Alvin said, shaking his head. "There are places within the caverns where we can make a fire. I'll show you."

"All right," I said, and lay down on my blanket.

"You'll want to cover yourself. Your body cools down quickly once we stop moving."

I thanked Alvin and made myself as comfortable as one could upon a hard stone floor, and not realizing my total exhaustion, I soon fell into a deep slumber.

*

When I awoke and opened my eyes, I found myself alone. "Alvin?" I called out.

Hearing no response, I let out a groan as I got to my feet. Not surprisingly, after sleeping without the comfort of a straw mattress, my lower back ached. I stretched a bit, trying to loosen up before venturing out beyond the confines of the secluded sleeping place. It was not that dark; I realized that a series of candles, secured to the stones with wax, lit the way down a short tunnel. I followed it out into a cavern where my guide was tending to a fire. The swirls of smoke looked as if they were being sucked through crevices in the cavern's roof. This, I understood, was one of those places where a fire was possible. "Alvin," I called out again.

This time he heard me, and without looking up, he lifted his hand and summoned me over with a crooked finger. "Coffee?" he said, offering me a cup.

Like a fish to a worm, I was hooked by the brew's tantalizing aroma. I took the tin cup, nestled it between my two hands, and sipped. "Oh, this is delicious," I said, marveling at the taste.

"I make a good cup of java," Alvin boasted.

"That you do," I said, and I got closer to the flame, enjoying its warmth.

"In a few hours, we should reach the spot where Lame Johnny supposedly entered."

"Oh, that's good, because I'm starving," I said, swallowing the last gulp.

"I'm sure; we'll find something to hunt," Alvin said, lifting his pack. "Why don't you go and get your things so we can head out?"

I nodded and walked back to my sleeping place. As I stepped onto the stone plateau, I stopped cold at the sight of a wolf pawing at my pack. Though the candlelight offered no more than a soft glow to the sight before me, I saw enough to know the danger of confronting a hungry wolf within an enclosed space. "Alvin," I said, though my raspy voice was barely a whisper.

The wolf looked up and saw me. Cautiously, it took a step backward, its golden eyes locked onto mine. Though it was hard to tell in the subdued light, the wolf seemed to sport red fur, almost the same color as my own hair and beard. Sensing danger, the animal snarled, displaying an impressive set of fangs. As I imagined those jaws of death sinking into my flesh, Alvin appeared, and before I could twitch a muscle, he let loose an arrow, striking the beast in its torso. It squealed in pain and spun round and round, as if it were chasing its tail. I watched, wide-eyed and slacked-jawed, as Alvin nocked another arrow and shot. This one pierced the animal's neck, swiftly ending its life.

As the wolf splayed out in a growing puddle of its blood, Alvin patted my back and said, "No need to hunt now."

I pointed and asked with a grimace, "You're going to eat that?"

Alvin nodded and said, "Oh, yes. *We* are. Red wolf is delicious."

CHAPTER 38
THE CHUTE

"This is something you should know how to do," Alvin said, slicing his blade deep into the bloody meat of the wolf.

I cringed and said, "I've hunted with my father, though we brought our kill to the butcher in town."

"Under the mountain, or out on these hills, you'll need basic skills to survive."

I sighed, knowing he was right.

"After we eat, we'll go to where Lame Johnny entered and see if we can pick up his trail."

"I'm curious," I said, watching as Alvin cut the meat into small cubes. "Why haven't you ever searched for the gold?"

Alvin looked up at me and smiled. "My riches lie here within the bosom of the Almighty. Though," he said, with a finger raised in the air, "if you should lead me to the bounty . . ."

I chuckled and wondered if Alvin would still call these caverns home, should we discover the gold.

*

"What do you think?" Alvin asked as I bit into the charred meat.

It tasted strange, leaving a bitter aftertaste, unlike the steak from a cow. But it wasn't awful, and I nodded my approval.

When we finished, Alvin wrapped up what was left over and burned the carcass remains in the fire. "It's best not to leave anything behind," he advised.

As we made our way down a passageway, narrow streams of daylight pierced through cracks in the ceiling, illuminating our way. "Occasionally we're just below the surface," Alvin said, gesturing overhead.

"Does that mean we're close to an opening?" I asked, squinting into the light.

Alvin shook his head. "Not necessarily. This way actually takes us deeper under the mountain," he said, pointing straight ahead. "We'll soon head down a chute and into a cavern."

"A chute?" I asked, sounding concerned.

"It's about twenty feet straight down. But not to worry, I built ladders."

"You've been busy," I remarked.

"This leads to a popular destination for my tours. That's why I built bridges and ladders—to help people get around. It's also where I believe Lame Johnny and his cronies ventured."

"Are you serious?" I said, wondering if this would be the place where the treasure had been hidden.

"Yes, so I've been told."

"Please, lead the way," I said, wondering if he knew more about Lame Johnny than he led me to believe.

*

I figured we had walked about an hour when we came upon the chute. "Is this it?" I asked, looking straight down a dark hole.

Alvin nodded. "I'll go first. Wait until I light the candles before you head down. When I reach the bottom, I'll call out to you."

Upon his descent, he paused to light candles and press them into crevices, allowing me to study the slender stone shaft, glimmering in a coating of wetness, and a ten-inch-wide wooden ladder, angling its way downward.

Once Alvin disappeared from view, it was only a short while before he shouted my name.

"All right," I yelled back, "I'm on my way."

Each narrow rung was just wide enough for either a foot or a hand, one at a time. With deep breaths and a racing heartbeat, I did my best, keeping focused until I reached the bottom.

"Ah, there you are," Alvin said, waiting for me. "Now, that wasn't so bad, was it?"

I exhaled and grimaced. "It was frightening," I confessed.

"That's nothing," he said. "There are spots that are much more challenging than that to maneuver."

"None where we're going, I hope," I said, wiping the sweat from my brow, though Alvin was buttoning up his coat.

"Let's light a few torches and allow me to show you something spectacular."

CHAPTER 39
THE JEWEL CAVE

With each torch lit, my jaw dropped lower and my eyes opened wider. "I can see why you call this the Jewel Cave," I said, gazing around at the enormous beds of glittering crystals encrusted into honeycombs, choking every inch of the cavern walls, along with a dense forest of delicate stalactites, dripping down from the ceiling.

"This alone," Alvin proclaimed, holding out his arms, "is worth the price of admission."

"Are these real jewels?" I asked, wondering at its value.

Alvin shook his head. "At first glance, everyone thinks they're diamonds. But it's only calcite crystals. Not worth anything to the outside world."

I climbed onto a stone shelf, bringing myself closer to an outcropping, and ran my hand across the jagged mineral. "This is a wonder," I said, marveling at the natural beauty.

"It certainly is," Alvin agreed with a smile stretching from ear to ear.

I continued looking around the massive, decorated cavern, then remembered why we were here. "Is this where Lame Johnny came?"

From behind a collection of stalagmites, Alvin stuck his head out and said, "Come here, Leo. I want you to see this."

I made my way over to Alvin, who had his back toward me, and asked, "What do you want to show me?"

"Is this what you're looking for?" Alvin said as he turned around, and in his hands was what I assumed was the Sacred Pipe.

"You found it," I said, doing my best to examine the details as I remembered them.

"Yes," Alvin said, shifting his brow.

"This is terrific," I said, clasping my hands together. "You knew where it was the entire time?"

Alvin nodded.

"But why didn't you tell me?"

Ignoring my question, he held the pipe out with both hands and said, "What makes this so valuable?"

"The Sacred Pipe is very old, handed down from generation to generation. It is revered as a holy object to the Lakota people. When smoked, it's their way of opening a channel of communication into the spirit world."

"Sounds important," Alvin said.

"To the Lakota people, it's treasured," I said, continuing to examine the pipe in Alvin's hands, until he turned away and laid it down.

"Did you find the gold too?" I asked.

Alvin twisted his mouth and shook his head. "Sadly, no, someone had gotten to the gold before me. I guess whoever found the gold had no interest in the pipe, and neither did I, until now."

"What are you saying?"

"I'm saying that you've enlightened me."

I scoffed. "The pipe is of no value to you," I said.

Alvin turned to face me, brandishing a gun he pulled from his pouch.

"What's this about?" I asked, holding up my hands.

"I didn't think it was worth anything until you came along. Apparently, this could be worth as much as the gold," he said with a sly smile.

"Don't be crazy. It's only worth something to the Lakota."

"I'm sure a Lakota chief, or someone else, would offer me a handsome reward for its return."

"That may be true. But let's go back together, and I'll give you the reward, whatever it is. All I want to do is return the Sacred Pipe to its people."

Alvin pointed the gun at me and shook his head. "I don't think so."

I swallowed hard and said, "So what are you going to do, kill me?"

"Pfft," Alvin sputtered. "I'm no murderer."

"Just a thief," I said.

"No, not really. Lame Johnny is the thief. I just found it."

"So, what are you going to do with me?" I asked, taking a step backward.

"You'll stay here," he said, waving his gun around.

I looked around the cavern wide-eyed and said, "Why would I do that? I'll just follow you back," and gestured to the ladder.

Alvin shook his head. "Sorry, I can't allow that," he said, carefully placing the pipe into his pack.

"Oh, come on, Alvin. You can't leave me here. I'll die."

He stared at me for a moment, then reached into his pocket and pulled out a folded paper. "Take this," he said, opening the folds. "It's a map of the caverns and passageways."

"You're joking, right?" I said, spreading out my arms.

"I'm sorry, Leo. But to show you I'm a nice guy, here are my beads," he said, tossing them at me. "With these and the map, you should be able to find your way out of here, eventually."

"Eventually?" I repeated, holding the string of beads in one hand and looking at the map in the other as a feeling of light-headedness washed over me. I searched for a place to hold on to. "I'm not feeling so well," I said, as the blood drained from my face and my head began to spin.

"Sit down," Alvin said and grasped my arm. But before I could reach the cavern floor, my world went dark.

CHAPTER 40
ALONE

When I came to, I got to my feet and took a moment to steady myself. Looking around, I saw the wonders of the Jewel Cave still lit by the flickering torches. Its glimmering array brought back my dizziness, though I didn't feel as if I would pass out this time. I sighed and rubbed my tired eyes.

"Alvin," I cried out, "are you still here?"

After the cavern swallowed my echo, the silence resumed. Though that's not to say that the cavern was still. There was a persistent, gentle whistling of a moist wind, as if it were blowing from down a narrowed corridor. I dismissed this observation and focused instead on Alvin. Where did he go? I ran over to the chute we'd descended and saw, to my dismay, no ladder. "Alvin!" I screamed, with nostrils flaring.

He had pulled up the last section of ladder, leaving in its place a slick, vertical tunnel of stone. "I can't believe this," I said with a growl.

I looked up again into the darkness, trying to find the next section of ladder. But beyond a few feet, the chute had soaked up every bit of light from the last measly candle melted onto a crag. I returned to the cavern and dislodged one of the torches. Once back within the shaft, I reached the flame up as far as I could, and there it was, perched on a stone shelf—the next section of an unreachable ladder.

"Dammit!"

I wandered back into the cavern and saw Alvin's map lying next to my pack. I reached for it and wondered, *Maybe there's another way to the surface*? I perused the drawing, which was filled with a confusing array of crooked and connecting lines.

I took a breath to steady my nerves. The first thing was to find my current location. After a quick read of the map, I found, written in the lower left-hand corner, the word ENTRANCE. This was where we had taken our first steps into these caves.

I followed the pathway, marked with the number 24. According to Alvin's bead system, I knew these were the number of paces. I traced my finger further along and recognized the last cavern we had crossed through. It was drawn as a wide space with a narrow corridor shown at its far end, where I read the word SHOOT.

"Aha!" I said aloud and saw solid double lines that led into an enlarged space that was labeled JEWEL CAVE. I smiled in relief, but knew finding my place on the map was hardly a cause for a celebration, as an escape from here would take more than following a few hand-drawn lines.

After perusing the map, I noticed what appeared to be another corridor leading out from the Jewel Cave with the number 20 marked. I held the diagram with the word *SHOOT* as if it were behind me, using it as a fixed point, and traced with a finger to the spot straight ahead. When I looked up, I gazed upon a solid wall of crystals and stones that did not offer any signs of an exit.

Sighing, I got to my feet, positioned the beads in my hand, and with each step, I slid one over. At twenty paces, I stood before a protruding wall, well-lit by a nearby torch, but darkness lay beyond its flanking wings. I hurried over, grabbed the torch, and held it out into the darkness, where, to my surprise, I discovered a stone passageway.

My heart thumped hard at the prospect of a daunting escape. I gathered my things and turned around one last time, hoping to see Alvin. But all I saw was the empty Jewel Cave, glittering a magnificent farewell. So, with a deep breath, summoning my courage, I proceeded into the unknown.

*

The stone corridor was a silent, silvery-gray passageway, with none of the Jewel Cave's splendor. With the singular purpose of finding my way out, I advanced boldly, though I knew caution should temper any enthusiasm, as a misstep could prove deadly.

While I tried to keep my focus on what lay before me, my mind drifted to Black Elk's words and his vision of what dwelled here.

They brought me deep inside the caverns of the Black
Mountains where both stillness and movement reside, to the
central axis point of the six sacred directions.

Just as I pondered my proximity to this holy place where north, south, east, west, above, and below meet, a gust of wind barreled down the narrowed passageway, extinguishing my torch.

I stretched out my arm, holding the snuffed-out end of the torch, trying to find the walls that encased me, but touched nothing. I remained blinded in the void, not knowing which direction I had come from or where I needed to go. My very next thought was—*Will I die here?*

My mouth went dry, while sweat poured down my beard, chest, and back. "Alvin!" I cried out. I dropped the torch, unhooked the straps from my pack, and laid it at my feet. While bent over, I placed my hands on my knees and began to cry. "Mother, help me," I said, sobbing.

While tears washed down my cheeks, I noticed a gentle vibration coming up through my boots. I got down to my hands and knees and placed a palm upon the chilled, wet stone, and the reverberations became noticeably more pronounced. I crawled a few feet, and as I did, the feeling turned into an audible humming sound. Drawn to its effect, I retrieved my pack and followed the pathway. No longer would counting my steps be useful, because I moved forward like a dog on all fours.

I advanced, no longer afraid of crashing into a stone wall or tumbling off into an unexpected crevice, but my knees soon ached from the pain, forcing me to stop. As I rubbed my tender kneecaps, I noticed a faint flicker of light, similar to a firefly, off in the darkness. With a burst of enthusiasm, I got to my feet and advanced.

With each step, the minuscule glow grew larger, eventually illuminating my way. The vibrations were also increasing in intensity to the point that I not only felt it, but could hear a deafening roar. Whatever lay ahead, be it good or bad, I was about to find out.

Chapter 41
Thunder Falls

Moments before reaching the light, I needed to cup my hands over my ears to silence the unrelenting, thunderous barrage coming from beyond. Accompanying this cacophony of sound and brightness was a gentle, cool mist, carried along by a breeze blowing toward me. I hoped whatever lay ahead included an escape from these ravenous caverns.

As I stepped beyond the confines of the stone passageway, I emerged into an enormous cavern, home to a towering waterfall. I look upward to its crest and stared in awe at its magnificence. The only waterfall I'd ever seen before was on a river in Carlisle, which I thought was impressive, but in comparison, it was only a ten-foot drop that would run strong in the spring and diminish to a pitiful trickle come midsummer.

These falls were hardly lacking in potency. As high as three two-story houses stacked upon one another, the waters rushed straight down and exploded into a cloud that drifted everywhere, coating me and the cavern in sheets of water.

I pulled out the map and quickly found that I stood at the foot of Thunder Falls, as Alvin had aptly named it.

I took a moment to drink from its bounty, at a pool of black water. As I continued to admire its splendor, I realized that this enormous cavern was not only filled by the rushing of the falls but also with daylight. Where was it coming from?

I peered through the vapors to the bright light shimmering through cracks in the stone ceiling. Could I be so close to the surface? But none of the openings seemed large enough for me to squeeze through, and even if they were, there was no way of reaching them without ropes to climb.

Frustrated, I sat down, pulled from my pack a piece of smoked meat, and bit into its bitterness. As I chewed, softening the chunk before swallowing, a chill washed over me, causing my body to convulse and shiver. The dampness of the cavern was seeping into my bones, and I knew this was no place to linger.

I surveyed the cavern, looking for an exit, but none was obvious. So once again, I consulted Alvin's map. Just as I unfolded it, a wisp of wind jerked it from my fingertips and sent it twisting away. I tried snatching it back, but it soared upward beyond my reach.

"Dammit," I cried out, as I knew without that map my chances of survival were slim.

My eyes darted about, following the journey of the map. It eventually landed, stuck like wallpaper, to a protruding rock about fifteen feet overhead. Though beyond my reach, it seemed possible to get close to it by climbing onto a stone shelf. But the problem was that every surface was slick as ice.

It seemed I had a decision to make. Either leave the map where it was and move on, trying to find my way out of this maze without it, or make an attempt to retrieve it. Deciding upon the latter, I stepped onto the shelf, trying to assess its texture. Certainly, a fall could disable me, even if it was from only a few feet up.

I took a deliberate step, placing my boot on the black rock. I felt stable enough to release my back foot and take another step. Swallowing hard, I judged it would take three more strides to put me in a good position to reach overhead for the precious map.

As I placed each foot on the slippery stone, I crunched my toes as if they were sharp animal claws digging in. After a few steps, I was close enough to reach for the map, still glued to the ceiling. I locked my legs, making sure to keep my balance, and stretched an arm upward, but I was still about two inches too short.

I took a deep breath and stood on my toes, raising me just enough for my fingertips to lift the wet map from where it clung to the stone. Carefully, I folded the drenched map and slipped it and the beads back into my pack.

Focused now on climbing back down, I turned around and retraced my steps. I smiled just short of the cavern floor, and that's when I slipped. My front foot slid out and I fell, hitting the ground hard on my already sore back.

"Ahh!" I gritted through clenched teeth.

I pushed to my feet, placed a hand on my hip, and moved about gingerly, testing the extent of my injury. It hurt, but not enough to keep me from walking.

Once I gathered my wits and felt ready to move on, my body convulsed again into shivers. The chill sank deeper into my bones. I realized I couldn't go far with these wet clothes. The persistent mist and spray had drenched me through and through. I would need to make a fire to dry my garments, though not here, due to the dampness as well as the lack of any kindling or wood. I hoped Alvin had stored some firewood in one of the caverns ahead. But first I would need to find my way out of the wonders of Thunder Falls.

I studied the cavern, but the walls were solid, offering no escape. I sighed my frustration. As I looked deeper into the downpour, I noticed a bright light flickering within. Could it be that the portal was through the falls itself?

CHAPTER 42
THE DREAM

Wanting to protect my pack, I laid it behind a stone outcropping and then stepped to the lip of the pool. Already soaked, I had no qualms about submerging myself beneath the falls. Slowly, I lowered myself into the icy water. My exposed skin felt as if it was under attack by thousands of pinpricks.

Standing waist deep, I gazed upward at the imposing rush of water while its tremendous force pounded on the frothy, bubbly surface churning around me. I reached out, placing my hand into the downpour, then held my breath and stepped into the falls. The force thumped hard upon my head, neck, and shoulders. Once I passed through to the other side and wiped the water from my eyes, I saw a small corridor leading into darkness.

I climbed out of the pool and onto the stone platform. With no other recourse, I stepped from the backside of the Thunder Falls into the unknown, while the roar and the light diminished behind me, and once again I was without sight.

With arms outstretched, my palms glided across the walls and I found my way forward, albeit slowly, worried I could crash into an obstruction.

At first, the rush of adrenaline warmed me, but as my body settled, the chill returned. With soaked clothes and wet hair, along with the frigid temperature of the cave, my body erupted into uncontrollable shivers. Unable to walk, I lowered myself to the cold stone floor, and curled up, bringing my knees to my chest, and in the pitch blackness, while my convulsions settled, I fell asleep.

I heard cannon fire, guns, and the shouts of men in battle. I looked around, recognizing the kitchen where I lived as a young boy.

"Leo," Mother called out.

"Mother?" I replied, finding her shoved against the stove. Her eyes twinkled at me. "Where are your legs?" I asked.

She cocked her head toward the table, where her lower portion remained, and said, "You mustn't rest here. Get up, Leo, and move on. You don't have much further to go."

"I want to stay here with you, Mother."

"No, it's not your time! You have a life yet to live."

"But everyone I've loved is gone. You, and now Father."

"You mustn't linger. Get up and walk, my son. There is still much to learn."

"But I can't find my way."

"Yes, you can."

I awoke and opened my eyes to darkness. "Mother," I said aloud, my dream still fresh in my mind. I got to my feet. Though still cold, I had a renewed confidence after seeing her in a dream. This had been the first time, in all these years since her death, that she came to me. "There is still much to learn," I said, repeating Mother's words. This was something to consider, but certainly not now.

Using my hands to guide me, I stepped forward and deeper into the darkness. Though it was only a dream, I felt Mother's presence, causing me to smile.

I didn't realize how far I had walked until I heard a whooshing sound. I paused, trying to pinpoint its location, and understood it was straight ahead. No longer afraid, I proceeded with vigor, and with each step, the distinctive sound of wind slicing through the air intensified.

I felt my way around a rocky diversion in the cave, and as I came around the other side, a sharp breeze smacked my face. Around me, many winds whipped and howled, layered in intensity and pitch. I stood lost in the void, wondering if this was where I would take my last breath.

CHAPTER 43
THE WIND CAVE

I stood in complete darkness, feeling like I was in the eye of the tornado, as the force of the winds encircled me. I tucked my arms tight against my sides. I dared not reach out into the turmoil for fear of being sucked into the ear-piercing, whistling, sharp winds.

Thoughts of the Lakota creation story Red Dog had told me entered my mind. Could this be where his people emerged from, and if it was, had I found a portal into their spirit world?

While I pondered the prospect of being in the presence of the supernatural, the whirlwind shifted, moving its protective cone away, and as it did, I was lifted off my feet. I rose like an autumn leaf freed from its branch, flailing and twisting until I was pulled further into the tempest, where I spun round and round at a speed so fast I lost consciousness.

When I awoke, I remained in the darkness, lying upon a cavern floor, with the swirling winds now reduced to a pleasant, gentle breeze. Lifting myself up onto my elbows, I realized that my clothes were now dry and I was no longer shivering.

Exhausted from the ordeal, I lay back down, yawned with heavy eyes, and drifted off again into a deep slumber.

*

I opened my eyes to the sight of a lone fruit tree. Lacking my bearings, I got to my feet and looked around. It seemed that I remained within the network of caves beneath the Black Hills, but unlike before, I was no longer within the tumultuous darkness of the Wind Cave.

Instead, a bright light shone from behind a tree, illuminating dozens of large, plump, red fruits that appeared to be apples dangling off branches. Unlike any tree I'd seen, this one had powerful, exposed roots clinging to the stone of the cavern floor.

I approached, reached out for one of the low-hanging fruits, and cupped it in my hands. I brought it close and gave it a sniff. Though similar in color and shape to an apple, this was not an apple. Instead, a sweet, tangy aroma filled my nostrils, causing my stomach to growl in anticipation of biting into it. Just as I was about to pluck it from its sturdy branch, a woman's voice called out, "Stop, Leopold."

Without hesitation, I released it and looked about to see who was speaking to me. "Who's there?" I called out.

As I peered into the brightness coming from beyond the tree, a silhouette of a body appeared. I stepped backward as the figure of a woman with piercing blue eyes emerged. She approached me and accompanying her, at her side, was a red wolf.

She offered her palms and said, "Do you not recognize me, son?"

"Mother?"

She smiled and nodded.

"Am I dead?"

"No, you are alive. But you're in a place where I can reach you," she said, stretching her arms outwards.

"But isn't this the origin of the Lakota creation story?"

"Yes, for the Lakota people, it is. But for us, this too is our holy place," she said, gesturing to the tree. "This is where your soul family dwells."

I looked at the tree, then at Mother, and said, "Soul family?"

"That's right," Mother said, holding out her arms, while her long black hair rippled in the gentle breeze. "These fruits are called pomegranates," she said, pointing, "and each one represents a soul yet to be born or reborn."

When I furrowed my brow, Mother explained, "During our time on the earth, we are surrounded by certain people we know from past lives. For example, during our brief time together, I was your mother. When we meet again in a life yet to come, you could be my mother, or perhaps my father."

I put my hand to my mouth and asked, "I can be your mother?"

"Sure, you can," she said, nodding. "Or you can be a friend or even my child once again."

I reached out, touched one of the fruits, and said, "Are you saying that there is a soul in here?"

Mother nodded. "When the time comes, and a child is conceived, an angel is called upon to accompany each essence to its ensoulment."

"Which one of these is Father?" I asked, looking at the ripe pomegranates.

Mother closed her eyes and shook her head. "All I know is he will reunite with you, and with me once again. In what form, I cannot say."

"This sounds hard to believe."

"What if I tell you that Sarah is among them?" she said, pointing.

"Is that because Sarah is dead?"

"Oh, you don't have to be dead. While alive, your soul still exists in the spirit world."

"You mean one of these is my soul?" I said, pointing to the tree.

"That's right, son."

I considered her words, then asked, "Do you know if Sarah is alive?"

"I don't know. In this form, knowledge flows to me in ways that are not understood. What I do know is that for some reason, you've been brought here by a powerful spirit, for no living man or woman visits their tree during a lifetime."

"Black Elk," I said, wondering if he could be the spirit she was referring to.

"You have been given a gift," Mother said, as she reached up and plucked a pomegranate and handed it to me. "Is Sarah someone you love?"

I swallowed hard, thinking of her. "I do, Mother. Very much."

"Then you must eat this to ensure your soul remains bound together with Sarah's into eternity."

I took the fruit and stared at it, then asked, "Are you saying Sarah and I will be together in this lifetime?"

"Eat the fruit, and swallow the seeds," she said.

"The seeds?"

"Yes. There are six hundred and thirteen of them, each one representing the six hundred and thirteen commandments of the Torah."

I brought the pomegranate to my mouth and bit into it.

CHAPTER 44
RESCUE

Gentle birdsong woke me, and when I opened my eyes, Abraham Lincoln was towering over me, staring back. "Abe?" I muttered, blinking my eyes into focus.

"That's right, Leo, it's me," he said, stretching out an arm.

We clasped hands, and he helped lift me to my feet. Standing behind him were Red Dog and Alvin. "Alvin, you bastard," I snarled at the sight of him. "You left me to die."

"I'm sorry, Leo," he said, holding up his palms. "But we came back for you."

"I don't understand," I said, shaking my head. "How did you get here, Abe?"

"Mother sent me to find you at the reservation and bring you home. She said you were in no condition to be on your own. You know, after what happened to Sarah."

"Sarah," I repeated softly, and pointed into the darkness of the cavern, as if I'd left something of hers behind.

"But just as I got to Pine Ridge, there was a commotion," he said, gesturing to Alvin. "He was trying to sell a pipe to the Lakota."

"The Sacred Pipe," Red Dog said, with narrowed eyes. "I recognized this thief right away and put a stop to him."

I looked over to Alvin, who offered a meager smile and shrugged.

Red Dog pointed and said, "He confessed to everything: leaving you behind and stealing the Sacred Pipe. But he promised to take us to you if we agreed to let him go."

Abe nodded and said, "That's when the three of us got into the wagon and came here. Alvin took us into caves and we found you sleeping before a tremendous waterfall."

"Thunder Falls," I said, nodding. "But that's not where I ended up. I passed through a long tunnel and came upon a tree."

Alvin scoffed. "There are no trees in these caves."

Ignoring him, I scratched at my beard. "But how did I get here?" I said, looking around at the brilliant green cover of the mountainside.

Abe put his arm around me and said, "The three of us carried you out."

"Where's my pack?" I asked, darting my eyes about, worried about Father's soul bundle.

"I have it," Abe said. "It's in the wagon. Now come on, we'll take you back to Pine Ridge."

I turned to Alvin, stuck an accusatory finger inches from his face, and said, "How could you just leave me? You knew I'd never find my way out."

"Don't be so sure. Many people do," Alvin offered.

*

While Red Dog attended to driving the wagon back to Pine Ridge, Abe and I sat in the back. Once we started down the trail toward Rapid City, I placed a hand on Abe's shoulder and asked, "Why have you come?"

Abe shrugged a bit, curled up the edge of his mouth, and said, "Like I said, Mother was worried. She wanted me to bring you home."

I scoffed and shook my head. "There's nothing for me in Carlisle anymore."

"You've done well, recovering the Sacred Pipe."

I nodded and said, "Did you see Chief Red Shirt?"

"No, I didn't," Abe said.

"What about Black Elk?"

Abe shrugged. "Black Elk? I don't know who he is."

Tugging at my beard, I called out to Red Dog, "What did Chief Red Shirt say about the pipe being returned?"

Red Dog twisted around to look at me and said, "He didn't say anything, because he's not at the reservation and neither is Black Elk."

"Where are they?"

Red Dog shrugged. "I'm not sure. Maybe when we get back, you can ask the Elders."

"Aren't you an Elder?"

"I am by age, but I'm not one of the Sacred Circle. They keep certain things private. But maybe they'll tell you, since you returned the Sacred Pipe."

"Not really, it was Alvin," I said, reluctant to take credit.

"Nonsense," Red Dog said, and turned back to the road ahead.

"How are your mother and Isaac Junior?" I asked Abe.

"The baby's good, growing. Mother seems happier living in the house. But it's weird being there without you." He grimaced. "After all, it's your home."

I shook my head. "I'm not ready to come back, Abe. What would I do there? Captain Pratt won't have me at Carlisle."

Abe sighed. "You always have your carpentry business. Maybe I can help you?"

"I would like that," I said, patting Abe's knee. "But it's not what I want to do right now. Why don't you stay with me at the reservation, at least for a little while?"

"Would that be all right?" Abe asked, looking up at Red Dog.

"Sure, I don't see why not," I said.

"It would be nice spending time with you, Leo."

I nodded and smiled.

"Oh, I almost forgot," Abe said, reaching into a pocket. "Mother found this at the house. It looks like a journal." He handed me a brown, leather-covered book.

I took it from him and opened it to the first page, where I read, in neat block letters—THE JOURNAL OF ANNE FOX. "This is Mother's," I said, looking up at Abe.

"I thought you might want it," he said with a smile.

"I never knew she kept a journal," I said, flipping through the pages.

"I hope you find some comfort in what she wrote."

"Maybe it will help me make sense of what happened in the caves."

"What do you mean?" Abe asked.

I bit my lower lip and said, "I saw something, but I don't know how to explain it."

Abe leaned forward, wrapped an arm around my shoulder, and said, "Try. You can talk to me."

I glanced up to Red Dog, whose eyes remained focused on the trail ahead, and said quietly, "When we get back to the reservation."

CHAPTER 45
RETURN TO PINE RIDGE

"Leo!" William shouted to us as the wagon rode into the Lakota village.

As we came to a stop and jumped out onto the dusty road, William ran and leaped into my arms. "How are you doing?" I asked, squeezing him tight.

"I'm so glad you're okay. Everyone was worried when that man came here with the Sacred Pipe. Did he really leave you lost in the caves to die?"

"I would have found my way out, eventually," I said, patting his back, though I still had my doubts.

"Thank goodness we found him," Abe said.

While it felt as if the eyes of the entire village were upon me, I gestured to a private place between the tipis where we could speak. William nodded as if he understood, and led the way.

Once far from prying eyes and ears, I asked, "What's this I hear about your father and Black Elk leaving Pine Ridge? Do you know where they went?"

"Father said he and Black Elk were going to become show Indians. I wanted him to take me, but he said it wasn't for children."

I put my hand to my chin and said, "Are you saying that your father and Black Elk joined up with a show about Indians?"

William nodded with a smile.

"That makes no sense," I said, shaking my head. "Why would the chief and Black Elk just go off and do something like that?"

"Black Elk said it's a way to learn more about the *Wasichus*."

"Wasichus?" Abe asked.

"The whites," William said.

"Isn't that what Carlisle was all about?" Abe asked.

My lips tightened at the thought. I said, "It's hardly a show when the mission of Carlisle is to kill the Indian."

"Such has been the burden of the Negro, too," Abe said thoughtfully.

I nodded, agreeing with Abe. I then turned to William and asked, "Do you remember the name of the show?"

"Buffalo Bill's Wild West Show," William said, with a wide grin.

"Wait, wasn't that where Tom went?" I said, remembering the advertisement he showed me.

"And I met him too—Buffalo Bill. He was here and spoke to the Elders, and to me. Though he didn't say much," he said with a grimace. "Just hello."

"You saw Buffalo Bill?" I asked, sharing a look with Abe.

William nodded. "He has a long white beard and wore a colorful jacket and a white cowboy hat. Father said he came to Pine Ridge to ask the chiefs and others to join his show."

"Who else went?" Abe said.

"Samuel's father, Chief American Horse, and a few others. They all rode out of here together," he said, pointing toward the road.

"Do you know where they were headed?" I asked.

"To a place Buffalo Bill called WASH-TON-D-C," William said, pausing after each syllable.

"Washington, DC?" I said, correcting the pronunciation.

"That's it," William said, jabbing a finger at me.

"You know it?" Abe asked.

"Yes, of course. That's where Sarah spent her summer with her uncle, Senator Cameron," I said.

"But what I don't understand is, why would Red Dog have pretended he didn't know anything?"

"Oh," William said, jumping onto his toes. "I know why."

I held out my hands, encouraging him to continue.

"It's because Red Dog was upset he couldn't go with them."

"Why not?" Abe asked.

"Because Buffalo Bill wanted only chiefs and special people, like Black Elk. But Red Dog said he too should be given the honor, since he helped with the rescue of the Sacred Pipe."

"The Sacred Pipe," I said, remembering the origin of my ordeal. "Did you see it?"

William nodded and said, "Yes, it was returned to the Keeper of the Sacred Pipe."

"So, it's safe now?" I asked, exhaling.

"Thanks to you," the chief's son said with a smile.

"Thank you, William," I said, with a long exhalation. "I suppose we should greet the others."

"Yes, come," he said, stepping through the open flap of the tipi, "the Elders want to honor you."

Chapter 46
Keeper of the Sacred Pipe

I ducked my head and entered the Elders' tipi, where I saw four men sitting around the fire. I recognized three of them from my first visit to the sacred ceremony, though this time Chief Red Shirt and Black Elk were not in attendance. The one man I didn't know had thinning, gray hair and a leathery face, and sat with the Sacred Pipe resting upon his lap.

The man swept his bony arm over the empty space next to him and said, "Leopold Wolf, welcome. My name is Elk Head. Please join us."

I sat down cross-legged and shared a brief look and a nod with each man.

"You have achieved Black Elk's vision," Elk Head said, raising the pipe.

I shrugged and said, "Not really, I sort of just stumbled upon it and—"

"No, Leopold," he said, interrupting me. "It was you, as the white man says, who stirred the pot."

I chuckled at the man's wit. "Are you the Keeper of the Sacred Pipe?" I asked, pointing to it.

He nodded. "Yes, I have this honor."

"I'm happy it's back where it belongs."

"Our people are grateful," Elk Head said and placed the pipe in front of him. "But before we smoke, I would like to ask what happened to you in the caves."

I took a breath and rubbed my chin. "You mean after Alvin left me?"

Elk Head nodded.

"I'm assuming Red Dog shared with you the discovery of the hole in the earth where we felt the wind."

"You mean the Oniya Oshoka, the breathing earth?"

"Yes, that is what Red Dog called it."

"But that's not all you saw, is it?" he asked, with a squint of his brown eyes.

I shook my head. "Once I passed through the Thunder Falls, something happened," I said with a sigh, and took a moment to make eye contact with each Elder. When my gaze returned to Elk Head, he cocked his chin, beckoning for me to continue.

"I ended up before a pomegranate tree and saw my mother and a red wolf."

"Your mother has walked on?" Elk Head asked.

I nodded. "She died—I mean, she walked on when I was eight years old."

Elk Head put his hand on my shoulder and said, "I am sorry, Leopold."

I offered a pained smile.

"Tell me, what is a pomegranate?"

I chuckled and shared what the fruit looked like, as well as my interaction with Mother.

Elk Head tugged at the drooping, aged skin hanging from his neck and said, "What you're saying is, you ate this fruit in order to bind your soul with a woman?"

"Yes. Her name is Sarah."

"Has Sarah walked on too?"

"I don't know," I said with a shrug. "The last time I saw her, she was shot and fighting for her life."

One of the Elders, a man with two long braids cascading over his shoulders, asked, "You say you saw a red wolf?"

"I did. It appeared alongside Mother."

The Elder scratched his head and asked, "This is most interesting. Do you have a connection with this animal?"

I thought a moment, then remembered. "Yes, we came across one in the cave. Alvin killed the wolf and we ate it."

The Elder shared a furrowed brow with the others, then looked at me and said, "It seems you have bound your eternal soul with the red wolf's."

"By eating him?"

"The wolf gave of himself to you. This is a great honor," the Elder said.

"I don't know," I said with a sigh. "All of it could have been just a dream."

The four men exchanged words in their language before Elk Head raised his palm, silencing them. He then turned to me and said, "This was no dream, Leopold. We have known since the time of our grandfathers' grandfathers that beneath the Black Hills is where the first humans emerged."

"Yes, your creation story," I said. "But Mother explained it was also our holy place as well. Where our soul family dwells."

"This is true," Elk Head said. "All people, of all tribes, share the same spirit world, though our visions of it change, depending upon our ancestry."

"So, it's a personal experience?"

"You can say that," Elk Head said, and leaned over to pick up the pipe. "Let's smoke to acknowledge your rite of passage."

"Rite of passage?" I asked with a furrowed brow.

Elk Head nodded. "Do you know why we are called Elders?"

I shrugged and said, "Because you are old?"

"If we are blessed, we all grow old," he said, smiling. "We have the honor of being known as Elders because we have witnessed, in one form or another, the Great Spirit."

I nodded, looking at each of the Elders.

"You have achieved this blessing as a young man."

"Like Black Elk?" I asked.

"Yes, that is so," Elk Head said. "Let us now smoke, as our way to offer our gratitude to you, Leopold Red Wolf."

CHAPTER 47
SHARING WITH ABE

Upon my return to the tipi, Abe was tending to the fire. "How'd it go?" he asked.

"I think I'm an Elder," I said, bending over to pick up a twig and tossing it into the flame.

Abe turned to look at me and laughed. "Aren't you a little young for that?"

"After what happened to me in the caves, it appears I've earned the honor."

Abe held out his hands and said, "I'm still waiting for you to tell me what happened."

I then shared my experience of the spiritual encounter with Mother and the red wolf before the pomegranate tree. When I finished, he stared at me and said, "Tell me again about this fruit."

"It was like an apple in size and color," I said, holding out my hands to demonstrate its size, "except not as shiny or as round, and it had this funny six-pointed stem at its bottom. Mother said there were six hundred and thirteen seeds inside, one seed for each of the commandments in the Torah."

"Torah?" Abe said with a grimace. "What's that?"

"It's the book containing Jewish wisdom and laws," I said.

"Wow," Abe said, nodding.

"Mother also said I needed to eat the fruit with all the seeds, as it would bind my eternal soul with Sarah's."

"Is that because she's dead?"

"No," I said quickly. "It doesn't matter. Each of us has a soul fruit, regardless of whether we're dead or alive."

"But I don't understand. How do you make a connection with someone by eating a fruit?"

"I don't know, but somehow this fruit has the power to join people in eternity," I said with a smile. "According to Mother, people I've known in my life will meet up with me again when I'm reborn."

"Like you and me?" Abe asked, pointing back and forth.

I nodded. "Except in my next life, you could be my mother or someone else."

"Your mother?" he said with a grin.

"Or I could be your girlfriend."

"God forbid," Abe said with a chuckle.

"That seems unlikely, but the point is, we're connected somehow."

Abe smiled and said, "I like that."

"Me too," I said, reaching out and patting his knee.

"Tell me about the red wolf," Abe said.

I explained what happened in the cave with Alvin and the Elders' reaction. "The Lakota are now calling me Leopold Red Wolf."

"Leopold Red Wolf," Abe repeated, with a sparkle in his eyes. "Wow, you have a real Indian name."

I chuckled and said, "I suppose I do."

"So, what are you going to do now?"

I took a deep breath, slowly exhaled, and said, "I need to find out if Sarah is alive."

"How will you do that?"

I stroked my beard, contemplating the question, then shrugged and said, "By going to Washington. That's where her uncle is."

"It's also where that Indian show is," Abe reminded me.

"That's right," I said, pointing a finger at him. "That would be a good place to start. I can also find Black Elk and tell him what happened in the caves. You should come with me."

He squinted and thought for a moment, then said, "I'd like that, but what about Mother? She'll be worried for the both of us."

"Once we get to Washington, we'll send her a telegram letting her know we're well."

"Excellent," Abe said, clapping his hands together. "We're off to Buffalo Bill's Wild West Show!"

*

"Will I ever see you again?" William asked, with streams of tears rushing down his cheeks.

"Of course," I said, ruffling his hair. "I'll be back to Carlisle in a few months."

He bit his lower lip and said, "But who's going to be my counselor now that you're gone?"

I shrugged and said, "I don't know. But you shouldn't worry. You know your way around there by now. If you need anything, go to Alice. She'll look out for you."

William turned to Abe, who nodded, then back to me. He hugged me tight around my waist and said, "Promise me, Leo, you'll come back."

I got down to my knees, put my hands on his shoulders, looked into the boy's bloodshot, brown eyes, and said, "I promise, William. I'll come back to Carlisle and we'll see each other again, very soon."

"You boys ready?" Red Dog asked as he pulled up the wagon through the throng of people gathered to see us off. Since my return from the caves, I was treated as an honored guest, with many calling out to me by my new name—Leopold Red Wolf.

Abe and I loaded our packs into the wagon and climbed aboard.

"Say hello to Father," William shouted as we pulled away.

I twisted around to wave and said, "So long, William."

CHAPTER 48
RAPID CITY

It was late afternoon by the time we reached Rapid City. Parched after the dusty eighty-mile trek from the reservation, we offered our farewell to Red Dog and headed into the Ruby Saloon. As our train was not due to leave for Sioux Falls until the next morning, Abe and I aimed to take a room and a bath, along with a hearty meal, before our departure.

We stood a moment on the wraparound porch and watched Red Dog's wagon disappear down Main Street, causing me to wonder if I'd ever make it back to Pine Ridge.

"You coming?" Abe broke in.

"Yes," I said, turning to the saloon doors.

I shouldn't have been surprised when nearly all eyes turned to us as we entered the bustling saloon—though it wasn't me, specifically, being gawked at. It was Abe.

We didn't take more than a few steps before a bearded man with bloodshot eyes blocked our path. "Your friend," he said, jabbing a finger at Abe's face, "is not welcome here."

"We're just looking for a room and a bath," I said, holding up my hands. "We don't want any trouble. We'll be heading out in the morning."

The man belched, sending out a waft of whiskey that caused me to jerk my head back. "Trouble is exactly what you're going to get if you don't—"

"Shut your mouth, Calvin," a voice called out from behind the crowd that had gathered to watch the affront.

The crowd parted, allowing a short, pudgy man wearing a white apron to approach. He offered his hand and said, "The name's Bennett Jones. I'm the proprietor of this fine establishment. Excuse Calvin here, he's an ornery drunk. Though come to think about it, he's ornery when sober, too."

A round of laughter swept through the saloon, disarming the tension as the crowd returned to their drinking, poker, and Faro games. Calvin scoffed at Bennett. "What the hell do you know," he barked and gave the layer of sawdust scattered across the floor a clumsy kick before leaving the saloon.

Bennett shook his head and sighed. "Let's get you boys checked in," he said, leading us to the bar.

As I filled out the registration card, Bennett asked, "Where you headed?"

"We're catching the train to Sioux Falls tomorrow," I said.

"Why don't you get yourself settled while I get a bath ready for you out back," he said, pointing to the door at the rear of the saloon. "Then after dinner, if you're so inclined, you can catch the Frank Butler Rifle Show. It's quite an exhibition."

"A rifle show?" Abe asked.

Bennett nodded. "Tonight's the last show before Mr. Butler heads out of town. I saw it yesterday and I'm going again. You can't believe what the man can do with a rifle. It's remarkable."

I shrugged and said, "Sounds good. What do you say, Abe?"

"Sure," Abe said, nodding. "We have nothing else to do."

Bennett leaned in, took a moment to size us up, then said, "You boys looking for some female companionship? I can send up two of my friendliest girls."

Though the offer sounded enticing, I didn't want to break my personal vow of being faithful to Sarah, so I politely declined.

"Very well," Bennett said. He handed me a brass key attached to a small wooden board marked with a number 4. "The show starts at six thirty. Admission is a nickel."

I had just enough money for the train ticket to Washington, and a little more for meals. I looked over to Abe, who nodded and said, "I have some money Mother gave to me. Enough for both of us."

"Thank you, Bennett, we'll be there," I said, shaking the man's hand and appreciating his hospitality.

*

Once in our room, Abe sat down on the bed and said, "I thought we were going to have a problem like we did at McClure's Pig Farm."

"Slavery may be over, but there's no changing the white man's ignorance," I said. "But thank goodness Bennett is more evolved than his customers."

"Did you see those girls downstairs?" Abe said, with his eyes bulging out.

I did catch a glimpse of three standing off to the side. Their faces were painted with color to accentuate their eyes. "I saw them."

"Can you imagine having one of them," he said, getting to his feet. "I've never been with a girl. Have you?"

I shook my head and said, "Not like that, but I did kiss Sarah."

"You did?" Abe said with a grin that stretched from ear to ear. "What was it like?"

I exhaled, thinking back upon that magical moment when our lips came together and our tongues touched. "It was amazing."

"Oh, what I wouldn't do to have a girl."

"Not these," I said, shaking my head. "It's not the same as being with someone you love."

Abe squinted. "And how would you know?"

"I don't," I said, lifting my brow. "But if you want to lose your seed to one of those, go ahead."

Abe scoffed, "Maybe I will."

CHAPTER 49
THE FRANK BUTLER RIFLE SHOW

After a warm bath and a hot meal, Abe and I found our way to the grand circus tent pitched on a field behind the Ruby Saloon. A large crowd had already gathered, nearly filling the bleachers, but we were able to find two front-row seats.

I looked around for Bennett and eventually, after twisting my neck from side to side, spotted him seated a few rows back. He noticed me too and offered a friendly wave.

"Ladies and gentlemen," a voice boomed, "welcome to the Frank Butler Rifle Show."

The audience responded with an enthusiastic cheer.

"In just a moment," the announcer continued, "Mr. Butler will dazzle you with amazing feats, proving that he's the world's greatest sharpshooter."

Again, the people applauded vigorously.

"But before we commence with the performance, let me stress the importance of staying in your seats once the show begins. Mr. Butler fires live ammunition. We don't want anyone wandering to places where they shouldn't, and accidentally getting shot."

A multitude of conversations commenced at once, causing the announcer to hold out his arms to quiet the crowd. "Ladies and gentlemen, if you please," he cried out. "We must have absolute silence."

Within an instant, the audience complied.

Satisfied, the announcer tugged down on his blood-red jacket, pulled back his shoulders, which were decorated with impressive gold epaulets, and said, "Allow me to introduce the man who has dazzled audiences with feats of marksmanship the world has never seen. Ladies and gentlemen, children of all ages, let's put our hands together and give a Rapid City warm welcome to the one and only Mr. Frank Butler!"

A deep blue velvet curtain at the far side of the grand tent was pulled aside and out stepped a tall, thin man wearing shiny, black knee-high boots with an equally black coat, the tails reaching down to the man's thighs. In one hand, he gripped a rifle stock, resting its barrel on his shoulder, and with the other, he waved to the audience. "Hello, everyone," he bellowed in a deep baritone.

People shouted back their hellos.

"I'm so grateful you all showed up," he said, looking at the bleachers sweeping across the long side of the tent. "I think I even see a few faces from yesterday's performance. Thank you all for your support."

A round of applause broke out.

He approached the stands and said, "Shall we get started?"

Heads nodded, including mine.

Mr. Butler stopped walking a few feet in front of me and Abe and said, "I'd like to begin my show with a volunteer from the audience."

Hands all around me shot up.

"You should do it, Leo," Abe said loud enough to catch Mr. Butler's attention.

Mr. Butler looked straight at me and said, "What do you say, son? It seems your friend here is urging you on."

I shrugged and said, "Sure, why not," and got to my feet.

"Wonderful!" Mr. Butler said, loud enough for the audience to applaud, providing me with additional encouragement. "What's your name?"

"Leopold Re—" I was about to say Leopold Red Wolf, my new Indian name, but thought better of it and simply said, "Leopold Wolf."

"Well, Leopold Wolf, right this way." Mr. Butler led me to the center of the tent. Once there, he grasped my shoulders with both hands and said, "Stand here with your back against this post."

"You want me to just stand here?" I asked.

"That's right," he said, and reached into his pocket and pulled out a plump, red apple. "Can you balance this?"

"Balance it where?" I asked, twisting my head to look at the hundreds of eyes glued upon me.

"Up here," he said, grasping my beard and tugging it so I faced forward. He then placed the shiny apple on top of my head. "Don't move a muscle."

"Okay," I said, trying to remain still.

Mr. Butler picked up his rifle and walked twenty long and deliberate strides across the expanse. He turned and looked down at the weapon in his hands and said, "This, ladies and gentlemen, is a Stevens Model 44 single-shot rifle. If all goes well, and if Leopold Wolf doesn't move, I will turn that apple balanced upon his head into applesauce."

Upon hearing those words, the audience burst into laughter while I swallowed hard. I felt the apple wiggle a bit, but it didn't roll off.

As the crowd hushed, Mr. Butler took his firing pose with the stock tucked into the cradle between his shoulder and neck and his other hand supporting the barrel. He squinted and took aim. After an elongated pause, he dropped his arms, and while still holding the rifle in one hand, he reached into his coat and pulled out a white hanky and wiped his eyes. "They're a little watery," he said. "Could be allergies."

A murmur of concern washed through the audience.

"Not to worry, ladies and gentlemen, I'm fine," he said, returning the cloth to his pocket. He once again took aim, and just as I thought he would pull the trigger, he stopped again, causing the spectators to release a collective moan.

Without moving a muscle, I was able to shift my gaze over to where Abe was sitting and noticed his hands covering his eyes, but he seemed to be peeking through open fingers.

Allowing the tension to build, Mr. Butler took a few steps over to a small table stationed nearby and grabbed something. "Let's make this more interesting," he announced and picked up a woman's silver handheld mirror. He showed it to the audience, causing quite a stir. Then he returned to the same spot and turned his back toward me. He reverse-gripped the rifle, placing its barrel on his shoulder so it pointed behind him, and with his other hand, he held the mirror out in front.

Is he going to shoot at me while looking into the mirror?

"Quiet, please," he called out. "For Leo's sake, I don't want to miss."

I could see in the mirror the reflection of his eyes locked onto mine, as the crowd hushed in anticipation. A cold sweat began to travel down the back of my neck and down my beard. Trying to remain calm, I shut my eyes. A moment later, the sound of a rifle shot exploded and at the same instant, the bullet lodged itself with a thud into the pole behind me, while the apple burst. After a breath of silence, the audience burst into applause and shouts of excited appreciation.

"Wonderful," Mr. Butler exclaimed, while I pulled off bits of apple clinging to my hair.

Frank shook my hand and offered his thanks, and I returned to my seat.

"That was great," Abe said, patting my back, along with several strangers sitting nearby. "Were you scared?"

"I was fine until he pulled out that mirror," I said.

We watched the rest of the show, in which Mr. Butler amazed the crowd with shots in all sorts of contorted poses, such as between his legs or bent over backward. He fired with perfect accuracy at birds and squirrels released within the grand tent and snuffed out ten candles in a row from fifty feet away.

At the show's conclusion, Mr. Roberts thanked the crowd for their patronage and said, "This is my last show before I catch the train tomorrow to head east, where I'll reunite with my wife Annie Oakley, whom many of you have heard of."

With the mention of his wife's name, the crowd cheered.

"She's currently performing her amazing feats of mind-bending, sharpshooting skills at Buffalo Bill's Wild West Show in our nation's capital."

Abe and I nudged each other, knowing we would be traveling cross-country with the performer Frank Butler.

CHAPTER 50
ABRAHAM'S NEWS

On the third day after our departure from Rapid City, Abe shared with me his plan to disembark at Harrisburg.

"I should go back to Carlisle to help Mother," Abe said, as we sat side by side on our third-class bench seat.

"But what about seeing the Buffalo Bill Wild West Show?"

Abe patted my knee and said, "You'll tell me all about it when you return home."

"Are you sure?"

Abe nodded. "It's not fair to Mother. She has Isaac Junior to take care of, along with her work at Captain Pratt's. I should never have left," he said, lowering his eyes and sighing.

"It's all right, Abe, I understand. But it won't be the same without you."

"I know," he said, offering me a warm smile.

I leaned in closer and whispered, "Can I tell you what happened last night?"

"Last night?" Abe asked with a furrowed brow.

I nodded. "After you fell asleep, I got up and wandered all the way up to the first-class cars," I said, pointing ahead.

Abe's jaw dropped and he asked, "And no one stopped you?"

"Nope," I said, shaking my head. "Mostly everyone was asleep, and when I got to the game room car, I saw Frank Butler sitting alone, playing solitaire. So I approached and introduced myself."

"Did he remember you?"

"Not at first. I think he'd had too much to drink. But once I refreshed his memory, he asked me to join him."

"What did you talk about?"

"I asked about how he became a marksman, traveling from city to city, and he shared some experiences. But what was most interesting was how he met his wife, Annie."

"The famous one who's with the Buffalo Bill show?"

I nodded. "A few years back, when he was in Cincinnati, he was approached by a group of farmers who enticed him into a contest against a local sharpshooter. Never shy to take on an opponent, he agreed to the challenge with the promise of a decent-sized purse.

"When he arrived at the designated spot, he saw his opponent was a teenage girl named Anne Moses. He learned later on she was only fifteen years old. Confident of his victory, he offered to double the pot, which the farmers accepted. The targets were twenty-five live birds, which were to be released one at a time. Frank shot all of them, except the last one. When it was the girl's turn, she never missed, killing all twenty-five birds."

"Wow," Abe exclaimed. "That's amazing; a girl beat Mr. Butler."

I held up a finger. "The story gets better. It seems that Mr. Butler became enamored with young Anne, and a romantic relationship ensued, and eventually, they married. Later on, she changed her name, becoming Annie Oakley. Now they perform an impressive array of sharpshooting acts together. He said she's the best he's ever seen. According to Mr. Butler, Annie still never misses."

"Sounds like the Buffalo Bill show is quite spectacular."

"Mr. Butler says it's the greatest show, with over three hundred people, from performers to stagehands, all involved in its production."

"I could see why Mr. Butler and Annie Oakley joined the show, but I can't understand why the Lakota chiefs and their holy man want to partake."

I took a deep breath and slowly exhaled. "I agree; it makes no sense. But I'll know soon enough."

"I suppose you will."

"I'm going to miss you," I said, putting my hand on Abe's shoulder and giving it a squeeze. "When I get back, we'll get Wolf and Son up and running again. You'll be my partner."

Abe smiled and said, "I'd like that."

CHAPTER 51
WASHINGTON, DC

"Leo! Over here," a voice called out as I disembarked at the Washington, DC, train platform.

I looked past the crowd and spotted Mr. Butler waving at me. I acknowledged him with a wave and made my way around the multitudes. "Thank you, Mr. Butler, for waiting to say goodbye," I said, offering my hand.

"Nonsense," he said, slapping my hand aside. "First of all, call me Frank. And second, you're coming with me. I have a stagecoach waiting for me out front. I assume you're going to the showgrounds?"

I nodded. "Yes, I suppose I am. Thank you, Frank."

"Let's go," he said, as I stayed close on his heels, following him through the train station. When we reached the street out front, a line of stages stood poised. "That's ours over there," he said, pointing to the stagecoach painted with the words *Buffalo Bill's Wild West Show* on its side.

We stored our valises on the back rack and climbed inside. I had never been in such a fancy stagecoach before and marveled at its decorated interior. Red velvet curtains adorned the windows, along with deeply tufted upholstery in a rich navy-blue fabric to sit upon. "Wow," I said, absorbing the luxury.

"Bill knows how to treat his people right," Frank said, across from me.

"You've met Buffalo Bill?" I asked as the stage pulled away from the curb.

"Sure I have. Annie and I did his show in Omaha two months ago. That was our first, and I would have moved on with them, but I had this prior engagement in Rapid City. Annie went on ahead without me, along with my horse, Lightning. But to answer your question, yes, I met Bill Cody."

"Bill Cody? That's his real name? What's he like?"

Frank nodded. "Bill's a good, decent man. You know he pays everyone in the show a fair wage, even the Indians."

"Is that right?" I said, "I'm curious to see the show."

Frank lifted his eyebrows and nodded. "It's quite an extravaganza. I've never seen a better show. Audiences everywhere love it."

"Sounds interesting," I said, trying to reserve judgment until I witnessed it for myself.

"What's your skill, Leo?" he asked, pushing back the curtain to gaze out the window.

"I'm a carpenter."

"Carpenter?" he said, turning to look at me. "Bill always needs carpenters. If you'd like, I can put in a good word for you."

"Thank you," I said with a nod, though my intention in going to Washington was not to get a job working for a cowboy and Indian show.

Frank returned his gaze out the window and pointed to the wide boulevard. "Have you ever seen architecture so grand?" he asked, as we passed by what I assumed were government buildings, built with enormous blocks of white stone.

"I'm from a small town where the largest structure I've seen was the local church."

"Oh, right. It's where we dropped off your friend."

"That's Harrisburg. We're actually from Carlisle, about twenty miles west."

Frank tapped his forehead and said, "Carlisle, that sounds familiar. Why have I heard of it?"

"Well," I said with a shrug, "it's not far from Gettysburg and it's home to the Carlisle Indian School."

"The Carlisle School," he said, nodding. "Sure, I know it. Isn't that the place where the Indians are sending their children to learn how to live like we do?"

"You mean like the white man?"

"Yes, like the white man. Such a wonderful idea. What do you know about it?"

I chuckled and said, "I worked there for two years as a counselor. That's how I ended up visiting Pine Ridge. Chief Red Shirt's son was in my group."

Frank leaned closer and asked, "Is it true what they say about that place, how they kill the Indian in order to save the man?"

I stared at him a moment, biting the inside of my lip and realizing his ignorance was not unlike that of most whites. "It's true, Frank, that the program at Carlisle is to wipe clean the Indian within each child. But it's not like there's a white man underneath waiting to emerge from the ashes, like a sapling after a forest fire. These children are forced to cut their hair, change their names, with the goal of stripping them of their ancestral identity. My feeling is that this is an experiment doomed to failure."

Frank sat back and studied me. "Wow, Leo, you're a deep thinker. I'm impressed."

I shrugged. "Doesn't take much thinking to observe the obvious. The white man is hell-bent on decimating a race of people, and I have a feeling I'm going to see more of the same at Buffalo Bill's Wild West Show."

CHAPTER 52

BUFFALO BILL'S WILD WEST SHOW

"There it is," Frank said, pointing out the stagecoach window.

I leaned over to his side and saw a red, white, and blue striped circus tent and imagined that it was large enough to enclose the Great Lawn at Carlisle, including its ten barracks. "It's gigantic!" I shouted.

"I'm sure it's a sellout," Frank said, as I noticed long, meandering lines of men, women, and children in front of dozens of ticket booths.

"How big is the crowd?"

Frank shrugged and said, "I heard it's around ten thousand."

"Ten thousand people?" I repeated while I gawked at the sea of humanity pressing their way through the gates. Our stagecoach rode around the perimeter of the giant tent, toward its rear.

"The show starts in thirty minutes. I don't go on until the final act. Why don't you find a seat, and we'll meet afterward? That's my coach over there." Frank pointed to where an animated young woman was arguing with a tall man dressed in a fancy coat.

I looked over and saw she was wearing a cowboy hat and a pleated skirt with a red rose embroidered on one side. "Is that Annie Oakley?" I asked.

"Yes sir, Leo. That's my pretty petunia," he said with a wide smile. "And that's Buffalo Bill himself," Frank said, and slapped his open palm on the roof of the stage, a signal for the driver to stop. "I'd better get out here and see if I can settle this. Annie gets herself into a tizzy every now and then."

"All right, Frank," I said, as he didn't wait for the stage to come to a full stop before opening the door and jumping out.

"I'll see you later, Leo. Enjoy the show," he said, as we continued on.

When the stage came to a stop, I disembarked and stood among dozens of men, women, and children, all dressed in costume. There were cowboys, army soldiers, Indians, and settlers of the west. I searched among the dozens for Chief Red Shirt, Black Elk, and even Tom, but didn't see any of them.

"Opening scene performers, take your places," a booming voice announced.

Within an instant, the performers dispersed into organized groups, which I took as my cue to find my way into the tent. I pushed back a flap of the canvas and found myself behind a giant curtain. The chatter of the thousands assembling just beyond the barrier silenced my footsteps along the wooden boards set up as a walkway. I peeked through the overlap in the curtains and saw that the stands were nearly filled.

Someone tapped me on my shoulder, causing me to jerk my head back and turn around. "You can't be here," a young man said. "Please go find a seat."

I smiled, nodded, and made my way around the backdrop to a front-row spot along the bleachers, between a young boy whose wide eyes expressed his exuberance and a grizzled old man with a long, unkempt silver beard.

Once seated, I twisted around and saw the bleachers stretching dozens of rows upward and reaching out as wide as the tent would allow. *So,* this *is what a crowd of ten thousand people looks like?* I mused.

Just as I contemplated the throng, the sound of music caught my attention, along with everyone else's. Toward the back of the expansive open field where the extravaganza would take place, a group of musicians was assembled, all wearing matching red coats and tuning their various instruments, which caused the audience to hush as they sensed the show was about to commence.

The band conductor tapped his baton on the music stand in front of him, signaling his players to stand by. Then, after a momentary pause, he swung both arms in the air, and the performance began.

As the opening number struck its first notes, the curtain parted, and out rode Buffalo Bill on a white horse. He wore a long, pure-white beard, a spotless white cowboy hat, and a fine-looking white leather jacket with a long fringe that danced along in tandem with his prancing white horse. The crowd cheered as the star of the show waved.

Once in the center of the ring, he brought a megaphone to his mouth and announced, "Ladies and gentlemen, boys and girls, my name is Buffalo Bill. Welcome to Buffalo Bill's Wild West Show!"

A cheer exploded, causing Bill's horse to buck.

"Whoa!" he said, settling his ride. "White Rocket is excited too!"

Like a tornado sweeping across the plains, a wave of applause spread from one end of the bleachers to the other.

"Friends, you are about to witness a live reenactment of exciting, heart-pounding, and dangerous frontier events involving real American

Indians, United States Army soldiers, authentic cowboys, and honest settlers from America's Wild West."

Thousands of conversations buzzed like a room of unsettled little children.

Buffalo Bill held up his hands, silencing the crowd. "Our first adventure begins as citizens of this great land, many like yourselves, decided to make a change in their lives and head west with hopes of a new life and prosperity for their families. The journey was hard and fraught with many unspeakable dangers," he said, while the band struck up an ominous tune. "Now, let us sit back and enjoy Episode One—The Wagon Train."

With that, the massive curtain pulled back and three horse-drawn covered wagons entered the show field.

CHAPTER 53
BILL CODY

Hours after the show concluded and the last of the lingering spectators departed, I joined Frank and Annie for supper, prepared by the show's cooking staff at a table in front of their stagecoach.

"Allow me to introduce my lovely wife and partner—Little Miss Sure Shot herself, also known as Annie Oakley," Frank said with a sweeping gesture.

"Little Miss Sure Shot?" I repeated, offering her my hand.

"Oh, well, that's a nickname Sitting Bull gave me back in eighty-four. You can just call me Annie."

"It's a pleasure to meet you, Annie. My name is Leo."

"So, Leo, what did you think of the show?" Frank asked, reaching for corn cob.

Turning to Frank, I said, "You were terrific." Then I looked over at Annie, whose warm brown eyes seemed to accentuate her cheerful demeanor, and said, "And, Annie, I can't believe you shot that cigar out of that man's mouth."

"Oh, thank you, Leo," she said, with a cheerful smile.

"It's exactly what's advertised," I went on, then added, "and it's a great show—but at whose expense?"

"That's what I said," Annie offered, pointing a finger at me. "You're talking about how the Indians are portrayed, right?"

I nodded and sighed. "Certainly the crowd loved it, but it doesn't seem fair that it's always the Indian who's the aggressor. Haven't they been blamed enough?"

Frank shook his head and pointed to the gathering of natives sitting by a fire about twenty feet from us. "They don't seem to mind."

I looked over to the group of Indians, hoping to see Chief Red Shirt and Black Elk, but they weren't among these men, nor had they been in the show. Jerking my thumb behind me, I said, "I don't know why they're content to perpetuate this myth. It certainly doesn't help their cause."

"Cause?" Frank repeated. "What cause is that?"

"Allowing them to live in their native lands, as they've done for generations."

Frank leaned in and whispered, "You should be careful of speaking like that. Especially around here."

"Frank's right," Annie said, nodding. "Not everyone is open-minded like us."

"Hey, Leo, would you like to meet Bill Cody?" Frank asked, trying to lighten the mood.

"Sure, I'd like that."

"Come on, let's go find him," he said, pushing away his plate and getting to his feet.

"Oh, sure," I said, and looked at Annie. "Are you coming?"

"No, I need to clean my guns."

We'd taken no more than a few steps before Annie called out, "What about your plates, boys? I'm not your mother."

Frank rolled his eyes and said, "Of course, sweetie, we got 'em."

After we stacked our dirty plates on top of the teetering piles in the mess tent, I followed Frank as he weaved around the army men eating their chow, most still in uniform, who acknowledged him with a greeting or a wave.

"Hey, Leo, would you mind if I paid my horse Lightning a visit? I haven't seen him in weeks."

"Sure, why not," I said.

I followed Frank to the corral where several horses were being fed or brushed down. "There's my fella over there," he said, pointing to a beautiful red and brown horse.

Just as we approached, all six horses' heads popped up, and they bolted to the opposite side of the corral, as if a gunshot had frightened them. It took several hands to settle them down.

"What the heck?" Frank cried out. "It's like they were spooked by a wolf or something."

"A *wolf*?" I repeated.

"They'll be fine," Frank said, patting my shoulder. "Come on, Bill's through here." He pointed ahead, between two coaches.

We emerged onto a scene with a large bonfire. At its center, surrounded by covered coaches forming a circle, sat Buffalo Bill, stroking his white beard in front of a campfire.

"Frank," Bill Cody called out. "Great show tonight. You and Annie were stars, as usual."

"Thanks, Bill, I appreciate that," Frank said, dropping a heavy hand on my shoulder. "Let me introduce Leo Wolf."

At the mention of my name, two men with their backs toward me turned around. It was Chief Red Shirt and Black Elk. "Chief," I said, holding out my arms. "Black Elk."

"Ah," Bill said, getting to his feet and approaching. "I see you know my friends."

"Sure," I said, reaching out to shake his hand. "I've been to Pine Ridge."

"Not just that," Chief Red Shirt said. "Leo's the one responsible for the return of the Sacred Pipe."

"Ah, so this is the man," Bill said, wide-eyed. "Leo Wolf, you are quite the hero."

I shrugged. "*Umm*, yes, thank you, sir," I said, still thinking of the horses who seemed less than pleased with my presence.

"The chief told me of your adventure into the caverns under the Black Hills. We should figure a way of getting your story into the show."

I looked over to Black Elk, who offered a nod and a smile.

"Come and join us," Bill said, gesturing to the empty chairs.

"I need to get back to Annie. But you stay, Leo," Frank said. "We'll catch up later."

"Sure," I said, shaking Frank's hand. "I'd like that."

"It's good to see you," Black Elk said, sitting down next to me.

"I was surprised to hear that you and the chief left Pine Ridge for this," I said, spreading out my hands.

"It's how we learn the ways of the Wasichu."

I nodded and said, "The land-takers."

Black Elk looked around, then whispered, "Why have you come?"

"Something happened to me in the caves," I said, staring into his eyes. "I was—"

Black Elk held up his palm, suggesting I pause. He leaned in closer and whispered, "You must first take part in the *Inipi* before sharing."

"Inipi?" I repeated.

"It's known as a traditional ceremony to cleanse our body and mind," he said, tapping the side of his head with his finger. "But it's also a spiritual purification ceremony, enabling our rebirth."

"Rebirth?" I said, latching on to the word.

Black Elk smiled as if he knew of my experience in the Wind Cave. "Tonight at sunset, in the field behind us," he said, gesturing beyond the coaches. "You'll come?"

I nodded. "Yes, I'll come."

CHAPTER 54
INIPI

Moments before midnight, I arrived at the field and saw a young Lakota man tending to a bonfire. It burned hot and bright, seemingly unaffected by the persistent light rain. Just beyond it stood a round-shaped hut structure, covered with layers of old and faded woven carpets. At its front, a flap was pulled open, offering a small entrance.

"Is this for the Inipi?" I asked the man.

"Yes," he said, fussing with the fire. "I'm heating the stones now."

I looked under the burning logs and saw a pile of cannonball-sized stones. "What are they for?" I asked, pointing.

The man tucked a strand of his long black hair behind his ear and simply smiled.

"Ah, Leo," Black Elk said, approaching me from behind. "You'll want to remove your shirt and shoes."

I turned around and saw the holy man leading an entourage of several shirtless, barefoot native men.

He pointed and said, "I see you've met Takoda. He's our Firekeeper."

"Is everyone taking part?" I asked, waving my hand toward the dozen people crouching their way into the hut.

"Oh, yes," Black Elk said, patting my back. "It's like the white man says—the more, the merrier."

"Not always," I contested, kicking off my shoes and removing my shirt.

"There's nothing to worry about," he said, giving me a gentle push.

Anxious to get out of the chilling rain, I needed no encouragement as I ducked within.

"Leo, you'll sit there," Black Elk said, pointing to a place on the earthen floor only inches from a three-feet-round, and just as deep, hollow in the hut's center. Black Elk sat directly across, next to the hut's open flap. The remainder of the men sat encircling us, forming three rows deep.

Quiet conversations ensued while a shiver of dampness coursed through my body. I wondered whether removing my shirt and shoes had been a good idea. Takoda entered, grasping a pitchfork where he balanced upon its rusty tines a glowing stone, hot from the fire. Once within reach of the hollow, he tilted the pitchfork and the stone, looking like a giant beating heart, rolled off and landed in the pit with a thud. Immediately, I felt its warmth penetrating the chilled air. More stones were added, and it wasn't long before I broke out into a vigorous sweat, while the native men were moved to silence.

As we waited for the return of Takoda, I looked across the pit of the living stones at Black Elk, who sat cross-legged, eyes shut, and hands resting upon his lap. Taking his cue, I closed my eyes. A moment later, an image appeared of Mother and the red wolf poised by the Soul Tree. As I contemplated this mystery, I heard Takoda's return. With curiosity, I opened my eyes and saw the Firekeeper setting down a wooden bucket filled with water and a ladle hooked on its edge, next to Black Elk. He then ducked out, closing the flap behind him, leaving us in pitch-black darkness.

Just as I was about to inquire about its purpose, I heard the ladle dipping into the bucket and water being slowly poured over the pulsating stones. After several pours, which I assumed were carried out by Black Elk, the heat, which had not been overbearing before, turned infernal—a living hell. Quickly I tried backing away from the pit, afraid my skin would melt off my bones, but the men seated behind me prevented me from budging even an inch.

While my heart pounded out a steady drumbeat, I was about to call out for help when Black Elk began praying in Lakota. Out of respect, I forced myself to remain silent until he finished. Just as I was about to speak, the flap opened, and light flooded the lodge. I looked over to Black Elk, who smiled and placed a finger over his lips, beckoning me to remain silent.

Once again Takoda entered with more stones and, as if he could read my mind, Black Elk said, "The Inipi ceremony consists of four rounds."

I swallowed hard, worried about how to get through this ordeal three more times.

"Ignore the pain, Leo. Keep your focus here and here," Black Elk said, tapping one finger on his forehead and the other upon his heart. "Imagine yourself in the womb of Mother Earth. A place where the doors to the six directions are opened for you. Where water, air, earth, and fire live as one. Where the past and present are united and where another reality is touched."

I squirmed, trying to summon the courage, though to be truthful, I considered getting to my feet and charging out into the soothing rain. But it helped to observe the other men, none of whom were complaining. They all must have participated in this ceremony before, and showed no visible effects on their skin from the scorching heat.

Once again, the flap closed, plunging us back into darkness. I did my best, suffering in silence while listening to Black Elk's chants. It wasn't until the fourth round that the holy man offered his final prayer, this time in English. "Great Spirit, I pray to him first. I shall live with all my relations; that is why I pray to him first. Grandfather, I pray to him first. I shall live with all my relations; that is why I pray to him first."

After a moment of silence, I again heard the water being ladled onto the stones. Knowing this was the last round, I did my best to remain calm and wait for the scorching vapors to dissipate. Once I heard the ladle returned to the empty bucket, I sighed with relief. At last, I felt able to follow Black Elk's guidance by focusing on my mind's eye.

It took no more than a breath for the fear that had been welled up within me to flood out, intermingling with my sweat, and soak into the already damp earth beneath me. No longer afraid, I opened my eyes and saw Black Elk glaring back. Looking around, I noticed we were alone. "Where did everyone go?" I asked.

Black Elk offered me a gentle smile. "Leo, we are still in the hut, still in the dark. You and I have risen above the others, so that we may speak."

"Above where?" I asked, looking around.

He shrugged and said, "Into this private space."

I tugged at my beard, trying to make sense of my whereabouts.

Black Elk leaned forward. "Tell me, Leopold. What did you see in the Wind Cave?"

I took a breath, slowly exhaled, and said, "I saw Mother and the red wolf standing by a tree."

"The sacred tree joining earth and sky," he said, holding out his arms.

"Yes, and it grew pomegranates," I said, wondering if he knew that too.

"Such a thing only matters only to you," he said. "What's more important is that you've completed your quest. It's now time to do something with this knowledge."

I shook my head. "Knowledge? What knowledge? Why did I learn?" I asked, wondering if I missed something obvious.

"Leopold, few are permitted to see what you have seen."

"Which is?"

"Your people's holy place. Where your grandfathers' grandfathers have journeyed."

"And Mother," I added.

Black Elk smiled. "She is your guardian angel, and the red wolf is your spirit animal."

"What does all of this mean?"

"Ah, that is the question only you can answer," Black Elk said, pointing at me. "You have been granted great knowledge, Leopold Red Wolf. What you do with it is up to you."

CHAPTER 55
SENATOR CAMERON

The next day, I watched Buffalo Bill's Wild West Show through a slit in the giant curtain. Today's show began with ten buffaloes grazing on hay scattered across the center of the arena. A few hours earlier at breakfast, I'd overheard a man telling others about how Bill Cody earned his moniker of Buffalo Bill.

Before he began, this man, who played the part of a settler in the show, clarified the difference between the buffalo and the bison. "The French word for a beef animal is *boeuf,* hence the name buffalo. But the actual buffalo live in Africa and look different from their American cousins, smaller in size, with heavier horns. What roams the plains in this country is the bison. But people have become accustomed to calling it buffalo."

With that understood, he explained how several years earlier Bill Cody was hired by the Union Pacific Railroad to hunt these so-called buffalo. For nearly eighteen months, Cody delivered twelve beasts a day to hungry rail workers. According to this man, Bill killed more than four thousand buffaloes in eight months, and once, according to legend, he once slaughtered forty-eight in less than an hour.

But that paled in comparison to former President Grant's order to eliminate every last buffalo from the plains. This mass killing was justified as a necessary solution to the country's Indian problem. It was said the intent behind the government's directive was the outrageous idea that with each buffalo killed, another Indian would perish.

I'm sure Bill would have loved for his buffaloes to stampede across the arena, but the all-white crowd was seemingly fascinated even with these nearly extinct beasts lazily lumbering about. Then, capturing everyone's attention, the music commenced, and out rode Buffalo Bill. The audience cheered wildly as he made a wide circle around the herd. He pulled back the reins, causing White Rocket to rear up and kick out his front legs.

The showman lifted his megaphone to his lips and announced, "Ladies and gentlemen, boys and girls, my name is Buffalo Bill. Welcome to Buffalo Bill's Wild West Show!"

As expected, a tremendous cheer shook the canvas tent that shaded the spectators from the autumn sun.

"Before we begin, I would like to acknowledge a very important guest seated in the audience. From the great state of Pennsylvania, let's welcome the honorable Senator Donald Cameron."

Upon hearing this, I grasped a handful of curtain and nearly pulled it off its rigging. "Senator Cameron," I said aloud, as the man stood up, removed his hat, and swung it outwards. Then I shouted, "Sarah!" Though as far as I could see from across the arena, she wasn't sitting next to her uncle, nor anywhere close.

Luckily, my outbursts were swallowed up by the crowd's exuberant cheer. I considered sprinting across the arena to face the senator and ask if Sarah had survived her gunshot wound. But I imagined that before he could answer, I would be swiftly removed by his security team and locked away in a coach until he'd been safely escorted away. So, without much choice, I decided to wait for the two-hour show to conclude before making my approach.

*

It wasn't hard to distinguish the senator's coach from among the seemingly endless line. Two well-groomed black horses stood poised in front of an elegant black Abbot & Downing carriage. The finest coaches built in America. A fact I learned from Frank, who pointed out several on our way through Washington. Its driver had a cloth in his hand, cleaning off the dust clinging to the polished exterior.

I thought about speaking to him, as the driver may have known of Sarah's fate. But I doubted he would have such knowledge, and thought that he might, in turn, consider me a threat and prevent me from confronting the senator. So, I waited for the show's conclusion, which was the Frank Butler and Annie Oakley performance—always a favorite.

I paced the showgrounds, thinking of what to say to the senator. He probably wouldn't recognize me, as the only time our paths crossed was at Carlisle, and my relationship with Sarah was not of such great consequence that he would have taken any notice. I'm sure she never brought up my name in any of their conversations regarding the Indian school, except, of course, she might have mentioned me when explaining how she was shot. That is, if she survived the bullet to her stomach.

The waiting ended upon hearing Buffalo Bill's farewell announcement, followed by a loud cheer. Once the spectators began filing out, I stood poised to confront Sarah's uncle. It didn't take long before I saw him walking alongside two rather large muscular men and a nice-looking, well-dressed woman, whom I hadn't noticed before while he was seated in the stands.

I waited until the entourage was about halfway toward the stagecoach before springing out in front. "Excuse me, Senator," I said, with a smile stretching across my face. "I'm a friend of Sarah's. I was with her at Carlisle when she was shot. Can you tell me how she's doing?"

The senator stopped walking, looked at me wide-eyed, and said to no one in particular, "Who is this man?"

"My name is Leopold Wolf, sir, and like I said, I'm the—"

"Stand clear," ordered a tall man, shoving me aside and causing me to tumble to my knees.

"But all I want to know is whether Sarah's all right," I called out, as they marched by.

The only person to turn was the pretty woman, who caught my eye and offered a smile and a nod. My heart leaped at her kindness, confirming for me what I had been hoping for since last June—that Sarah had survived.

I got to my feet and followed the senator and the woman, whom I assumed to be his wife, along with their bodyguards, as they climbed into their stagecoach. Once all were inside, a curtain was pulled back and she looked at me once more. I think, though I was too far away to be sure, she gave me another smile. Regardless, I smiled back and sighed. Now all I had to do was find out where the senator lived and figure out a way to get to Sarah.

CHAPTER 56
FAREWELL TO THE CHIEF

"Leo, I never had the chance to thank you," Chief Red Shirt said, as we walked in the field past where the Inipi ceremony was held.

"Oh, that's all right," I said. "I'm happy I went."

"From what Black Elk told me, it seems you found more than just the Sacred Pipe."

"The caves beneath the Black Hills are indeed special," I said.

Chief Red Shirt rubbed his chin and said, "I've never thought of it as being more than the home to our creation story."

"Perhaps it's proof we're all connected to the same Creator."

The chief nodded slowly, and said, "You've come a long way, Leo, since we first met at Carlisle."

I chuckled and said, "I suppose so."

"So, what's next? I don't see a place for you here," he said, jerking his thumb behind him.

"I'm not sure," I said with a frown. "But there's a young lady whom I anxious to find."

"Ah, do you mean Senator Cameron's niece?"

I squinted and asked, "How do you know about Sarah?"

"My son told me," the chief said with a grin. "William said you two kissed at the lake."

I felt my cheeks blush. "Yes, it's true. We have feelings for each other," I said with a sigh. "Did you know she was shot?"

The chief furrowed his brow and said, "No, I didn't. Is she all right?"

"It happened while rescuing Abe from these pig farmers who wanted to hang him because he was a Negro. I didn't know she had survived until just an hour ago," I said, pointing to where I'd seen the senator.

The chief embraced me and said, "That's good news, Leo."

I sighed and said, "It is."

"I'm afraid it's going to be difficult getting close to her while she's under the care of the senator."

"I know," I said with a grimace, "but I have to try."

"You're aware Senator Cameron is no friend of the Indian."

"Oh yes, I'm well aware of the crimes he committed against your people."

The chief stared off into the distance, seemingly lost in thought.

I turned to him and asked, "Chief, can you tell me why you're here? This show doesn't portray you or your people in a good way."

He rubbed his chin and grimaced. "I'm ashamed to admit it," he said with a furrowed brow, "but I've come for the money. Cody pays me fifty dollars a week. That's a lot, and I need it to support my family."

"I understand," I said, nodding.

"This is the world my people live in now," he said with a sigh.

"What will happen to William?"

The chief shrugged. "Our way of life is over. He'll need to learn what he can at Carlisle and figure out how to make his way. No longer will our young people have their path laid out for them. Sadly, our future is unsettled."

"If he wants, William can work alongside Abe and me as a carpenter."

"Wouldn't that be something," the chief said, smiling. "A Jew, a Negro, and an Indian working side by side."

I laughed at the thought of it. "A real collection of misfits."

"But I have a sense you are destined for something greater than carpentry."

I lifted my brow and asked, "And what would that be?"

The chief shrugged, shook his head, and said, "Who can say? But from all that I have learned during my twenty-five years as chief, it's that it's best to be master of one's own destiny, rather than depending upon other people's choices."

I patted the chief's shoulder and said, "Wiser words have never been spoken."

CHAPTER 57
THE PRESIDENT IS SHOT

It was an hour's walk from the showgrounds to downtown Washington, which I figured would be the best place to begin my search. Knowing not a soul in the nation's capital, my plan, as crazy as it sounded, was to ask strangers in the street if they knew of the senator's residence.

But this plan came to an abrupt end when, several blocks from the White House, I came across a boy selling newspapers and hawking the headline. "President Garfield Shot!" he cried. "Read about the latest. Only a nickel."

I had about a dollar left, but with such big news, I felt I had no choice. I dug a coin out of my pocket and paid the newsboy. With paper in hand, I found a bench under an oak tree and read the news.

Sunday, July 3, 1881

President Garfield, less than four months into his term, was shot yesterday by Charles Guiteau, who waited for the president to arrive at the Washington, DC, train station. The assailant fired twice with a .44 caliber pistol. The first shot grazed President Garfield's right arm, and the second struck deep into his right side, near the eleventh rib. The president was rushed to the hospital, where he's being attended to, and at the time of writing this article, was alive, alert, and resting quietly.

The article went on to describe how the president's ordeal began, along with the background and motive of the delusional gunman. I put down the paper and considered the consequences. While saddened at the attempted assassination of a president only sixteen years since an assassin took Abraham Lincoln's life, I needed to stay focused on finding Sarah.

I thought for a moment. Perhaps this crisis would consume Senator Cameron, resulting in long days and nights away from home and leaving his wife as sole gatekeeper. I assumed, by her friendly demeanor at the show, that she would not prevent me from making contact with Sarah. Now all I had to do was locate the senator's home.

*

My original idea of asking people on the street was a failure. Most refused to speak with me, and those who did offered grimaces and frowns, assuming I was either up to something nefarious or mentally deranged.

Following the promenade, I eventually made my way to the steps of the United States Capitol building. While the caverns under the Black Hills were an incredible, magnificent creation by the Almighty, this architectural marvel, built by the hands of mortal men, seemed, dare I say, equally impressive.

While gawking at the Capitol's glory, I imagined the senator held up in a smoke-filled room, conferring with his colleagues about the succession of power, should the president perish. Though the current vice president, Chester Arthur, would assume the presidency under the terms of the Constitution, it was in the lack of his replacement, a new vice president, where the power vacuum presently lay.

While admiring the large dome, feeling dwarfed under its presence, I noticed a construction crew replacing marble blocks on the seemingly endless rows of steps. There were about two dozen men cutting slabs and laying them into place. Perhaps someone here would be familiar with the comings and goings of the senator. I approached and asked for the foreman in charge.

"What do you want?" barked a graveled voice from behind me.

I spun around and saw a bushily mustachioed man with a cigar stub tucked into the corner of his mouth. I said, "Excuse me, sir, I was wondering if you've seen any of the senators coming and going."

The man scoffed. "What's it your business if I do?"

"I'm looking for—"

"Hey, baby, you need a papa?" one of the laborers cat-called a young woman as she descended the steps. The offended woman lifted her chin, grimaced, and continued on her way.

The laborer's rude behavior prompted an idea. It was obvious these men would hardly notice an old man, even if he held a seat of power within the United States government; but a young, pretty lady—certainly that would arouse their interests.

"The man I'm looking for is usually accompanied by an attractive blonde woman, his niece."

The man nearly coughed the cigar out from his mouth. "His niece? We thought she was one of his babes."

"Babes?" I repeated, recoiling slightly. "So, you do know who I'm talking about?"

"Sure do. That's Senator Cameron. We got a crew over at his brownstone doing some work."

"I'm a friend of Sarah; that's the pretty blonde. Can you tell me where to find her?"

"*Pfft*, I don't think so," the foreman said.

"But it's true," I insisted. "We met at the Carlisle Indian School. Trust me, she'll be happy to see me."

"They'll can my ass if I allow a lowlife like you into their home. Now be off with ya."

"I'm no lowlife," I protested and continued asking. But nothing changed his mind. I sighed, gave up, and walked away, while the workers laughed and mocked my pitiful groveling.

Chapter 58
The Brownstone

After the foreman dismissed me, I found a park bench within view of where the men were working on the Capitol steps and considered ways of tracking down Sarah. One thought was to keep watch for the next time the senator exited the building and follow his T coach home. It could be days before such an opportunity occurred. While weighing the idea, a wagon filled with construction supplies pulled up.

"Not here, you imbeciles. That goes to the Camerons' residence on Jefferson!" the foreman yelled, running down the steps, his face twisted into a snarl.

The driver held up his hands, seeming to apologize. He snapped his whip at the horses, and the wagon creaked away from the curb, heading away from the Capitol. Without hesitation, I recognized my good fortune and ran in pursuit, while doing my best to avoid the foreman's notice.

Trying to keep up with the wagon, I dodged around the strollers, horses, and street vendors until, about twenty minutes later, the wagon pulled up to a brownstone along a street filled with similar homes.

It wasn't apparent where the work was being done—perhaps in the back of the house, I presumed. Not that it mattered, for all I cared about was to find the Camerons' home, and now I was standing before it. I took a breath to gather myself and climbed the ten stone steps to the large double doors of carved wood.

Before lifting the tarnished brass knocker, I tried conjuring up an appropriate greeting, depending upon who answered the door. Realizing the possible scenarios were endless, I relented, lifted the knocker, and slammed it down twice. Then, as if someone had cupped my ears, there was utter silence. No longer did I hear the street sounds of coaches and wagons clicking across the cobblestones or the chatter from the busy sidewalk a few feet below. This eerie silence broke with the sound of footsteps approaching from within. The clip-clapping stopped when the door creaked open, causing me to take a cautious step backward.

I assumed I'd face someone at my eye level; instead, I needed to look down into the face of someone staring back up at me. "Who are you?" a young boy with an abundance of brown curls asked.

"My name is Leo," I said, trying to peek behind him into the dark vestibule.

"What do you want?" he asked, demanding my attention.

"Is Sarah at home?"

He turned and shouted, "Sarah, someone is here for you!"

And before I could protest, he slammed the door in my face.

I stood there again, this time with the street noise at full pitch. For a moment, I considered turning and running, but before I could weigh the consequences, the door reopened and Sarah stood before me. Not sure to trust my eyes, I rubbed them vigorously. But there she was, the love of my life, appearing healthy. Her blonde hair seemed even more golden, her cheeks flushed, and her blue eyes sparkled from the sunlight spilling in through the open door.

"Leo?" she said, gaping at me. "What are you doing here? How did you find me?"

Suddenly I felt dizzy and grasped the door frame. "I didn't know what happened to you after you were shot," I managed to say.

"Are you all right?" she asked, reaching for my arm. "Do you want to come inside and sit down?"

I shook my head. "No, I'm okay. In fact, I've never been happier," I said.

"One moment," Sarah said and ducked behind the door, then reappeared. "Let's take a walk."

I nodded, and Sarah closed the door behind her. I watched as she bounded down the steps, her blonde hair bouncing, while I stood there frozen, unable to move. When she reached the bottom, she turned around and asked, "Are you coming, Leo?"

"Yes, of course," I said, and quickly joined her.

As we walked on the busy sidewalk, I couldn't stop staring.

Noticing my odd behavior, she said, "What are you doing?"

"I'm sorry, Sarah," I said with a shrug. "I didn't know what happened to you after leaving Carlisle. I thought you were dead."

"As you can see, I'm fine," she said, sweeping her hands downward. "Now, stop acting crazy. I know a quiet place where we can talk."

We walked without speaking until we reached a park. Once there, she led me to a stone wall that ran alongside the pathway until it veered off into a collection of large pine trees. "It's through here," she said, staying close to the wall.

"Where're we going?" I asked.

Sarah pointed to an archway forming a tunnel within the stone wall and stepped inside. I followed closely behind. Taking no more than a few steps, we emerged into an enclosed courtyard with stone benches surrounding a statue of some sort of fairy nymph.

"How did you find this place?" I asked, watching a bird land on the statue's outstretched marble hand.

"I take long walks," she said, sitting down, "and one day I stumbled upon this place. It's peaceful."

I looked around and said, "It's like a secret garden."

Sarah reached out, grasped my hand, and gave it a squeeze. "Now tell me, Leo, why are you here, and what's happened since I've seen you last?"

CHAPTER 59
THE SECRET GARDEN

With birdsong accompanying me, I shared my ordeal with Sarah. She sat still, focused on every word. Occasionally she would interrupt with a question, asking me to clarify a detail I may have skimmed over. Of all I shared, she marveled most at my adventures within the caverns of the Black Hills, especially my encounter with Mother, the red wolf, and the pomegranate tree in the Wind Cave.

"Mother said the fruit was called a pomegranate, and each one represents a soul, either alive or dead, and one of these red fruits was your soul."

"My soul?" she said, placing her hand on her chest.

I nodded. "And Mother asked if I loved you."

Sarah touched her cheek and asked, "What did you say?"

I took a breath and said, "Yes, I love her."

Sarah's eyes welled with tears.

"She then instructed me to eat the fruit in order to bind our eternal souls."

Sarah took a breath and asked, "And did you?"

"I did, and swallowed all the seeds."

"The seeds?" Sarah repeated with a furrowed brow.

"Yes, Mother said there are six hundred and thirteen seeds, each one representing the six hundred and thirteen commandments in the Torah."

"The Jewish book," Sarah said.

"You've heard of it?" I asked.

"Of course, Leo. I studied theology in college."

I sighed and tried to smile.

"Why the red wolf?" she asked.

"Black Elk said that after I ate the wolf in the cave, it became my spirit animal."

"No wonder," she said, reaching out to stroke my red beard, sending shivers down my spine.

I told her how I traveled from Pine Ridge to Washington and spotted her uncle at the Buffalo Bill Wild West Show, and how I followed the supply wagon to the senator's front door.

Sarah stood up, took a few steps toward the statue, turned around, and said, "What you've said is touching, and I would be lying if I said I wasn't moved. But as I explained before, Leo, we can't be together. My uncle will never allow it."

"Why are you so afraid of him?" I said, shaking my head. "We're destined to be together, not just in this lifetime, but for an eternity."

Sarah squinted her blue eyes and stroked her chin. "How do you know what happened to you was more than a dream?"

I jumped to my feet, walked toward her, and grasped her shoulders. "It was no dream, I'm sure of it," I said, and noticed her earrings. "What are these?" I asked, releasing my grip and gently touching one of the dangling red earrings.

"Oh, do you like them? My aunt got them as a gift at a dinner party from this man. He had a funny name," she said, pausing to think. "Oh yes, his name was Hajji. He's a diplomat from Persia."

"Persia?" I said, shaking my head. "Where's that?"

"It's a country in the Near East."

I looked again at the earrings and asked, "What do you think these are?"

Sarah scrunched her sweet face into a grimace and said, "They're apples, of course."

"These are not apples," I said, taking note of the shape. "These are pomegranates."

Sarah scoffed. "That's not possible."

"Sure, look at the six-pointed stem at its bottom."

"Where do pomegranates grow?" she asked, folding her hands across her chest.

"I suppose in Persia," I said with a shrug.

Sarah fondled one between her thumb and her index finger.

"Do you still think what I saw in the cave was just a dream?"

"This is weird," she said, wide-eyed.

"After what I've seen, believe me, this is far from weird," I said wrapping my arms around her waist and pulling her in tight. "This is something else."

"What?" she asked, her eyes locked onto mine, our lips just inches apart.

"It's proof of our spiritual journey, Sarah," I said, and kissed her.

She pushed me away and said, "What are we going to do?"

"Come back with me to Carlisle. We'll marry, have children, and I'll—"

"Oh, Leo, I want to, but we can't."

"But you're a grown woman, not a child," I pleaded. "How can he stop you?"

"I can't! I just can't," she cried out and shoved me aside.

Before I could reach out to stop her, Sarah ran from the secret garden, through the archway, and out into the park. I followed, but quickly lost sight of her among the foliage.

As I stood on the pathway, under the shade of an oak tree, I wondered how to break Sarah free from the clutches of her uncle.

While pondering my predicament, I heard a cheer coming from just beyond the hillside. I followed the sounds and as I crested the landscape, I saw a crowd huddling around a man who stood upon a wooden crate. He was pontificating about the plight of the Indians.

I made my way to the outer edges of the group of twenty or so people and asked a young man listening, "Who's that?"

While keeping his focus on the speaker, he said, "That's Thomas Sloan. People are calling him the Indian's man in DC."

CHAPTER 60
THE INDIAN'S MAN IN DC

It was only several minutes more before Mr. Sloan concluded his speech. In that brief time, he impressed me with his ability to connect with the audience, who, upon his conclusion, responded with vigorous nodding of heads and robust applause.

I waited while several people approached, asking the speaker questions. Upon their departure, I stepped forward. "Excuse me, Mr. Sloan," I said, offering my hand. "My name is Leopold Wolf. I just heard the tail end of your talk and thought it interesting."

The man smiled. He had barely a whisker on this smooth, tanned face, and neatly combed brown hair. He said, "Tell me, Mr. Wolf, what fascinated you?"

Unprepared for the question, I stammered, and said, "*Um*, your words about ending the government's abuse of the natives. I, too, support this cause."

He looked me over, then said, "Is there Indian blood in you? Though I doubt it, with that red hair and luscious beard."

"Me, no," I said, tapping my hand on my chest. "I'm a Jew."

"Is that right," Mr. Sloan replied, nodding. "So why does a Jew care about the plight of the Indian?"

"Well, Mr. Sloan, I—"

"Thomas," he said, interrupting me. "Please call me Thomas. I've just turned eighteen, and find it hard being addressed like my father."

I nodded and said, "And you can call me Leo."

Thomas smiled. "Please, Leo, continue."

I told him about my observations of the ongoing social experiment involving Indian children during my time as a counselor at the Carlisle Indian School.

"This is most interesting," he said.

"Why do you do this?" I asked, pointing to the wooden crate lying by his feet.

"To educate people on the Indian's plight," he said.

"But why?" I asked with a furrowed brow. "You don't look like a native either."

"Actually, I'm mixed. My father was born to a woman of the Omaha tribe in Nebraska. But he died when I was young. My white mother also died many years ago. I have no memory of either one. I was raised by my grandmother on the reservation in Omaha."

"Oh, I'm sorry," I said. "I also lost both parents. My mother when I was eight, and Father was murdered last year by a soldier of the South."

"My condolences," Thomas offered.

"Thank you," I said. "Tell me, why do you do this? You're so young."

"I want to go to law school. This is a way to hone my skills for admission," he said.

"Law school?" I said.

Thomas nodded, pinched the bridge of his nose, and said, "I read about this Carlisle School."

"Where?"

"In a journal supporting the cause. Did you know that since Carlisle opened its doors, dozens of similar schools have been springing up across the country?"

"I had no idea," I said, shaking my head. "I thought Carlisle was the only one."

"It's tragic, and from what I hear, the Senate is poised to pass a law making attendance compulsory for all Indian children."

"A law?" I said, shaking my head once again. "I bet Senator Cameron is behind that one."

Thomas tilted his head. "What do you know of the senator?"

I chuckled. "For starters, I'm in love with his niece. We met at Carlisle. That's why I'm here, in Washington."

Thomas blinked and shook his head. "That seems like a tall mountain to climb, you being a Jew."

I sighed. "Apparently, everyone but me seems to have a problem with it."

"Cameron's a bigot," he said, "and he's set his sights upon destroying what's left of the Indian. Before becoming senator, he was the Secretary of War, sending the army to fight the Lakota for control of the Black Hills gold."

I nodded with a grimace. "I know what he's done."

"Then why don't you do something about it?" Thomas insisted, holding out his hands.

"What can I do?" I said and scoffed at the absurd suggestion.

Thomas bent down, grabbed his wooden crate, and handed it to me. "Start with this," he said. "There's a story within you, Leo."

"You think standing on a box and shouting out to the world how unfair life is will change anything?"

Thomas dropped the crate and stared at me. "Maybe you're right," he said. "After what you've witnessed, you need a larger platform, and I know just the man."

CHAPTER 61
TIMOTHY FORTUNE

I was to wait in a park across from the White House. Thomas had instructed me to sit by the fountain, where an associate of Mr. Fortune would approach and direct me next. When I questioned the need for secrecy, Thomas said, "Mr. Fortune is not a popular figure in Washington. His newspaper articles in the *People's Advocate* offer less than flattering accounts of some of the nation's most powerful men. He needs to be careful when out in public."

The benches surrounding the fountain were empty, as an autumn morning chill kept strollers from lingering. With a brisk westerly wind spraying the benches on the east end, I chose to stay dry by parking myself on the opposite side.

I waited no more than a few minutes past ten before I felt someone tap my shoulder. Though forewarned, I was surprised at the stealthy approach. When I turned, a young boy stood before me, looking no more than twelve. Not knowing if this was the contact sent by Mr. Fortune, I glared at him, and before I could utter a word, he reached into this pocket and handed me an envelope.

Without waiting for a thank you, the boy turned and ran. I watched him as he disappeared down the pathway, then refocused my attention on the envelope. I took a breath, broke the wax seal, and removed the note. After unfolding it, I read:

Good day, Mr. Wolf. I understand that you have interesting observations to share about your time when employed at the Carlisle Indian School. If you're willing to take a risk by exposing yourself, I would be amenable to publishing your story. I am waiting for you now at Potter House. It's a saloon two blocks north of where you're seated. If you don't show up within the next twenty minutes, I'll assume you've decided not to come. Either way, I advise you to burn this note before leaving the park.
~Timothy Fortune

I reached into my pocket and removed my lighter. But before flicking it open, I looked around to make sure I was still alone. Satisfied, I lit the note and watched its ashes catch the wind and float into the fountain.

As I got to my feet, I hesitated, thinking of Timothy's dire warning, which in turn reminded me of Alvin's words in the caves, of being at a crossroads. It was apparent that I was about to make another life-altering decision. Certainly, I could walk away, thereby avoiding the risks; I had no idea what they may be, though they seemed ominous. But, if my life was to have a purpose, I needed to summon the courage and speak out regarding the abuse of the children at Carlisle. I swallowed hard, pulled back my shoulders, and headed north to the café.

*

I arrived a few minutes after the sun set over the massive government buildings to the west, leaving Potter House covered in shadows. Looking through the dirt-encrusted windows, I saw the flickering of candlelight illuminating the interior. Not knowing what Mr. Fortune looked like, I figured he would reach out to me in some subtle manner.

I'd taken no more than a few steps into the café when I heard my name being called out. "Leo, over here!"

I gazed into the dark shadows for the source and saw a dark-skinned man with brown curls and spectacles perched on a hawk-shaped nose. "Mr. Fortune?" I asked.

"Yes, Leo. Please come and sit," he said, gesturing to the empty chair across the table from him. "And I must insist you call me Tim."

I looked around and asked in a subdued voice, "*Um*, I thought we were supposed to be discreet."

"In here?" he said, his eyes traveling around the room. "There is no need; these are my people."

I turned my head side to side and saw that, indeed, all the patrons and the barkeep were Negroes. "Ah, okay," I said.

"This is a safe place, Leo," he said, gesturing for me to sit. "We can speak freely here."

I offered a pained smile and nodded. "So, what do you want to know, Tim?" I said, pulling out the chair.

"Tell me everything about your time at Carlisle. How you got the job, your responsibilities, what you saw, and I'll write a blistering exposé on what's going on there."

"Before I do that, you said in your note I'd be taking a risk, exposing myself, by speaking with you. Can you be more specific?"

Tim nodded with a grimace. "From what I hear, this grand experiment at Carlisle is just the beginning. More schools are popping up at an alarming rate across the country. The government is hell-bent on passing a law making it compulsory for native children to attend these boarding schools."

"Yes, Thomas said the same thing."

"We probably can't do anything to stop it, but we can try to raise awareness and you can lead the charge; once I make you famous," he said, raising his brow.

"Famous?" I repeated with a grimace.

"But it's true, there will be risks," he said, with a slight tilt of his head. "Senator Cameron may come after you. After all, he's the one sponsoring the bill in the Senate."

I ran my fingers through my beard, considering the consequences.

"You're worried about his niece?" he asked, cocking his chin toward me.

"Thomas told you?"

He nodded. "This is one way of getting her attention," he said with a sinister smile.

"But not in the way I want," I said with a scoff. "She'll despise me for it."

"I don't know about that," he said with a squint. "Wasn't she working at Carlisle at the same time as you?"

I nodded. "That's how we met."

"Like you, didn't she express her disdain at how the children were treated?"

I nodded. "She was just as adamant."

"Well, Leo, if this is the woman you want to spend the rest of your life with, have children with, then she should support the cause, regardless of who her uncle is."

"That's not the issue keeping us apart."

Timothy furrowed his brow. "What is it, then?"

"It's because her uncle would never allow her to marry a Jew."

"Ah, I see," he said. "It seems the senator's daughter has some soul searching to do."

"Soul searching?" I repeated with a smile. "That's a perfect way of putting it."

CHAPTER 62
THE PEOPLE'S ADVOCATE

ABUSE AT THE CARLISLE INDIAN SCHOOL
BY TIMOTHY FORTUNE
OCTOBER 25, 1881

Not far from the bloodstained battlefields of Gettysburg, where our beloved, late President Lincoln spoke those immortal words honoring the wartime dead, a travesty of epic proportions is being inflicted upon the innocent children of the oppressed Native American people.

The Carlisle Indian School in Carlisle, Pennsylvania, under the auspices of Captain Henry Pratt, the school's founder, is promoting cultural genocide, evident through its self-proclaimed mission of 'killing the Indian, in order to save the man.'

Here, children ranging in age from as young as five to as old as sixteen years are being forced to assimilate into the white man's culture by forbidding the use of their native languages and traditional practices. According to Leopold Wolf, a former counselor to the five- through seven-year-old boys, there have been numerous accounts of humiliation, abuse, beatings, and victimization.

I stopped reading, dropped the paper onto my lap, and stared out onto the street. Scratching deep into my beard, I shouted, "Dammit!"

While what I had shared with Timothy was accurate, he also included additional accounts from other unnamed sources, the truth of which I had no idea. This was a problem, because as I was the only named witness, a reader could assume the additional accusations were all coming from me.

The rest of the article continued in a similar manner, concluding with the pending federal law set before Congress, making attendance at schools like Carlisle compulsory for Indian children, and describing hundreds of similar schools now opening up across the country.

Timothy even suggested that the Bureau of Indian Affairs, a government agency in charge of distributing food, land, and other provisions, planned to withhold items and services from those tribes refusing to send their children to the schools, and to commission officers

270

to visit the reservations and forcibly remove children from their families.

Clutching the paper in my hand, I got to my feet and walked the four blocks to Potter House. Unlike last time, the place was empty except for the barkeep.

"Do you know where I can find Mr. Fortune?" I demanded.

The barkeep, with a brownish dishcloth in his hand, looked at me with a squint and said, "Sorry, I don't know."

I approached the long wooden bar hugging the wall and slammed the paper down on it. "You don't understand," I said, with nostrils flaring. "He used me to give legitimacy to this article."

The Negro man looked at me, shook his head, pulled out a bottle of whiskey along with a glass from behind the counter, and poured a drink. He pushed it toward me and said, "It's on the house."

I squeezed the damp glass and threw back the shot. As its warmth coated my throat, I sighed, allowing my tense shoulders to drop. "Thank you," I said, "I needed that."

"Not a problem."

"What's your name?" I asked him.

"His name is Nathanial," a voice called out.

Turning my attention to the back of the saloon, I saw Timothy emerging from the shadows. "You're here," I said, holding out my hands.

"You must learn discretion, my friend, if you want to survive in this business," he said, pulling out a chair and gesturing for me to join him.

"Business?" I said, sitting down. "What does that mean?"

Tim raised a hand to Nathanial, who nodded, ducked under the counter, and emerged on its other side. He walked over to the front door and locked it.

"What's going on?" I asked, gripping the wooden armrests of my chair.

"Relax, Leo, I'm not here to harm you. I want to help you, and in turn, perhaps you can help me."

I scratched at my beard and said, "I don't understand. How can I help you?"

"When I say business, I'm referring to the newspaper business. The *People's Advocate* is widely read and has provided me with enough income to open this place," he said, sweeping out his arm.

"You own Potter House?" I asked, wide-eyed.

Timothy nodded, pushed back his chair, and got to his feet. "Come with me. I want to show you something."

CHAPTER 63
THE PRESS

Timothy directed me to the supply room, where, alongside stacks of wooden crates, an old, decrepit blanket hung off a rusted iron curtain rod. He pushed the drape aside, exposing a darkened doorway, reached for a lantern, and said, "It's down here."

Timothy descended the stairs, with me following closely behind. Once down the single flight, we were in a cellar where a large iron contraption took up most of the cramped space. "What's this?" I asked.

Timothy placed the lantern down on a small table pushed up against the wooden wallboards, placed a hand on the machine, and said, "This, Leo, is called a printing press. It's where I create the *People's Advocate* and where I'll print your paper."

I looked at the massive, black iron machine, constructed of wheels, large round tubes, and an array of gears, and said, "My paper?"

"Yes, your own newspaper. You think you'll cause change by standing on a box and expressing your outrage to a handful of strangers. With a newspaper, you can reach hundreds of people at a time, maybe thousands, if you have a story to tell and write well."

"I'm sorry, but I don't understand," I said, shaking my head. "You want me to start a newspaper? Where would I get the money to buy something like this? It must cost a fortune."

"It does, but you don't need to," Timothy said, lifting his brow. "You can use this one."

I squinted, suspicious of the offer, and said, "Why would you be so generous?"

"Trust me, I'm not," he said, shaking his head. "My intention is to profit from your enterprise, and so will you."

"How's that?" I asked.

"My paper reaches a specific audience—mainly those interested in the plight of the Negro. Sales have been decent enough to pay back the bank for the loan and the rent for the saloon. But I'd like to have the press working seven days, instead of the four days it is now. My idea is to print a new weekly paper, with a different perspective from mine, speaking to a fresh audience."

"And you think I'm able to write for a newspaper?"

"Sure, and I'll be your editor," he said, tapping his chest. "After a few rewrites, you'll get the hang of it."

I grimaced and shook my head. "I don't know."

"As for the business end of things, we'll split profits fifty-fifty."

"Fifty-fifty?" I repeated, and wondered if this venture deserved to be pursued, as it appeared more rewarding than swinging a hammer. Allowing for the possibility, I asked, "What would I call it?"

Timothy rubbed his chin, thought for a moment, and said, "How about *The Observer*? It means one who observes without participating. I've always believed that's the essence behind honest journalism."

I pointed and said, "I like it."

Timothy clapped his hands. "Great, let's get started. We have lots to do."

A rush of enthusiasm sparked a multitude of ideas. "What do you think about writing my first piece about the Buffalo Bill Wild West Show? I know several people performing there, including Chief Red Shirt and Frank Butler—that's Annie Oakley's husband."

"Great idea," he said with a grand smile, displaying his perfect white teeth. "You should get started on the interviews right away."

"Interviews?" I said.

"Sure, you need to quote credible sources if you plan on convincing your readers."

I gave my beard a tug, wondering whom to approach first.

Picking up on my musings, Timothy suggested, "Buffalo Bill himself would be a wonderful feature story for the inaugural issue."

"He would be great," I said, biting my lower lip at the challenge set before me.

*

Later that night, Nathanial served me supper in the saloon and offered me a place to sleep in the cellar, alongside the printing press. I didn't mind the unusual accommodations, as I was getting used to spending my nights wherever I could find a quiet spot. This vagabond lifestyle was helped by traveling light with nothing more than the clothes on my back, and a few things tucked away in my pack, like Father's soul bundle and Mother's journal.

This thought gave me pause, accompanied by a touch of guilt, as I realized I had yet to read Mother's words. Perhaps reading her entries would be a way of connecting with her, as I did within the Wind Cave.

CHAPTER 64
MOTHER'S JOURNAL

I could only manage twenty minutes in the basement because the odor of the ink, which can best be described as a toxic blend of turpentine and soot, caused the inside of my mouth to itch and my eyes to water. So, I slung my pack over my shoulder and climbed back up the stairs to the saloon.

Nathanial had already shuttered the place for the evening, leaving the saloon dark except for moonlight spilling in through the large windows, providing enough illumination for me to find my way to the front.

Just as I gripped the door handle, I hesitated. Venturing out into the night made little sense with the few coins left in my pocket, certainly not enough to let a room at a nearby inn. Reconsidering my options, I turned around, surveyed the saloon, and found a spot where I could remain hidden from view should anyone peer in through the windows.

I settled along the wall opposite the bar and, with legs stretched out and my back propped up, I removed Mother's journal from my bag. By the glow of the moonlight, I read.

June 1, 1863–I dreamed last night I had one month left to live.
But what frightened me the most was not my impending doom,
but leaving my precious son Leopold without a mother to
raise him.

I looked away from the handwritten pages and shook my head. How could Mother foresee her demise thirty days before it happened? Anxious to learn more, I dropped my eyes to the journal and continued reading.

June 2, 1863–I awoke just moments ago after another nightmare. Whatever was about to happen to me, it appeared Leopold would be witness to my violent death. But I hadn't been able to see what killed me or why my son was present. Though it was still hours before morning, I got out of bed, careful not to wake Isaac, and checked on my eight-year-old boy. Seeing him sleeping peacefully, I sighed, bent over, and kissed his forehead.

June 13, 1863–If I could scream aloud, I would. But again, it was the middle of the night and both Isaac and Leopold were fast asleep. Not wanting to forget a detail of my nightmare, I slipped on my housecoat, dropped my journal into a pocket, and tiptoed into the kitchen, where I lit a lantern and took a breath. Tonight, as foretold in my dream, I learned how my life would end.

While the war has been raging on for the past four years, it had until yesterday remained elsewhere. But according to Isaac, the fighting had arrived forty-five miles to the south in Gettysburg, and was expected to reach Carlisle any day. Which is why my husband departed this morning, rifle in hand, to join up with the local militia in our fight against the Rebels. It was during this upcoming battle, taking place in the streets of our small town, I dreamed not of Isaac's death, but of my own.

I read her words about how she foresaw her death with me as witness. But she did not describe the gory details of how it would occur—though I needed no reminder of that moment when the cannonball tore through the walls of our home, ripping her body in two.

June 20, 1863–I spent the past few days fussing over Leopold, attending to his needs and telling him incessantly how much I loved him. I would have probably done the same even without my nightmares, as the sounds of approaching cannon fire rattled the windows in our home.

That was the last entry. Ten days later, Mother lost her life. I flipped through the pages of the leather-bound journal, searching for more writings, but except for a lovely pencil drawing of a white dove sitting on a branch, the remaining pages were blank. I furrowed my brow, considering how Mother's dreams had foretold her violent death.

I closed the journal and brought it to my heart, wondering about its intention. Did Mother leave it for me to discover? Where did Alice find it and why did it remain hidden all these years? Did Father know of it, and for some reason decided never to show it to me?

While considering the abundance of unanswerable questions, my eyes became heavy, and I drifted off to sleep.

CHAPTER 65
BIDZIIL

Upon reaching the showgrounds, I saw several crews of men releasing thick ropes from iron posts hammered into the earth, thereby allowing the giant canvas tent to be lowered to the ground. It was an impressive display of coordination, obviously not their first time packing up the show and making it ready to move on to the next city.

Careful not to get into anyone's way, I weaved around wagons and coaches being loaded and backed away from men hauling bins filled with trash. I crossed the path of a foreman barking out orders who took notice of me, planted a strong hand on my chest, and asked, "Who the hell are you?"

"My name's Leo Wolf. I'm a journalist with *The Observer*. Can you tell me where to find Buffalo Bill?"

"A journalist?" he asked with a sneer.

"That's right," I said, nodding. "I'm here to interview Buffalo Bill."

"Mr. Cody is gone. He left for New York City a few hours ago."

"New York City," I repeated. "Why?"

"It's our next stop," he said and gave me a gentle shove. "Now, if you don't mind, we have work to do."

"Sure, thank you," I said, and walked away.

Disappointed, I tugged on my beard, wondering what to do next. I assumed the performers had also ventured on, leaving the moving crew to their work before meeting up in New York City. Just as I was ready to head back to Potter House, I heard a commotion.

I hurried over to where a crowd had formed around what appeared to be two men in a brawl. Pushing my way through, I saw one of the combatants was shirtless, his massive physique glistening in sweat. As his body spun around, after a bone-crunching punch to his opponent's jaw, I saw it was Tom, the young Navajo who'd killed Major Lawrence in Carlisle.

"Tom?" I called out, though my voice was swallowed by the shouts of the spectators, who were champing at the bit for more fists to fly.

But before Tom could finish off the man, who was now bent over, grasping at his knees, and spitting out a wad of blood onto the dirt-packed ground, the same foreman who'd reprimanded me reappeared. "That's enough, you two," he barked. "I told you, Injun, one more fight and you're done."

Tom rolled back his broad shoulders, cocked his chin toward the foreman, and said, "That's fine with me."

The foreman waved his hand in the air and said, "Grab your stuff and get the hell out of here."

Tom scoffed and walked away, while the man he'd pummeled was having his broken nose attended to.

"Tom!" I shouted as I ran toward him. "It's me, Leo."

Upon hearing my name, he stopped cold and looked over his shoulder. "Leo?" he said, wide-eyed. "What are you doing here?"

"I'm here to interview Buffalo Bill for a newspaper article."

"You're writing for a newspaper?"

"Not just any newspaper," I said with a proud smile. "It's my own paper, though I have a partner."

"So you're living in Washington?"

I grimaced and said, "I'm not living anywhere for the moment, but that's a long story. What are you doing?"

Tom looked over my shoulder at the foreman, who had returned to his duties, and said, "I suppose I'm heading to the train station once I get my things packed up."

"Where are you going?" I asked.

He shrugged and said, "I really don't know."

I leaned in and whispered, "Have they come looking for you? You know, for what happened to Major Lawrence."

"I haven't seen nobody," he said, shaking his head. "Anyway, I'm not worried. Major Lawrence was a soldier of the South. The police in the Union states couldn't care less."

I gazed into Tom's sad, brown eyes and saw a beautiful young man, the son of a chief, whose life had been derailed by the white man's ambition. Acting on impulse I said, "Hey, why don't you join up with me?"

Tom furrowed his brow and said, "Doing what?"

"Work with me on the newspaper. You can help me write articles, speak out in public forums, help the Indian cause. Having a Navajo on staff would provide a credible voice."

"Come on, Leo," he said with a scoff. "Who would care what I have to say? I'm nobody."

I looked around, making sure we were alone. Then I poked a finger into his muscular chest and said, "You're not nobody. You're Bidziil, the Navajo warrior."

CHAPTER 66
FIRST ISSUE

The dozen or so patrons fell silent the moment we entered Potter House, stupefied by Tom's presence. We made our way to the bar, where Nathanial, his eyes bulging out of his head, asked, "Who's your friend, Leo?"

"Nathanial, this is Tom," I said, reaching up to pat the young man's shoulder. "But his Navajo name is Bidziil, which means strong."

"I can see that," Nathanial said, offering his hand. "It's good to meet you, Tom, or should we call you Bidziil?"

"Tom's fine," he said, shaking Nathanial's hand.

"Do you know where Timothy is?" I asked.

Nathanial jerked his thumb. "He's down in the cellar."

"Thanks," I said, and told Tom to follow me.

As we made our way across the saloon, I could feel the floor vibrating, a sign the press was in action. By the time we reached the cellar, the vibrations evolved into a deafening roar. Watching the press at work reminded me of a railroad car chugging along. Tom, needing to duck under the low ceiling, stared in awe, his mouth hanging open at the unearthly machine.

Feeding large sheets of paper into the press was Timothy, assisted by another Negro man who turned the crank, keeping the machine in action. Both men remained oblivious to our presence until I took a step closer and caught Timothy's attention. Noticing me, he held up a hand.

After a few more sheets passed through, the assistant stopped cranking and the press fell silent.

"Who's this?" Timothy asked.

I introduced Tom, explained our history at Carlisle, and how we reunited at the showgrounds. "I think he can give *The Observer* an authentic voice."

Timothy agreed and encouraged me to get started right away. "A newspaper doesn't exist without words."

"I need to find a place to stay," I said, gesturing to the cramped space.

Timothy considered my predicament, then said, "I can get you a room at the Rosebud Inn, but I'm sure Tom won't be allowed. However, he's welcome to stay here."

"Okay," Tom said without hesitation.

I grimaced and said, "Are you sure?"

Tom shrugged and nodded.

"If it's okay with Tom, it's fine with me," Timothy said. "Having him around will certainly give troublemakers pause."

"Great," I said. "I suppose we should get started."

"We'll print the inaugural issue of *The Observer* this Friday," Timothy said, looking at his assistant.

"Friday!" I said, jerking my head back. "That's in two days!"

Timothy nodded. "I can see the headline," he said, holding up his hands. "Navajo Warrior Exposes Carlisle Indian School!"

I looked at Tom's furrowed brow and nodded. "All right," I said with a sigh. "I suppose we should get to work."

Over the next several hours, Tom and I composed ten pages of a detailed exposé describing the multitude of abuses at Carlisle. Tom's accounts, coming from the perspective of a sixteen-year-old boy on the cusp of becoming a man, were especially thoughtful, moving, and disturbing. In one passage, we wrote about the time he stood upon the table in the dining hall while the entire school watched and proclaimed, "You can cut my hair, take away my clothing, but you cannot take away the generations of great warriors who have come before me."

By the time the clock tower bells from a nearby church struck midnight, we were done. The first issue of *The Observer* was ready to be typeset and printed the next day.

Timothy said the best place to sell papers was in the park, where I'd met Thomas Sloan. "Get up on a wooden crate and give your speech. If you're good, and have your Navajo Indian alongside, trust me, you'll gather a crowd and sell papers."

With that done, I said goodnight to Tom and headed for my room at the Rosebud Inn.

CHAPTER 67
MAN OF THE YEAR

When Tom and I arrived at the park with several dozen folded newspapers tucked into my pack, we stumbled upon a fairly large crowd gathered in front of a stage for what appeared to be some sort of political rally. Swags of red, white, and blue bunting were pinned to the front edge of the platform. Upon it, a decorated podium stood poised in front of a single row of chairs stretching across the width of the stage. A large American flag hung as a backdrop. Off to one side sat a group of six musicians tuning their instruments.

We joined the audience, trying to blend in, though Tom, with his impressive height, physique, and skin tone, became a curiosity. But those stares ended when the band struck up a tune, redirecting everyone's attention to the stage. Several well-dressed men with tall black hats climbed the steps and took their seats.

The music stopped when another man stepped before the podium and smiled. "Good afternoon, ladies and gentlemen. My name is Alphonso Taft," he said, and paused, his gaze sweeping across the audience. "For those who may not know me, I was once Secretary of War under President Grant, a position I was honored to serve. When I stepped down to pursue other interests, I was succeeded by a man who had, as one of his first duties, to contend with the discovery of gold in the Black Hills and its consequences. Once word spread, it didn't take long for thousands of gold seekers from near and far to flock to the Black Hills in the southern

Dakota territory, which the Sioux claimed as their ancestral homeland. The arrival of the prospectors stirred up the Indians, who did their best to oppose the intrusion. To quell the unrest, Secretary of Interior Zachariah Chandler, spearheaded negotiations with the Sioux, only to be thwarted by Chief Sitting Bull and Chief Crazy Horse, who, after long and arduous negotiations, refused to compromise. With no place to turn, the problem was referred over to the War Department. Under the auspices of today's honoree, the United States launched the Great Sioux War, the results of which we're all familiar with."

While a round of applause forced the speaker to pause, Tom elbowed me and directed my attention to the side of the stage, where Senator Cameron was waiting, with Sarah standing by his side. My first instinct was to run to her, but instead, I quickly returned my attention to the stage as Mr. Taft resumed his introduction.

"Ladies and gentlemen, let's give a warm DC welcome to the winner of this year's Humanitarian Man of the Year award, from the great state of Pennsylvania, the honorable Senator Donald Cameron."

The moment the senator stepped onto the stage, Tom bolted through the crowd, shoving people aside. "Tom!" I cried out and chased after him. But I was too late. He had already soared several feet from the grass field and landed on the stage, inches from the senator, who cowered, holding out his hands.

"Murderer!" Tom shouted, raising his powerful arms in the air.

While the crowd watched in awe, a man bolted across the stage and buried his shoulder in Tom's chest, knocking him to the platform, and in an instant, three more men jumped onto the stage and piled on, pinning Tom down.

"Get him the hell out of here!" screamed the senator.

By the time I reached the edge of the stage, Tom was being escorted away with tears washing down his cheeks. Before I could begin to worry about ways of getting him freed, I too was grabbed by the senator's men, dragged to a coach, and pushed inside, where I was seated next to Tom. Across from us sat two men, one of which was brandishing a Colt .45.

"I'm sorry, Leo," Tom said with a sigh.

I patted his leg. "It's all right, I understand."

"Keep quiet," one of the men ordered.

"Where're you taking us?" I asked.

"I told you to shut the hell up," the other snarled.

*

About a half-hour later, we pulled up to the back of a dilapidated brick building near a railroad. I swallowed hard. Would the senator do us harm?

With our hands cuffed, Tom and I were pulled from the coach. I missed the step and stumbled to my knees onto sharp gravel. "Get up," one of them barked.

Tom and I were pushed along to where two more men, dressed in black overcoats, were waiting by a large wooden door that hung upon wrought iron hinges. As we approached, the door swung open, and we were shoved inside, into a dark, open space.

Though it took a few seconds for my eyes to adjust, I could taste the mustiness of what appeared to be an abandoned warehouse.

"Tie them up," a familiar voice said.

Before I could protest, I was pushed against a pole and bound to it with heavy rope. They did the same to Tom, though his pole was a distance away from mine.

Out of the shadows, one of the men in the black overcoats appeared. He had what I could best describe as a boxer's nose, apparently broken more than a few times. He stuck his face an inch from mine and gave me a sniff. As if I smelled putrid, he jerked his head back and grimaced.

Before I could utter a word, the man reared back and threw a punch that connected with my chin, causing my head to slam hard against the wooden post, and all went dark.

A splash of frigid water across my face brought me back to consciousness, though my vision took a moment longer to focus on the man standing before me—Senator Cameron.

"Who the hell are you?" he demanded, though it was hard to see his lips moving under his bushy mustache.

"Leopold Wolf, sir," I said with a raspy voice. "We met at the Carlisle School."

He squinted at me, stroking his mustache, and said, "At Carlisle? I don't remember."

"I was a counselor to the five—"

"Doesn't matter," he said, interrupting me. "Why were you and your Indian friend causing a ruckus at my ceremony?"

I looked over to Tom, who remained tied up like me, though still unconscious. His head hung like a rag doll's with a drool of blood dripping from his mouth onto the wooden floorboards below. "What have you done to Tom?"

"Never mind him. Just answer my question."

"We stumbled upon your event. I guess Tom was angered by Mr. Taft's introduction glorifying your role in the Indian massacres."

"Is that so?" he said with a furrowed brow.

I nodded.

The senator squinted as if he was sizing me up and asked, "Why are you in Washington?"

I certainly didn't want to tell him I was a journalist with papers in my pack criticizing the Carlisle Indian School, so I said, "I'm traveling with Buffalo Bill's Wild West Show. That's where Tom and I met. We're spending a few days in Washington before catching up with the show in New York City."

The senator looked over at Tom, who was now shaking his head, regaining his consciousness, then back to me. "All right, Leopold Wolf. Just keep your Indian under control, and away from me." He turned away.

"Yes, sir," I said, and exhaled.

"Cut them loose," the senator said to one of his men in the long black coats, "and make sure they get on the next train to New York."

"Sir!" One of the senator's security men had opened my pack and was removing its contents. "You should see this."

Senator Cameron was handed one of the newspapers. As he unfolded it and began to read, I looked over to Tom, whose bruised face hardly diminished the pent-up anger in his eyes.

"So, you lied to me, Leopold Wolf," the senator said, staring at the paper. He read the headline aloud. "Navajo Warrior Exposes Carlisle Indian School, by Leopold Wolf."

I tried to speak, but my mouth went dry.

"Isn't this convenient. We have both the Navajo and the journalist."

The senator took a few minutes to read the article, then looked up at me and said, "Who printed these for you?"

A cold sweat trickled down the back of my neck as I stared into the senator's dark eyes. Not wanting to give up the location of the printing press in the cellar of Potter House, I devised a lie and said, "I did, in Carlisle, where they print the school newspaper."

"Why would Captain Pratt permit this?" he asked, smacking his palm against the paper.

"He didn't. I snuck in at night and printed them without his knowledge," I said, surprising myself with the quick-witted deception.

Senator Cameron grimaced, turned away, and whispered what appeared to be instructions into the ear of one of his men, who nodded as if he understood. Then, as he headed for the door, he made a dismissive gesture with his hand in the air and said, "Drop these two off at the station and make sure you see them getting on the next train to New York."

*

The senator's goons forced Tom and me onto the northbound train heading for New York City. We traveled as far as Baltimore, the next stop, where we disembarked and boarded a southbound train back to Washington. As we exited the station, Tom said, "That seemed too easy."

"Maybe they thought we wouldn't have the nerve to return," I said, rubbing the tender bump on the back of my head.

"Are you all right, Leo?" Tom asked.

I nodded. "I have a nice bruise from that goon who punched me. What about you?"

"Oh," Tom scoffed, "I'm fine."

"I hope we don't run into them again," I said.

"Not me," Tom said. "I would love to make things right."

"We should get back to Potter House and tell Timothy what happened," I said.

Tom stopped walking and turned to me. "I'll tell you something, Leo," he said, pointing a finger at me. "If that newspaper of yours is as powerful as it seems to be, I'll see that they make their way into the hands of every person in this city."

"Thank you, Tom," I said, patting his shoulder. "But regardless of your taste for revenge, I doubt the senator would be so inclined to give us just a warning the next time our paths cross."

CHAPTER 69
A MESSAGE

After sharing with Timothy the details of our encounter with the senator and his entourage of hoodlums, I left for the Rosebud Inn, while Tom settled down for the night in the cellar of Potter House. We agreed to meet in the morning to discuss our plans for distributing the paper in a more discreet way.

When I arrived at the front desk and asked for the key, the manager also handed over an envelope with my name written on it. "What's this?" I asked.

"Someone dropped this off," he said and took a puff of his cigar. "I can't tell you who, since I was out picking up supplies and found it sitting on the desk when I returned."

I thanked the man and headed up to my room on the third floor. Once inside, I sat on the edge of the bed, opened the envelope, and withdrew the folded letter. Before reading it, I dropped my eyes to the signature and saw it was from Sarah. Feeling my pulse quicken, I read the letter written in her beautiful cursive script.

Dear Leo,

Since our meeting in the park, I haven't stopped thinking about your words. While I tried dismissing them as some sort of fantasy of yours, I can't seem to deny the stark truth behind them. Especially the part about the fruit you saw in the Wind Cave. After many sleepless nights, I've come to the conclusion that my unusual pomegranate earrings are more than a coincidence.

If, as you say, our love is eternal, based upon you eating the seeds of this fruit, I would like to see this tree for myself. This would be the ultimate proof of our mutual eternal destiny. Leopold Wolf, would you take me to the Black Hills?

I will await your reply at the secret garden tomorrow morning at seven, ready with my valise.

All my love,

Sarah

I stared at the letter, pulling hard on my beard. Could this really be happening? I reread the letter, admiring the stylish scoops and swirls of her expert penmanship, making sure I didn't miss a word, especially her signature—All my love, Sarah.

A litany of questions flooded my mind. How in the world would I sleep tonight, knowing my life was about to change in a big way in the morning, and even more perplexing, was how did Sarah know to find me at the Rosebud Inn?

I wondered about purchasing two train tickets to Rapid City. But would the ticket office be open at this late hour? What about Tom? Would he want to come too?

It wasn't until the wee hours of the morning, after these thoughts bombarding my mind lost their energy, that I was able to fall asleep. After what seemed only a moment, I awoke at ten minutes before seven, and in a panic, I flung my belongings into my pack and charged down the stairs, tossing the room key into the hands of the manager as I flew by.

I ran as fast as I could manage and made it to the park just as the clock tower struck seven bells. I slowed down for a moment, trying to remember the way to the secret garden. Then I saw through a gap in the foliage the stone wall and charged ahead until I reached the tunnel. As I emerged onto the secret garden's clover ground cover, I saw Sarah with her back to me.

"Sarah," I called out.

When she turned, I saw tears flowing down her cheeks.

"What is it?" I asked. "Has something happened?"

"Oh, Leo," she said, running to me. "Potter House was firebombed late last night."

"What?" I cried out. "How do you know?"

"I overheard Uncle speaking of it this morning. Apparently, he had something to do with it."

"Oh no—Tom," I said.

"I doubt Tom was there, as this was done late at night after the place closed."

I bit my lower lip and shook my head. "He was sleeping in the cellar," I said, grasping her arm. "I must go see."

"I'm coming with you," Sarah said.

I held up the letter and asked, "How did you know where to find me?"

"My uncle knew," she said. "You were followed there."

                                    *

We could see the smoke from several blocks away, and by the time we reached Potter House, dozens of firemen had extinguished the remaining fires. There appeared to be nothing more than a smoldering pile of charred wood.

"Leo," Timothy called out.

I turned and saw him standing next to Nathanial. "You're all right," I said, embracing him.

"I am, but I'm afraid Tom isn't," he said, shaking his head.

"What do you mean?" I asked. "Is he hurt?"

"He's dead," Timothy said. "His body was burned in the flames."

"Oh my lord," Sarah said, placing a hand over her mouth.

"Who would do such a thing?" Timothy asked, shaking his head.

A wave of dizziness, along with a profuse sweat, washed over me, dropping me to my knees.

"Leo!" Sarah cried out, grasping my shoulder to steady me.

"Your uncle," I said, looking up at Sarah. "His men must have followed us from the train station. Tom said our return was too easy. Looks like we led them here."

"Are you all right?" Sarah asked, bending over to look at me.

"I'll be fine," I said, trying to gather myself.

Timothy exhaled and said, "The senator is certainly not subtle with his messages."

"This is awful," Sarah said, helping me to my feet. "I've been living a lie for too long."

With the nausea passed, I wiped the sweat from my brow and said, "Maybe we all have."

"Me more than most. I've been living and working for this man for years now. People think they know him, but he's far worse than his public persona. He's truly a monster, and this is proof," she said, pointing to the smoldering remains.

We all stood a while in silence until Timothy suggested, "We should at least honor the Navajo with a ceremony."

I nodded, but worried that if Sarah and I lingered too long, the senator would learn of his niece's disappearance and prevent her from leaving. Tom deserved some sort of ceremony, though, even if it was brief. I said, "I know of a good spot."

*

After a short walk, the four of us gathered around the fairy nymph statue. Her gentle, serene face offered a stark contrast to the memory of Tom's square, strong, and serious features. "Tom may be gone, but the great warrior Bidziil will live on within me," I said, as tears welled up in my eyes.

"Can you read the Navajo prayer for the dead?" Sarah asked, reminding me of the words Tom asked me to read at Father's funeral.

I nodded, went to my pack, and withdrew the folded paper. "It's as if he foresaw his death," I said.

Timothy, Nathanial, and Sarah bowed their heads while I read, "As I walk, as I walk. The universe is walking with me. In beauty it walks before me. In beauty it walks behind me. In beauty it walks below me. In beauty it walks above me. Beauty is on every side. As I walk, I walk with beauty."

We remained silent for a while, allowing the birds to fill the quiet. During this interlude, I reflected upon Tom's demise and how he didn't deserve to die this way.

"May I use that passage?" Timothy asked, interrupting my musings.

"In your paper?" I asked.

He nodded. "I'd like to write a story about what happened."

"But how? You lost everything."

"Not everything. We're still here," he said, patting Nathanial's shoulder. "I'm not a quitter, Leo. Plus, the printing press, though damaged, seems salvageable."

"That's good to hear," I said.

Timothy pointed to the valises and said, "Where are you two headed?"

"We have something to do in the Black Hills," I said, grasping Sarah's hand.

"Do you need any money?" Timothy asked.

I looked over to Sarah, who shook her head. "No, we're all right," she said. "Thank you."

"Really?" I said, relieved, as I hadn't a penny.

"Consider it reparations from the United States Senate," she said with a sinister smile.

I opened my eyes wide at Sarah's unexcepted audacity.

"I going to miss you, Leopold Red Wolf," Timothy said. "Perhaps our paths will cross again one day."

"And I you," I said, shaking his hand. "Hopefully, I can continue in the newspaper business. You whetted an appetite I didn't know I had."

"You can always wire me articles. I'd be happy to print them as soon as I get my press back up and running again."

"I admire your fortitude. I may take you up on that offer."

"Keep writing, Leo, you have a story to tell."

I smiled and said, "People keep telling me that."

CHAPTER 70
SOULMATES

"What do you think your uncle will do when he realizes you're gone?" I asked Sarah, as our train sped off into the countryside. We were already several miles beyond the city limits of Washington.

"Aunt Elizabeth will tell him I went home to Harrisburg," she said, with a tilt of her head. "Honestly, he couldn't care less about me. Uncle only agreed to have me shadow him around Washington as a promise to my father, who upon his deathbed asked him to watch over me. He'll be relieved I'm gone."

"Does your aunt know about us?" I asked.

Sarah nodded. "Oh sure, I tell her everything. She's the one who gave me the money," she said, patting the purse that hung around her neck. "You know, she saw you at the Wild West show."

I nodded, remembering our interaction, and asked, "But how did she know who I was?"

Sarah reached out and stroked my beard. "You have a way of making yourself noticed, my Red Wolf."

I smiled and said, "But can you trust her?"

Sarah laughed. "Of course. She hates him just as much as I do."

I took a deep breath and sighed. "I still can't believe this is happening."

"What's that?"

I held out my hands. "That you're no longer resisting me. Ever since we first met at Carlisle, I've longed for you."

"I've noticed," she said with a smile.

"But, to be truthful, not until my experience in the Wind Cave, did I realize the significance of our relationship going beyond our connection in this lifetime."

Sarah nodded slowly and said, "And I have to admit, Leo, I never thought the definition of the word *soulmate* was literal."

"What did you think it was?"

"I don't know," she said with a shrug. "I suppose it means finding the love of your life, but certainly not a relationship that lasts an eternity."

"But don't you believe in the journey of the soul—you know, what happens after we die?"

"Of course I do," she said. "I guess I never thought about how we stay connected once we pass on."

"As I understand it, each of us is part of our soul family that interacts with one another over and over again during our lifetimes, though it may be in different forms," I said, stroking my beard. "Mother said that in her next incarnation, I could be her mother, or a friend, or someone else."

"That's weird," Sarah said with a chuckle.

"No, it's not," I insisted.

"What were we in our previous lives?" she asked mockingly. "Brother and sister?"

I shook my head. "Nothing. This is our first life together. That's why Mother said I needed to eat the pomegranate in order to bind our souls. Our journey together is just beginning."

"But what about me? Shouldn't I also eat of this fruit?"

I paused to think about it. "I don't know. Maybe."

Sarah squinted and said, "It seems only fair that I have a say as well in this binding of our souls. Don't you think?"

"Yes, you're right. You must also agree, but I don't know if that means eating the pomegranate."

"All right," she said and took a deep breath. "But we should at least go and try to find this Wind Cave."

"I agree," I said. "I'll take you there if that's what you want."

Sarah smiled, looked into my eyes, leaned in, and said, "I do."

I reached out to touch one of her pomegranate earrings and fondled it between my fingers. With a deep breath, I dropped my hand to her neck and gently pulled her close. As we kissed, my heart pumped out a joyful warmth that cascaded deep into the recesses of my soul.

*

We were about an hour out from Rapid City when I finished telling Sarah the story of what brought me to Washington and my experience at the Buffalo Bill's Wild West Show.

"But why would someone like Black Elk subject himself to such humiliation?"

"He said he's using it as a learning experience. Trying to better understand the white man."

"*Pfft,*" Sarah blurted out. "If he's as wise as you say, shouldn't he have figured that out a long time ago?

"I know, but Black Elk's different. As a young boy, he had visions that have since guided him."

"What sort of visions?"

"He saw himself as the one to restore his people's strength, their sense of purpose and ancestral traditions, to make his nation live as it once did before the invasion of the white man."

Sarah looked out the window onto the vastness of the Dakota plains, and when she turned back to face me, she had tears in her eyes. She said softly, "This is all so sad."

I sighed and nodded. "There's nothing more Black Elk can do except not give up. That's why I want to write about what's happening at places like Carlisle. It's the least I can do to help these poor people."

Sarah grasped my hand and gave it a squeeze.

Chapter 71
Return to the Black Hills

With Sarah's money, we purchased a horse and wagon, several woolen blankets, six torches, and a can of pitch from a stable not far from the Rapid City train station. "If I remember correctly," I said, studying the map leading into the mountains, "we head due west up into these hills."

Sarah, sitting alongside me, looked up and said, "They look slightly more imposing than hills."

I chuckled. "That they are."

"Does the map take us directly to the caves?"

"I believe so," I said, giving the horse's hind end a sharp snap with the crop.

With the morning sun rising behind us, illuminating the face of the mountains, its trees donning the warm colors of autumn, we headed toward the Black Hills. It was the tail end of summer the last time I ventured into these mountains, and at least twenty degrees warmer. I worried that the caves, though cold in midsummer as Alvin warned, would now be more like a human ice box.

*

Two hours later, while driving the wagon up the steep trail that Red Dog had also followed, we came upon the bluff where I recognized the bald-faced cliffs soaring above the entrance into the caverns. "It's just up ahead," I said, pointing with an outstretched arm.

"Do you think we can find our way without Alvin?" she asked.

I sighed and said, "With his map, I'm sure we can find our way at least to Thunder Falls."

Sarah nodded, but with a grimace.

"Are you scared?" I asked, as this was the first time she showed any fear of venturing underground.

She took a breath and said, "A bit. I've never been in a cave before."

"We don't have to do this, Sarah."

"No," she said, shaking her head. "I want to go. I'll be fine as long as you're by my side."

"Every step of the way," I said, but wondered if that was possible once we passed through the Thunder Falls and into the Wind Cave, where I lost consciousness and awakened before the pomegranate tree.

During the last few feet up the trail, a wave of anxiety rushed through me as I considered venturing back into the caves without Alvin as my guide. It was true he couldn't be trusted, but knowing that, I could make sure he didn't leave us in a precarious situation like he did the last time.

"Here we are," I said, announcing our approach to the entrance.

Sarah reached over and grasped my hand. "It's magnificent," she said, wide-eyed.

I scoffed. "Wait until you see what's down there." I brought the wagon to a stop, jumped down, and tied up the horse to a sturdy branch.

Just as I reached into the wagon to gather my pack and the torches, I heard my name being called out. "Leopold Wolf! Is it really you?"

I turned and saw Alvin walking toward me.

"You've returned," he said and looked over to Sarah. "And you brought a friend. And a pretty one, too."

"Hello, Alvin," I said plainly.

"I suppose you're not here for a tour?" he said, with a cockeyed smile.

"Is this the man that abandoned you?" Sarah asked with a scowl.

I nodded and said, "This is Alvin."

"Welcome to my underworld," he said and turned to me. "I hope you don't hold any grudges, Leo. What happened last time was just a misunderstanding. I planned on coming back for you all along."

"Why am I having trouble believing you?"

"Well, if it means anything, I'm truly sorry," he said and walked over to Sarah. "Let me make it up to you and give you two a tour for free. I'll take you anywhere you want and promise not to leave you until you're back on your wagon, heading home."

I looked over to Sarah, who rolled her eyes.

There was no doubt that with Alvin guiding us, the tunnels and caves would be less worrisome than they would if we tried to find Thunder Falls on our own. Also, with no Sacred Pipe to recover this time, there was no financial reward to entice his mischief, and therefore no reason for him to do us harm.

"All right, Alvin. I'll give you a second chance. But know this." I walked over to him and stopped with my face inches from his. "If you even think of trapping us down there, I'll—"

"I know," he said, interrupting me. "I swear on the life of my mother and father not to leave either of you down there alone."

I tugged on my beard with both hands and asked Sarah, "What do you think?"

Sarah shrugged and said, "It's up to you."

I stared at him and said, "All right, take us to Thunder Falls and then wait for us until we return."

"You're planning on going through the falls, like you say you did last time?"

I nodded. "That's right."

"Very well, Leo and Sarah, follow me," Alvin said and led us into the first cavern.

With my pack strapped to my back, I grasped Sarah's hand and took a step. But she held tight and stood still. "What's wrong?"

She closed her eyes, took a deep breath, and said, "Okay, I'm ready."

I leaned in, kissed her lips, and said, "Let's go."

CHAPTER 72
THE DOVE

"I've never seen anything like it!" Sarah shouted loudly enough to be heard over the waterfall rushing down into a pool of churning water.

"It's a marvel," I agreed.

"Well," Alvin hollered, "this is it."

"I'm supposed to walk through the falls?" Sarah asked, pointing.

"We'll go together," I said.

"I'll wait here for you," Alvin called out from behind us.

"Sounds good," I said and looked at Sarah. "On the count of three."

With a furrowed brow and a deep grimace, she nodded.

"One, two, three," I cried out, and we climbed down into the pool.

"It's freezing!" Sarah yelled.

"Ready?" I said, taking her hand.

She nodded and squeezed my hand. We stepped forward into the deluge.

The falls pounded just as hard as before, and after a few steps, we emerged on the other side of the falls in a small protective alcove. I rubbed the water from my eyes and looked for a passageway like last time, but besides the wall of rushing water behind us, we were encased by stone.

"Which way do we go?" yelled Sarah, pushing back strands of her hair.

I shook my head. "I don't know. It wasn't like this last time," I said, wringing out the water from my beard.

Wide-eyed and holding out her arms, Sarah asked, "What should we do?"

I shook my head, confused. "I suppose we return the way we came," I said, gesturing back to the deluge.

"But what about the Wind Cave and the tree?"

I sighed and said, "I don't know. Come on, let's go back."

Sarah nodded.

We again clasped hands, immersed ourselves in the pool, and pushed back through Thunder Falls.

"That was fast." Alvin was standing in the same place we'd left him a few minutes earlier. "What did you see?"

"Nothing," I said, helping Sarah with a hand as we climbed up onto the stone floor.

"We need to get into the sun," she said, wrapping her arms across her chest.

I too felt the chill seeping through my bones, causing me to shiver, and realized that without Alvin to guide us, Sarah and I might not have made it out of the caverns without a great deal of suffering. "What's the quickest way out?" I asked Alvin.

"This way," he said, turning. "We'll be out of here in a few minutes."

Following a passageway that I assumed was the same one Red Dog and Abe carried me through when they found me asleep by the falls, we emerged into bright sunshine and welcoming warmth.

"Sit here," Alvin said, gesturing to a rocky outcropping. "You'll feel better soon."

"Are you all right?" I asked Sarah, whose shivering lips had turned blue.

"I've n-n-never b-b-been s-s-so c-c-cold before," she said, trying to push the words out.

"I'm so sorry, Sarah," I said, removing my soaked shirt, shoes, and socks. "I don't know what to say."

"It's okay, Leo."

I ran my fingers through my hair and sighed. "I guess you don't believe my story about what happened down there."

"Honestly, at this moment, I don't know what to think," she said. "But what I do know is I'd like to dry off. So, if you don't mind—can I have some privacy?"

"Oh, sure," I said. "I'll go with Alvin and fetch the wagon."

Alvin led me along the trail, heading to where we left the wagon. On the way, he put a hand on my shoulder and said, "I suppose what you saw the first time was meant just for you."

I stopped walking, scratched at my beard, and said, "I don't know, Alvin. All of a sudden those memories feel like dreams now. Maybe none of it really happened."

"Perhaps you're not allowed to share what you saw."

I shrugged. "I don't know. Maybe you're right."

A few minutes later, we arrived at the wagon and I offered my farewell to Alvin. I thanked him for guiding us through the caves.

"I hope you'll forgive me for leaving you there last time. Greed got the better part of me."

"Yes, I forgive you, Alvin," I said, and we shook hands.

As he turned and disappeared back into the cavern, I climbed aboard the wagon and made my way back up the trail to the clearing where Sarah, already dressed, was staring up into a tree.

"Are you warmed up?" I asked.

"Would you look at that, Leo," she said, pointing.

I followed her hand and saw sitting on a branch a white dove, cooing its song.

"That's strange," I said. "I've never seen a white dove in these mountains before."

"Doves are symbols of the Holy Spirit," she said, keeping her eyes focused on the cooing dove.

"Why is this familiar?" I said, racking my brain. Then it occurred to me. I retrieved my pack and rummaged through it until I found Mother's journal. Quickly, I skimmed through the pages and landed on what I was looking for—the pencil drawing she did of a white dove.

"Look at this," I said, running over to show Sarah. "Mother drew this in her journal."

Sarah took the book and stared at the drawing, then back at the dove and said, "Remarkable." She then reached out, and with one hand gently touched the page while with the other she tapped one of her earrings. "Doves and pomegranates, Leopold Wolf. I believe our destiny awaits."

*

We gathered our belongings and climbed onto the wagon. Sarah sat close and laid her arms loosely around my neck. "So, what now, my Red Wolf?" she asked, gazing into my eyes.

I took a breath and said, "*Um*, I'm not sure."

"Well, we can't stay here. Unless you want to be cavemates with your friend Alvin."

"Cavemates?" I said with a grimace. "Definitely not."

"So why don't we go back to Carlisle and move into your home?"

"And live there together?" I asked, wide-eyed.

"Of course; how else?"

"But shouldn't we marry before we do that?"

"Are you asking me to marry you?" Sarah asked with a smile that brightened her face.

"Yes, *um*, Sarah Cameron, I guess I am," I said, stumbling over my words. "I mean, we appear to be bound to one another for eternity, shouldn't we at least tie the knot during this lifetime?"

Sarah laughed. "Yes, Leopold Wolf, I will marry you," she said and kissed my lips.

"I'm happy for you both, and honored you would ask me to preside over your nuptials," Black Elk said. "But there's no traditional wedding ceremony among our people."

"So how do you marry?" I asked.

Black Elk shrugged. "A man would offer say, five horses to the girl's father, and if he accepts, then that's it, they're married."

"Five horses?" Sarah repeated. "Is that all a woman is worth?"

"We don't assign a monetary value to things like the white man does," Black Elk explained. "We view marriage as a mutual state when a couple is together and stay together as long as they're happy until they decide they are no longer happy."

"You mean like a divorce?" I said.

Black Elk nodded. "Yes, except unlike in your culture where ownership of property exists, when we separate, we simply pick up our few things and move out of one tipi and into another."

"We do want a marriage in our own tradition," I said, reaching out and grasping Sarah's hand, "but we would like you to perform the ceremony."

Black Elk sighed and took a moment to look at Sarah and me. "I'd be happy to do so, but you should know it won't be recognized in the eyes of the white man."

"We're aware. We plan to visit the justice of the peace in Harrisburg upon our return home and take our vows under Pennsylvania law," I said.

While we stood before the tribe, I said, "I wish William was here."

"At our civil ceremony, we'll invite Alice, Abe, and William," Sarah said.

"Don't forget Isaac Junior."

Sarah laughed. "Of course not."

We waited for Black Elk to make his appearance on the grassy knoll not far from the river where I first met the holy man. Surrounding us was a circle of the Elders, all seated cross-legged, and around them standing in concentric circles were the people of the village, three or four deep, twisting and tilting their necks, trying to catch a glimpse of us.

"Will the chief attend?" Sarah asked.

I shook my head. "Chief Red Shirt remained with the Buffalo Bill show. They were headed to New York City."

Then, without any fanfare, the people in front of us stepped aside, creating a pathway for Black Elk to emerge. He wore his brown fur hat with an assortment of feathers atop like a flower arrangement.

"Oh my," Sarah said, at the sight of the shirtless holy man wearing a beaded necklace and a skimpy loin cloth tied to his waist, decorated in red, blue, and green.

Once Black Elk passed through, the circle closed and the chatter ceased. As we stood before him, Black Elk instructed us to hold hands. He then reached out and lifted our clasped hands for the crowd to see. From a pouch tied to his waist, he removed a long braid of sweetgrass and wrapped it around our wrists, binding them together. "I saw this done at an Irish wedding when I was with the Buffalo Bill show in Washington," he whispered. "Though the sweetgrass was my idea."

Sarah and I laughed at the whimsical touch.

"We all know Leopold Red Wolf," Black Elk began, loud enough for the community of his people to hear. "He first came to Pine Ridge as counselor to Chief Red Shirt's son at the Carlisle Indian School."

Heads nodded, and a bit of chatter ensued. Black Elk continued, "Two summers ago, during his visit, we sat by the river under that tree," he said, pointing to the very spot where we first met. "It was then that I shared my vision of Leopold Red Wolf's purpose to find the lost Sacred Pipe and return it to our people. This quest he accomplished last summer."

While Black Elk spoke, Sarah gazed upon the congregation who had gathered to honor us. Then she turned to me and smiled. I squeezed her hand.

Black Elk continued, "But it was during this search into the caverns deep beneath the Black Hills that he was led to a special tree where he observed a vision of his mother, who had walked on when Leopold was a young boy. He also was greeted by the red wolf, his animal spirit."

Upon those words, a wave of commotion swept across the gathering. Those who could understand English were now doing their best to translate for their clueless friends and family. Once they understood, silence was restored.

"Standing before us is Sarah Cameron, also former counselor at the Carlisle Indian School. She, too, glimpsed into the spirit world by witnessing the white dove, a symbol of the Christian Holy Spirit. It was then she understood her connection to Leopold Red Wolf. It is their wish that I bind them as soulmates in this lifetime, so they are able to walk on, unified, into the spirit world when called upon."

He then clasped his hands over ours, closed his eyes, and said, "Great Spirit, teach these two souls to trust their hearts, their minds, their intuition, their inner knowing, their sense of their bodies, and the blessings of the spirit. Teach them to trust these things so they may enter the sacred space and learn to love beyond fear and walk in balance with the passing of each glorious sun."

With that, the holy man concluded. As the crowd dispersed, I took notice of the joyous looks on their faces, filled with bright smiles and laughter.

*

Later that night, while sitting by the fire, we offered our gratitude to Black Elk for his kind and thoughtful words. Though we were not yet considered husband and wife within the eyes of the law, Black Elk offered us something the government was unable to provide, a connection to the spirit world.

"Can I ask you something, Black Elk?" Sarah said. "Why do you suppose the white man feels entitled to take what he wants, regardless of the devastation he leaves behind in his wake?"

Black Elk took a deep breath, straightened his spine, and paused a moment, then exhaled and rested his elbows on his knees, gazing into the campfire. He said, "It's obvious they believe the earth is here to serve them. Take the gold, for example. We have lived with it for generations, never thinking of picking it up off the ground and turning it into great wealth. Our people believe that anything that the Great Spirit has placed in the ground should stay in the ground, where it was meant to be."

"I agree," Sarah said. "Somewhere in our history, we became an arrogant race, out of touch with the natural world."

"Let's hope, before it's too late," Black Elk said, opening his palms to the sky, "that the earth does not decide to reclaim what is rightfully its own."

CHAPTER 74
RETURN TO CARLISLE

"It feels good to be home," I said, stepping onto the front porch.

"Is anyone here?" Sarah asked.

I shrugged and called out, "Alice, Abe!"

Before I could reach for the front door, it swung open and Alice appeared, holding Isaac Junior. "Oh, my lord," she said, "I can't believe my eyes. Abraham, come quickly."

"It's good to see you, Alice," I said and reached out to touch Isaac's arm. "Look at you. You're such a big boy."

"This is a surprise," Alice said, leaning forward to kiss Sarah and me.

"It's good to see you, Alice," Sarah said, and ruffled Isaac's curly brown hair. "How old is he now?"

"He's almost seven months," she said. "Come on in. You must be thirsty and hungry. I was just preparing dinner for me and Abe."

"Are you sure there's enough?" Sarah asked.

"Oh, don't you worry, there's plenty," Alice said and hurried into the kitchen.

"Is that you, Leo?" Abe shouted, and he charged down the stairs and jumped into my arms, nearly knocking me over.

"Hello, Abe," I said, embracing him with a laugh.

"What are you doing here?" he said, releasing me and looking over to Sarah. "It's good to see you, Sarah."

"You too, Abe," she said, giving him a hug.

"Come, let's sit down and I'll tell you everything," I said, gesturing to the table. "I'm starving."

*

There was much to share since Abe and I parted at the Harrisburg train station. Not until we had eaten the last of Alice's delicious fried chicken did Sarah and I finish our long and winding tale. "But even after all that, I can't tell you how happy I was coming down our street and seeing the house."

Abe lifted his arms in the air and said, "This all is wonderful. When's the wedding?"

I looked over to Sarah and said, "Well, we sort of got married at Pine Ridge."

"Sort of?" Abe asked with a furrowed brow. "What does that mean?"

"It was a ceremony performed by Black Elk. We intend to make it legal with the justice of the peace in Harrisburg. Sarah and I would like to ask you all to come as our witnesses."

"We'd love to," Alice said, and tickled Isaac's belly. "Wouldn't we, Isaac?"

"Have you seen William?" I asked.

"Oh yes, every day," Abe said. "He asks about you all the time."

I tugged on my beard and said, "Do you think you could sneak him over so I can see him?"

Abe grimaced and said, "I don't know, Leo. They're keeping an eye on the children more than ever. We've had numerous problems with runaways."

"Is it true that Captain Pratt is paying bounties to get the children back?"

Abe frowned and said, "I'm afraid so."

"What's your plan?" Alice asked. "We can move back into Captain Pratt's house if you need us to."

"Absolutely not! You're all welcome to stay here. There's plenty of room."

"Yes," Sarah said, nodding. "We want you to stay."

"Do you plan on starting up Wolf and Son Woodworking?" Abe asked.

"Not at the moment," I said. "I'm in the newspaper business now."

"Newspaper business?" he repeated.

"That's right, I've started my own paper called *The Observer*. Timothy, a friend of mine back in Washington, is printing it for me. That is, once he gets his press up and running again. Which reminds me," I said, and rubbed the back of my neck. "I'm sad to say that Tom is dead."

"What?" Abe said.

"Oh my," Alice said.

"He was in the basement of Timothy's saloon, where the paper is printed, when it was firebombed by Senator Cameron's men." I looked over to Sarah, who bit her lower lip and nodded.

"Why would he do that?" Alice asked.

"I'll explain everything after dinner. Right now, Sarah and I need to wash up and get settled."

CHAPTER 75
SOUL BUNDLE

Early in the morning, an hour before reveille sounded at the Carlisle School, I sat on the front porch sipping my coffee when Alice opened the door and joined me.

"Good morning, Alice," I said. "Is Isaac still asleep?"

She turned her head to look at the house and said, "Oh, heavens, no. He's been awake for hours. Abe has him."

"What do you do with him when you go to work?"

"Captain Pratt began a free childcare service for the locals. He allows parents to drop off their little ones into the care of the older Indian girls. It's part of the school's child-rearing classes."

"That's convenient. Does Isaac like it?"

"He's fine, and close by in case he needs me."

I smiled.

Alice reached out, grabbed my hand, and said, "Do you know what today is?"

"I do," I said, gently squeezing her callused palm. "It's one year since Father's murder."

Alice nodded. "Is it possible to have a small ceremony at his gravesite later today?"

"I would like that," I said and thought of the soul bundle still tucked inside my pack. "But we should wait until the captain retires for the evening. I'd prefer not to run into him."

Alice pointed a finger at me and said, "It's only a matter of time until he discovers you and Sarah are back. Then, you know, he'll wire word to the senator about Sarah."

"There's not much he can do," I said with a sneer. "We've committed no crimes and have every right to live in peace."

"You're being naive, Leo," she said. "Once he learns his niece is back in Carlisle, he'll stop at nothing—"

"I won't be intimidated by that man," I said, interrupting Alice. "I'm going to write an article about what he did to Tom at Potter House."

"You're playing with fire, Leo. You have no idea how powerful the senator is. I've heard him speaking with the captain. He's set on destroying the Indian, and everything and everyone standing in his way."

I sighed, put an arm around Alice's shoulder, and said, "And I won't rest until I find ways to stop him."

*

By the time we crossed the Great Lawn to the cemetery, it was pitch dark. The heavy cloud cover blocked any moonlight, requiring us to navigate our way with lanterns. I led the way, followed by Alice holding Isaac in her arms, and Abe and Sarah in the rear. I would have liked to include William, but that wasn't possible without making our presence known to the Carlisle community, which would have included Captain Pratt.

Upon reaching the cemetery, I noticed that in the year since Father was buried, there were at least twenty more headstones. Holding the lantern close, I read the names of boys and girls, along with their tribes and the dates they died.

"Isaac is over here," Alice said, pointing to the grave.

We joined her at the foot of the grave. This was my first time seeing Father's headstone, and like Mother's at the Jewish cemetery in Harrisburg, there was no epitaph, just the dates of his birth and death.

ISAAC WOLF
BORN - APRIL 21, 1835
DIED - NOVEMBER 2, 1880

I would have liked to have added a literary note to the engraving, offering some sense of the man. But, as I observed, none of the other headstones offered anything more—though Father's forty-five years of life seemed like old age compared to the children buried beside him.

I unhooked my pack with Father's soul bundle inside and placed it on the grass. I took a breath and said, "Alice, would you like to say a few words?"

She nodded, and I stepped aside, allowing her the spot facing Father's headstone. Alice lowered her head and sighed, and when she looked up, tears were flowing. "My words are not just for Isaac, but they're meant for you as well, Leo," she said, looking at me.

I smiled, acknowledging the honor.

"Isaac was a man who faced adversity with an abundance of courage. When called upon during the war, he fought bravely with the militia, keeping our town of Carlisle safe. Though not a religious man, he was a righteous one. Someone who the Almighty would look upon and say, *This is a good man,*" Alice said firmly. "And he was a good man, and he was good to me. Not because he gave me a child," she said, stroking Isaac's cheek, "but because he saw beyond the color of my skin, to a woman

324

whom he connected to on a deeper level." Alice paused, looked directly into my eyes, and said, "It's as if our souls were destined to meet, even if it was only for a brief time."

Alice's words caused my jaw to drop, and Sarah whispered, "Oh my."

"That is all," she said and took a step away from the grave.

"Thank you, Alice," I said, giving her and Isaac a hug.

"A year ago," I said, taking my turn, "Father was murdered not far from where we're standing. A senseless death caused by the white man's hatred. Strangely, both Mother's and Father's demise could be traced to this desire for control of the Negro." I looked at Alice, who continued to weep. "Though they are not the only victims of such brutality, as you can plainly see by taking a moment and looking around you at the others buried here."

Alice was now bawling and heaving. "Maybe you can say something nice about your father," Sarah suggested while trying to comfort Alice.

"I'm sorry," I said. I got down on one knee, opened my pack, and removed the soul bundle. "I was given this by the Lakota last year when I was in Pine Ridge," I said, laying the bundle on the grass and unwrapping it. "Tucked inside is a lock of my hair, cut during the Sacred Pipe ceremony with the Elders. It was meant to be Father's hair, but as I had none of his, they used my hair instead."

I pinched the bundle between my thumb and forefinger and lifted it into the air while I got to my feet. "I was told that I needed to live a harmonious life for a year, and at the end of it, to take this bundle outdoors and release the cuttings into the air. If the hair is caught by the wind and blown away to the right, then Father's soul will be judged worthy and will be permitted to walk on with the Great Spirit. If, however, the wind takes it to the left, Father will be unable to take his soulful journey."

"Are you saying your father's eternal soul is dependent upon which way the wind is blowing?" Abe asked with a grimace.

I looked at the hair, bit my lower lip, and nodded.

Abe licked a finger, held it in the air, and said, "I'm sorry to say, Leo, but there's not a breath of wind."

"What do you think?" I asked Sarah.

"Are you sure it's exactly a year?" she asked.

"Yes, November second. One year ago today."

"Well then," Abe said, patting my back, "have you lived a harmonious life?"

I swallowed hard. "We're about to find out," I said, stretching my arm overhead and releasing the bundle. As it left my hand, it fell straight down to the grass and lay there. No one spoke while we paused for the wind to carry it off in any direction. But none came.

Chapter 76
William's Toothache

"Are you sure you want to send this?" Sarah said with a grimace, after reading my article entitled *Murder at Potter House*.

"Of course I do. That's why I wrote it," I said. "Little good it will do, going unpublished."

Sarah handed the pages back to me, shook her head, and sighed. "This will bring the wrath of my uncle, not to mention Captain Pratt. Seriously, do you want to take them both on?"

I held out my hands and said, "How do I write for a newspaper if I'm frightened of the consequences?"

"All right, Leo," she said with one hand on her hip, "but don't say I didn't warn you."

"I can't very well ignore it, Sarah. For God's sake, Tom was killed."

"My point is, you don't walk into a tiger's cage with red meat in your hands," she said, holding out her own hands to demonstrate. "You're asking for trouble, and you know what my uncle is capable of."

I pulled on my beard. "So, what should I do?"

"Don't use your real name," she said with a shrug. "Come up with an alias."

"*Pfft,*" I said, holding out my hand, "then no one would know I wrote it."

Sarah released an exasperated sigh and said, "Is this about your ego, or giving a voice to the voiceless?"

I stopped and stared at Sarah. Of course, she was right, but I knew Timothy would never print a story with an alias. Instead of admitting that to Sarah, though, I shrugged and said, "All right, I'll send it off and insist he keeps my name off it."

Sarah squinted at me. "Really?" she asked.

I nodded and said, "Really."

*

While waiting for a reply from Timothy, I spent my time working around the house. Since Father's death, simple things he would have attended to were left in disrepair. There was a bookshelf that had pulled out of the wall from too much weight, requiring me to reinforce it with new studs, as well as rotten boards on the back porch that needed replacing.

As I attended to these chores, I couldn't help thinking about Father and that disappointing day of the soul bundle ceremony. What did it mean that the hair, instead of it being taken by the wind, fell like a stone to the earth? Yes, it was true it wasn't Father's hair, as the Lakota tradition prescribed, but Chief Red Shirt said my hair would serve the same purpose. Could he have been mistaken?

Anyway, I felt assured that Father's journey was well underway, as I didn't feel his presence in the house—though each time I picked up one of his tools, I couldn't help but hear his voice in my head, instructing me how to do things properly. He would often tell me how he learned the carpentry trade from his father, who emigrated with his family from Russia when he was ten years old.

"These tools are older than I am," he would explain, holding up a coping saw. "Your grandfather brought them over with our trunks and valises on the steamship."

There was also comfort in knowing we lived in Father's house. He had built it after the cannonball ripped the old house apart, killing Mother in the process. "We don't need to be reminded of what happened every day," Father said, choosing a lot four miles away.

*

It was during one of these late autumn days, with the trees dropping leaves at a steady rate, when I saw William for the first time since my return to Carlisle. Abe brought him over under the guise of taking him into town to see the dentist.

"Do you really have a toothache?" I asked William, upon his releasing me from a bear hug.

"Not really," he said, opening his mouth and sticking his finger inside to wiggle a loose tooth. "See, it's about to come out."

"That's why you're going to the dentist? I can take care of it right now," I said, picking up a pair of pliers from my toolbox.

"Oh no," William said, covering his mouth.

"When the captain asked me to take him into town, I thought a small detour would be perfect," Abe said. "But we can't stay long."

I patted Abe's shoulder and got down to my knees to look into William's eyes. "How've you been?"

"You know," he said with a shrug. "Some days are good."

I nodded. "Hang in there, William. Before you know it, it will be summer and maybe we can find a way to spend it together."

From the front porch, William looked through the open window and asked, "Is Sarah here?"

"She's upstairs bathing Isaac," Abe said.

William turned to me and motioned for me to come closer. I leaned in and looked into his eyes, and asked, "What is it?"

"The other day," he began in a whisper, "there was this boy—Danny; he's ten, I think. During mathematics class a few days ago, he was talking too much and the teacher, Mr. Conrad, got mad and smacked him in the face."

William paused a moment. Tears filled his eyes.

"It's okay, William," I said, putting my hands on his shoulders.

"He hit Danny so hard, he knocked him over. He fell, and he hit his head on the floor and he died. There was so much blood."

"I haven't heard about this," Abe said.

William shook his head. "We were told not to speak of it, or we would be in trouble."

"I'm glad you told me," I said.

"I'm scared, Leo," he said, with tears now flowing. "Can I please stay here with you?"

"Oh, William," I said, hugging him. "I wish you could."

CHAPTER 77
MURDER AT POTTER HOUSE

"Have you seen this?" Sarah said with a snarl and shoved a folded newspaper at me.

"What is it?"

"That newspaper of yours, *The Observer*. It was in today's mail," she said. "Look at the front page."

I unfolded the paper and read the headline aloud, "MURDER AT POTTER HOUSE by Leopold Wolf."

"He used my name," I said, staring at the paper. "But I told him not to."

"Did you?" Sarah said with a suspicious squint.

"Of course I did."

"Read it, then we'll talk," she said, turning on her heel and heading back into the house.

Sweat ran down in trickles through my beard, even though Carlisle was experiencing its first frost of the season. Anticipating the worst, I sat on the front porch rocker and read.

*

MURDER AT POTTER HOUSE
BY LEOPOLD WOLF

With his long, black hair restyled and traditional dress replaced, he chose a new name off a list written on the blackboard. By pointing to one, the warrior Bidziil lost his identity as the son of a Navajo chief and simply became Tom. So began the attempted assimilation of this troubled then fifteen-year-old boy into the United States of America as a law-abiding citizen.

Tom's story is not unlike that of many of the other children attending the Carlisle Indian School, where a misguided mission has resulted in twisting the minds of these native children. Upon their arrival at Carlisle, they were comfortably well-versed in their traditional cultures; Carlisle soon made them into confused and frightened citizens of this great country, a far cry from school founder Captain Richard Henry Pratt's benevolent professions. The stated purpose of Carlisle is to kill the Indian in order to save the man. As the captain is known to have said, "We are not born savages; it's the environment one is raised in that determines such an outcome. There's a civilized man to be uncovered beneath this native savagery."

Tom's trouble began when he made an oath of vengeance against a certain Major Lawrence, a former officer of the South and counselor at the school. Lawrence was being held for transfer in the Carlisle stockade for the cold-blooded murder of my father, Isaac Wolf, when Tom broke into the stockade and strangled him to death.

Arrested for this revenge killing, he was detained in the same cell where, the day before, he'd slain the major. But Tom broke free, escaped, and eventually joined up with the extravagant Buffalo Bill's Wild West Show performing in Washington, DC. That was where I caught up with the fugitive and offered him a place by my side, assisting me as publisher of this newspaper, a publication dedicated to publicizing the plight of the Indian.

At the outset of our first investigation, we stumbled upon a political rally held by Senator Donald Cameron of Pennsylvania, where the speaker introducing the honorable man highlighted his role in the Sioux wars. As Tom is never one to shy away from a fight, he forced himself on stage, confronting the senator with his crimes as a mass murderer.

It wasn't long before Tom and I found ourselves accosted by the senator's security team and brought by force to a ruined warehouse, where we were beaten by thugs and questioned by Senator Cameron himself.

After this violent interrogation, we were forced to leave Washington. Two men with guns escorted Tom and me on the next train to New York. Once we reached Baltimore, though, we disembarked and returned to Washington. Unbeknownst to us, the senator's men anticipated our move and followed us back to Potter House, where in the cellar a printing press was secretly producing this fledgling paper and where Tom had spent his nights.

It was the next morning that I learned of Potter House being firebombed and the subsequent death of my dear friend Tom.

*

I was all too familiar with these words, as Timothy had published them without edits or changes. I put the paper down and summoned the courage to find Sarah in the house.

"I guess it would have been obvious who wrote it, even if my name wasn't on it," I confessed.

"It hardly needs your byline," she pointed out.

I sighed. "I know, and I'm sorry. But I couldn't let him get away with it."

Sarah dropped her gaze to her hands, which had curled into fists. "An eyewitness account?" she said, gritting her teeth. "Do you think that's going to shield me from my uncle's wrath?"

"I'm sorry," I said, reaching out for her hand, which she snatched back.

"Hopefully, Captain Pratt hasn't seen this."

"Do you think he—"

"I don't know what to think," she shouted, interrupting me. "What I do know is we need to get out of here before it's too late."

I thought a moment, then said, "We could go to Pine Ridge. Chief Red Shirt will protect us. We'll take William too."

Sarah took a deep breath and nodded. "Okay, Leo, we'll leave first thing in the morning. You and Abe will need to sneak William out from his barrack before morning reveille."

"All right," I said. "I'm so sorry, Sarah."

"*Pfft,*" she said, turned on her heel, and walked away.

<h1 style="text-align:center">Chapter 78
Taken</h1>

While everyone slept, I stayed awake on the front porch, even though the air had turned frigid, forcing me to bundle up in my winter coat, hat, and boots. As the hours passed, I thought about Captain Pratt, wondering why he hadn't confronted Sarah and me upon our return from Washington, now over a month ago. Perhaps he knew of our presence but decided to ignore us, though after the publication of *The Observer*, that would be hard to do. Most likely, the senator had wired the captain, demanding some sort of retribution for my accusation of him as Tom's killer. If this were close to the truth, our decision to depart from Carlisle in the morning would be prudent.

I don't know when I fell asleep, but I must have been in a deep slumber, as I never heard the horses approaching nor the men who grabbed me, shoved a gag in my mouth, bound my arms and legs, and threw me into the stagecoach.

As we pulled away from the house, I struggled with my bindings, trying to push the gag out with my tongue, which triggered a coughing fit.

One of the men reached out and removed the cloth. "Don't die on us," he snarled, tossing the rag to the floor.

"Who are you?" I demanded of the two men who sat across from me, one pointing a gun.

"No talking or I'll shove it back in."

"Wait," I said, remembering, "you're the senator's men. We met in the warehouse."

"One more word and I'll put you in the rear boot," the one with the boxer's nose said.

I shook my head and turned my gaze out the window into the darkness as we traversed the road into town. What would happen when Sarah awoke and found me gone? She would have no idea I was taken by her uncle's men, and I had no clue as to my fate. Would they take me to some desolate spot and kill me?

I pulled again on the rope binding my arms, but the knots were tied too tight to budge. Even if I was able to break free, I wouldn't get far as the skinny man kept his gun gripped in his bony hand pointed at me.

"Are you going to kill me?"

"Shut up," Broken Nose said.

Resigned, I sat back and stared out the window.

*

By the time morning came, we'd arrived at the Harrisburg train station.

"Where're we going?" I asked, as my arms and legs were freed.

Skinny jammed his gun into my ribs and said, "You do anything except walk between us quietly and I'll shoot to kill. You understand me?"

"Okay, I get it," I said. "But can you at least tell me where we're going?"

"To New York City. Now shut the hell up."

"New York City?" I repeated. "Why not Washington?"

"I told you, Wolf, not another word," he said, giving me a push.

Once inside the station, we sat side by side on one of the long wooden benches, waiting for our departure. I contemplated making a run for the set of doors across from us, doubting they would shoot me in a public space. But even if they didn't, it wouldn't take them long to chase me down. Hopefully, there would be a better opportunity to escape once we moved toward the platforms.

While sitting in silence, watching the passengers arrive and depart the terminal, my mind drifted to Sarah, who would have awakened by now. She would be ready for our departure to Pine Ridge, but find me gone. I imagined she would ask Abe about me, and when he could not explain my absence, panic would set in.

No doubt she would suspect her uncle and confront Captain Pratt, demanding an explanation. I doubted that the captain would confess to any knowledge of my whereabouts.

While I lingered on my thoughts of Sarah and my machinations of an escape, I was jarred back to the present moment by an elbow to my ribs. "Let's go," Broken Nose said.

I got to my feet and the three of us, still marching side by side, headed up the stairs to the train bound for New York City. I looked around the crowded platform, again considering an escape, but as before saw no viable options.

"This is crazy," I said, as the train pulled into the station. "Why can't you let me go? Tell the senator I got away."

"Quiet," Skinny said, as the train came to a stop and the doors were pulled open.

"All aboard!" the conductor announced.

Skinny gave me a shove and said, "Let's go."

We climbed into the car, made our way to a bench seat, and as we pulled away from the Harrisburg station, I wondered if I would ever see Sarah again.

Chapter 79
Steamship

Four hours later, we arrived in New York City. Without saying a word, Broken Nose and Skinny escorted me through the terminal to a waiting stagecoach. I had never been in America's largest city before and realized any chance of my escaping was back in Harrisburg, much smaller, and one I was familiar with.

The stagecoach took us through winding, narrow streets, and across wide boulevards filled with street vendors, their wooden carts chock-full of wares and foodstuff. Eventually, we made our way down to the waterfront, where a series of piers hugged the coastline as far as I could see. Once close enough, I made out several large steamships in a line stretching out into the harbor beyond the length of the piers.

The stagecoach pulled up to the curb, and we exited and headed toward one of these ships. This one featured a large black smoke tower that soared seemingly into the gray clouds above us. Along its hull, written in large block letters, was the ship's name—*State of Nebraska.*

There were dozens of men loading all sorts of crates, trunks, and boxes. I even saw a lineup of horses being led into the ship's hold. Confused by the activity, I said, "What's going on? Why are animals boarding the ship?"

Without bothering to answer me, the men ushered me across one of many narrow, elevated walkways connecting the wooden dock to the steamship. Halfway across, I looked over the railing and saw, dozens of feet below, the blackish water crashing against the ship's hull. Could I jump from here? I considered it for a moment, but thought how easy a target I would be for Skinny. And even if he missed shooting me, I would have a hard time swimming to freedom in the frigid water.

Instead, I walked sheepishly on, looking at the looming steamship and the small, opened doorway straight ahead. Once we reached the hatch, we were greeted by a man wearing gray overalls and holding a clipboard. "Who we got here?" he asked, looking at us above his reading glasses.

"He's on the list," Broken Nose said. "His name is Leopold Wolf."

The man in the overalls scanned the paper, dropped a finger at the spot, looked at me wide-eyed, and nodded. "All right, one minute," he said, and walked away down a darkened corridor.

"What do you mean I'm on the list?" I objected while we stood there and waited.

"Quiet," Skinny snarled.

Less than a minute later, the man in the gray overalls returned with another man and said, "Benny will take him from here."

"Good riddance," Broken Nose said, giving me a farewell shove.

I stumbled a bit, but Benny steadied me by grabbing my arm. "All right, Mr. Wolf," he said, "please follow me."

I took a last look behind me at my kidnappers, who were already halfway along the walkway. When I turned back around, Benny was a dozen steps ahead. I ran to catch up and asked, "Where you taking me?"

"Down below with the livestock," he said, keeping his eyes straight ahead.

"Livestock?" I repeated. "What kind of livestock?"

"Um, I believe there are horses, buffaloes, a few elk, deer, moose, and a bear."

"A bear!" I called out. But Benny had no further interest in conversing. He ducked through low hatches and scampered down narrow metal staircases while I followed.

For the life of me, I couldn't figure out why Senator Cameron had exiled me on this steamship, heading to a foreign destination with a zoo of animals. "Can you at least tell me where the ship is going?"

Benny stopped, turned around, and, before I could raise my hands to defend myself, he grabbed a handful of my coat and shoved me hard against the ship's hull. "You need to shut the hell up and stop asking questions. Do you understand me?"

I swallowed hard and nodded.

Satisfied with his position of power, Benny gestured for me to follow. I did so, while my thoughts drifted to Sarah, Abe, and Alice, who were likely distraught by my disappearance. Did Captain Pratt have knowledge of my whereabouts? Would he share it with them?

I smelled the animal dung before we entered the ship's cargo hold. Once inside the cavernous space, I saw a lineup of cages housing the animals, separated by species. At least a dozen horses were held in an enclosure seemingly the size of my house in Carlisle. As we passed by, the horses became agitated, bucking and whinnying their displeasure.

"What's got into them?" Benny said.

I wanted to say they sensed the presence of the Red Wolf, but instead I followed in silence. Beyond the horses were four more cages, holding the six buffalo, two moose, two elk, and lastly a large black bear, bound by chain to one of its hind ankles.

"This one's for you," Benny said, stopping at the smallest cage, where a blanket and a bucket were waiting.

"You want me to go in there?" I asked, with a grimace.

He unhooked a ring of keys from his belt, unlocked the gate, and said, "Get in."

"But why? What have I done to be treated like an animal?"

Waiting for me to duck through the doorway, Benny closed it behind me and squeezed the lock together until it clicked, then said, "It appears you have angered the wrong people."

"You mean Senator Cameron?"

Ignoring my question, he said, "I'll be down once a day to bring you food and empty your waste bucket."

"But you can't leave me here," I shouted after him, as he vanished from my view. "I'm no animal."

CHAPTER 80
ANGUISH

The vibrations of the engines stirred me awake. The cages, including my own, rattled loudly, causing the animals to cry out. I wanted to scream too, but that seemed futile.

I imagined the engine room was close by, as the fumes were now seeping through, blending a sharp, biting odor with the stink of the animals.

My cage was just tall enough for me to stand. The neighboring cage was that of the black bear, who sat with his back resting against the metal bars and seemed to take an interest in me, as he stared without seeming to blink for hours at a time.

While the incessant humming and vibrations continued, I thought I heard human voices. From what I could make out, though I couldn't see anyone, two men were feeding the animals and cleaning out the cages.

By the time they reached the large cage with the elk, just one beyond the bear's cage, I was able to see them. "Hey, can you help me?" I shouted.

But they ignored me. So, I continued to make my presence known. Finally, one of the two men acknowledged me with a wave.

"Please, sir, let me out of here," I begged.

While they continued on with the bear, Benny appeared, carrying a tray of food. "I hope you like this. It's what we're serving in steerage," he said and slid the tray through the gap under the door.

To my surprise, I smelled coffee. It offered such a pleasant aroma compared to the overwhelming stench coating my clothing, skin, and hair.

"Hand me your bucket," he said while pushing a clean one in to take its place. "Make sure you don't leave any leftovers. And for God's sake, don't feed the bear."

"Can you please tell me where we're going to? I have a right to know."

"Listen to me, Leo," he said, holding the pail filled with my waste, seemingly undisturbed by its stink, "you're considered a prisoner by the captain, and since we have no brig, there's no other place to keep you until we reach England, and—"

"England," I said, interrupting him. "So that's where we're going."

Benny sighed. "I said too much. Just behave yourself. We'll be at sea for two weeks."

"Two weeks! I can't live like an animal for that long," I said, but my words were drowned out by the wailing of the disturbed animals and the incessant humming of the ship's engines.

*

With plenty of idle time, I pondered many things. One reflection in particular that brought on an abundance of self-loathing was Black Elk's vision of me recovering the lost Sacred Pipe, and how, upon my return from the Black Hills, the Lakota people honored me. If only they could see me now—what would they think of their illustrious hero?

I wondered how young William was doing, as well as the other precious children at Carlisle. Were they all petrified of being the next victim of the school's abuse? I vowed that if I was able to get myself freed from this interment, I would double my efforts to speak out for these innocents.

Of course, I couldn't help thinking how perturbed Sarah was after reading my article in *The Observer*. Though I tried blaming it on Timothy, she knew my intention was to take full authorial credit, even if that meant putting us in harm's way, which it obviously did, at least for me—and it was well deserved.

I worried if this incident would give her pause about completing our marriage nuptials with the justice of the peace in Harrisburg. That is, if I ever made it back to America from this banishment.

*

With no portholes in the cargo hold, I had no idea whether it was night or day, and eventually, I lost track of the number of days as well. The stench had thickened to stew-like, weighing upon my soul like a heavy blanket, though that is not to say I ever felt warm. The temperature dipped below freezing, and the condensation on the hull's interior formed abstract sculptures of ice.

The only escape from my torment were my dreams. In one, I was back in the Wind Cave, standing before the pomegranate tree. Mother had instructed me to eat the fruit and swallow all of the seeds. Though I kept gnawing at its core, I was never able to consume all six hundred and thirteen seeds, as they seemed to be multiplying in number.

"I can't eat anymore," I complained.

"You must, Leo, if you're to bind your soul with Sarah's," Mother insisted.

"But it's too late now. Her uncle has taken me from her."

"It is not too late," Mother said, undeterred. "He hasn't the power to keep you apart."

"But look at me. I'm an animal in a cage, no longer a man."

"What he does to you in your earthly form means nothing, my son. Your essence in the spirit world remains as it ever was."

Suddenly, despite Mother's assertion, I was no longer in my human form. Instead, I had become the wolf. I was the Red Wolf, sinking my fangs into the nectar of the pomegranate, its blood-red juices running down my snout as I licked it up with my wet, long tongue.

It was dreams like this one that consumed me, and at the same time, my body was weakening. Soon, sickness took hold. It started with a cough, and then a fever. This brought on a delirium that left me in a state of both hot and cold, unknowing of whether I was awake or asleep. Death, I thought, more than once, would be my only escape from such anguish.

CHAPTER 81
DELIVERANCE

"Wake up, Leo," a voice said, piercing through the winds that whistled and swirled about me.

I peered into the darkness and asked, "Who's there?"

"You're going to be okay, Leo," the voice said. "Give me a hand and let's get him out of here."

Like a hand reaching for a drowning man, my mind was pulled out from the dream world and awakened to a familiar face, inches from mine. "There you are," he said with a smile.

It took me a moment to recognize the man. "Frank? Is that you?" I asked, trying to push myself up onto my elbows.

"You stay put," he said, patting my chest. "We're taking you to the ship's infirmary, and I'm going to find out who put you in this cage."

"But I don't understand. Why are you here?"

"We're all here. The entire show. Didn't you know?"

"Know what?" I asked, my head pounding as I tried to make sense of things.

"These animals here are for the show. We're heading to England to perform for Queen Victoria. The Buffalo Bill's Wild West Show is going international."

"What?" I said, not fathoming the words.

"Like I said, we're all here. Annie, Bill Cody, and your Indian friend too—Chief Red Shirt."

"The chief?" I muttered.

"That's right," he said, grabbing my legs, while someone Frank called Billy pulled on my arms. They lifted me onto a stretcher.

As they carried me past the cages, we paused a moment by the horses. "It's all right, Lightning," Frank said. His horse seemed agitated, along with the others. "I don't get it. They were fine when I came down here a few minutes ago."

I reached out and squeezed Frank's arm, and said, "It's me, Frank. They're frightened of the Red Wolf."

"Red wolf? I don't see any wolves," he said, and they carried me away.

*

It took a few days under the watch of the ship's doctor, and some foul-tasting medicine, before I was able to get to my feet and take rejuvenating walks along the top deck as we sailed the North Atlantic to England. During this time, I had visits from Frank Butler, Annie Oakley, and Bill Cody, who all wished me well. Mr. Cody even offered me a position with the show. "You can be the official show correspondent."

I appreciated the opportunity, but told him that as soon as we reached our destination, I intended to return home as soon as possible.

It was during these visits I learned of Queen Victoria's upcoming Golden Jubilee. It was to be a celebration of her fifty years on the throne, with all sorts of extravagant events planned, including Buffalo Bill's Wild West Show. Frank, excited about the prospect of meeting the queen, read to me an excerpt from a British newspaper he found on board.

Buffalo Bill's Wild West Show is an extraordinary exhibition that has created a fury in America, and it's easy to understand why. It's not a circus, nor is it acting in the theatrical sense, but it is an exact reproduction of daily scenes in frontier life as experienced and enacted by the very people who lived it. Such a phenomenal undertaking could be carried out only by a remarkable man, William Cody, also known as Buffalo Bill, guide, scout, hunter, trapper, Indian fighter—and a remarkable man indeed. He is the perfect horseman, an unerring shot, a man of magnificent presence and physique, ignorant of the meaning of fear or fatigue. His life is a history of hairbreadth escapes and deeds of daring, generosity, and self-sacrifice, which compares very favorably with the chivalric actions of romance, and he has been, not inappropriately, designated the Bayard of the Plains.

"Now that's what I would call an exaggeration," I said, as Frank finished and smiled ear to ear at me.

Frank laughed. "I know, but it sounds wonderful!"

*

One late afternoon, a few days out from docking at Liverpool, Chief Red Shirt caught up with me while I strolled topside.

"I've heard what happened," he said, laying a heavy hand on my shoulder. "I'm sorry for what you've been through."

"Thank you, Chief," I said, offering a smile. "We planned on leaving the next morning for Pine Ridge when I was taken."

"Do your people back home know what happened to you?"

"Hopefully by now they should. Frank Butler had the ship send a wire on my behalf, letting them know I'm all right."

The chief sighed. "It seems you made a powerful enemy in Senator Cameron."

"How can a man be so ruthless?"

"*Pfft,*" the chief said. "That man has no qualms about doing whatever it takes to get his way, nor about wielding his sword of power. You need no more proof than to see what's left of my people."

"I'm well aware," I said with a deep sigh. "You should know, Chief, that I was planning on sneaking William out with us."

The chief furrowed his brow and asked, "Why would you do that?"

"William came to me a few days before I was taken, telling me he was frightened. Apparently, an older boy was struck by a counselor and died."

The chief gestured to a bench and said, "Would you mind some advice?"

I nodded and sat down, and the chief sat beside me.

"You shouldn't run away to Pine Ridge with Sarah and William," he began, leaning forward and resting his elbows on his knees. "Though I am grateful that you are looking out for the welfare of my son."

I, too, leaned forward, turned my head, looked into his eyes, and said, "What should I do, then?"

"Book passage on the next steamship back home, marry Sarah, and then the two of you move to Washington. The senator can't touch you once you're married to his niece. You'll be what the white man likes to call a thorn in his side."

I nodded, listening to his words.

"Once there, get that newspaper I've heard about up and running. Speak out for the Indian cause. Maybe even run for political office. Who knows, perhaps one day you can challenge the senator for his seat. After all, you're from the same state."

"But what about William?" I asked. "He's frightened at Carlisle."

The chief patted my knee, offered a knowing smile, and said, "William's journey is not yours. My son will learn, grow, and stumble, and be better off for it. In a way, this is his rite of passage."

I sighed and shook my head. "I'm not so sure."

"No one is," he said with a shrug. "All we can do is serve the Great Spirit the best way we can, and if we're lucky, as you have been, be allowed a glimpse into the spirit world while still within our earthly body."

"Speaking of that," I said. "On the anniversary of my father's death, I released the hair in the soul bundle."

The chief nodded and held out his hands. "What happened—which way did it blow?"

"It didn't," I said with a scoff. "There was no wind, not even a breeze. But I tried anyway and as I released it, the bundle dropped straight down to the grass and just lay there."

The chief took a deep breath and slowly exhaled. "Well, I wouldn't be too concerned. I'm sure your father is well on his journey by now," he said, dismissing my concern.

"I'm not worried," I said with a shrug. "But looking back, it seemed a convenient way of convincing me to search for your lost Sacred Pipe."

"What do you mean?" the chief asked with a furrowed brow.

"When I asked if finding the pipe would prove my worthiness in the eyes of the Great Spirit, Black Elk said—*most certainly*."

The chief rubbed his chin, thinking for a moment, then said, "Do you think we deceived you?"

I shook my head. "Deceived? No. It's more like you encouraged me in a certain way."

"Maybe we did. But not without the best of intentions," Chief Red Shirt said with a smile. "You should understand that all of our prayers, our ceremonies, and our way of life are far from perfect. For generations, our people have lived simply by honoring our ancestors, the animals, and the earth, and up until the arrival of the white man, we trusted in our beliefs. I'm sad to say, though, they no longer seem to be working."

"Oh, but it worked on me," I said, tapping a finger on my chest. "That's what convinced me to search for the Sacred Pipe."

"I'm sorry we disappointed you, Leo."

"Oh no, I'm not disappointed. In fact, I'm grateful for everything. Searching for the Sacred Pipe brought me before the great Thunder Falls and the marvels within the Wind Cave. I would have never experienced any of it without going on my quest."

"I have a feeling, Leo, that you have many great quests yet to come."

"Yes, and much more to learn."

The chief smiled, grasped my shoulder, and said, "It would seem that the education of Leopold Red Wolf is just beginning."

TO BE CONTINUED . . .

About the Author

Beginning with his debut novel—*A Cobbler's Tale,* followed by *Moon Flower, The Righteous One, The Bomb Squad, Hope City, Sadie's Sin, Cape Nome, Otzi's Odyssey, Denali* and most recently—*Thunder Falls,* Neil Perry Gordon has established himself as a well-respected and prolific historical and metaphysical fiction novelist. His storytelling ability has earned him high editorial praise from the likes of Kirkus, Midwest Book Review, Book Viral, and others, including hundreds of four and five star reader reviews on Amazon and Goodreads.

Neil attributes his love of the writing process from his formative education at the Green Meadow Waldorf School, where he understood that classes such as music, dance and theater, writing, literature, legends and myths, were not simply subjects to be learned, but lessons to be experienced.

His creative writing methods and inspiration have been described as organic, meaning he begins his work with a premise for his characters, rather than working within the confines of a formal, detailed outline. This encourages his writing to offer surprising twists and unexpected outcomes, which readers have celebrated. His novels have the attributes of being driven by an equal balance between character development and fast-paced action, which moves his stories along at a swift page-turning pace.

Learn more at www.NeilPerryGordon.com